Aydy's Fiddle
The Memory Thief
By Edward C. Curnutte

Aydy's Fiddle
The Memory Thief

Text copyright © 2016 Edward C. Curnutte

No part of this book may be reproduced or transmitted in any form or by any means, electronic or mechanical, including photocopying, recording, or by any information storage and retrieval system, without permission in writing from the author.

All Rights Reserved

ISBN 9781519020802

"This world is not a perfect place, but it is filled with love, hope, and endless wonder."

For Delilah

In 1887, the precocious twelve-year-old daughter of a café manager aspires to be a concert violinist. She inherits her grandfather's violin and begins to play it with rapid and stunning progress. However, music has the power to draw memories from people and she soon realizes she can see these memories in the people who hear her play.

As she plays over time, her visions become stranger and she learns a disturbing series of family secrets. She must try to make sense of what she sees, reconstruct events from her early childhood, grasp at the barest fragments of memory – and solve a mystery. Is her uncle responsible for the death of her beloved grandfather? She is soon faced with the choice of moving her career forward or finally solving the mysteries contained in the visions.

Through all this, there's the music – always the music. Such power music has; it wraps itself around you, it transports you. It can only bring about pure magic.

Prologue

Essex County, Canada, 1879

One early morning in May, Joseph Delmott stepped off the carriage at the foot of the tree-lined driveway to the old family homestead. It was a modest farm owned by his father, Delphis, a few miles to the south of Windsor. He thanked the driver and walked along the dusty laneway, the heavy smell of spring hanging in the air. Joseph was pleased his father had seen fit to keep the place up even after his mother passed on. As he approached the house, he could hear violin music coming from the kitchen, as always. He rapped on the door, the music stopped and in a moment the door swung open. His father stood there, a broad grin making his spreading moustache seem even larger.

"Joseph! I was just thinkin' about you, c'mon in!"

The two men sat in the kitchen. Delphis ran his aged fingers across his moustache. He paused a moment. In his other hand he held a well-worn violin on his lap.

"You know, I'm pleased, yes real pleased you could come back down here and help me finish up. I think we should have it all done today."

"Well, Papa, I couldn't very well let you manage the spring planting alone! Have you given any thought to retiring? You could move to Windsor and come to the café and play your fiddle all the time. Everyone would love it – but no one more than our little Alexandra."

The old man's eyes lit up.

"*Heh heh,* well that little protégé of mine is puttin' her all into that fiddle of hers, I'll tell ya that!" He placed the violin on his shoulder and adjusted it in the crook of his neck, but then returned it quickly to his lap. "I'll tell ya this too; that's always been the plan of mine to retire there, y'know, ever since I opened it a way back in '54."

"Same age as the town."

"Darn straight, boy!" the old man said as he smacked his hand on the table and grinned. "Plus the best darned coffee in Canada! Don't you ever forget that!"

"You tell me all the time," said Joseph, winking.

"How's Helen doing? Does she get anxious when you come down here to help?"

"She's doing fine, Papa, always busy, I swear she's a miracle worker. Alex has been a bit fussy lately but Helen seems to be managing. I explained that you really needed the help here and she told me to go, so, here I am."

"Well remember, son, I can always get myself a farm hand or two to help out. Don't work your wife to death! Now if your brother would come by and help that'd make things so much easier!"

"I asked, and he said he's too busy."

"Well that don't surprise me none. Pity he can't tear himself away for a few hours!" Delphis said as he raised the violin back up to his shoulder.

"I suppose. Helen always says, 'George was here again complaining about this or that business deal and client,' and so on. I don't like him going there and telling her all those things."

Delphis ignored the remark and grinned. He looked at Joseph with crystal clear blue eyes and began playing an old French-Canadian folk song. Joseph listened and watched as his father's bow danced and twisted across the strings. Those eyes never left him and the smile on his father's face never dimmed. After several minutes, he stopped and placed the violin back down in his lap, a look of satisfaction on his face.

"I'm *very* proud of you, son, did you know that? Now, can you take a run in to town? We need some seed for the last five acres. Let's get you hitched up."

* * *

Delphis and Joseph hitched up the horse and wagon and soon Joseph was off. Delphis returned to the kitchen and sat down. He took up his violin and played many songs, some slow, some fast. He particularly liked this time when he could play alone and without distraction, having come to prefer the solitude of the farm house to the hustle and bustle of the café. His mind was clear. He could enjoy his music.

He closed his eyes as he played. The peaceful sounds were captivating for him, and with no one to listen for miles around, he played the instrument with energy and vigor.

His thoughts soon drifted away to a warm, breezy night in downtown Windsor. The streets were deserted, except for a man who ran out of a little shop.

An unnatural glow flickered in the window of the shop until it shone with unnatural radiance.

Moments later, an explosion. Windows shattered.

Hungry flames tore through the structure, forming into a column that reached high into the starry sky.

Panic. Bells clanging. The wooden frame of the building, weakened and ravaged from the searing flames, leaned sideways and collapsed onto the neighbouring building in a massive shower of flying sparks and debris. That building, too, was soon set aflame.

"That'll serve him right!" said the young man from the street corner.

Delphis opened his eyes. He sighed heavily. At that moment, there was a knock. He placed his violin down on the table and walked to the side door. He opened it wide.

"Hello, George," he said, frowning.

Chapter 1

At the outskirts of Windsor, Ontario, 1887

On a bright day in May, twelve-year-old Robbie Stuart dropped his schoolbooks near the road and raced through the forest woodlot. Ferns whipped his legs as he sped through the dogwood trees and the thorns of wild rose bushes scratched his arms. Shouts and curses grew louder behind him; they were getting closer. If he could only make it another half mile or so, he'd be out of the woodlot and into the safety of his farm home, but he was smaller than his pursuers and knew he was reaching the end of his endurance.

From behind, an unfriendly hand clutched his shoulder and clawed at his shirt. Robbie twisted sideways, the hand lost its grip, and he heard the heavy sound of someone tumbling down among breaking twigs. Ahead in the distance he could see the forest opening up. He leaped wildly over fallen logs and sped over lichen-covered ground, shielding his face against the low-hanging branches of the sugar maples. His undoing came from the wild grape vines that spread across the forest floor; they caught his foot and sent him headlong to the ground. He scrambled back to his feet and tried to run again, but his five pursuers surrounded him.

"Rabbit Stew! Rabbit Stew! I'm finally going to get my wish!" yelled the boy with murky green eyes and sandy hair.

"Please, Owen, don't!" Robbie said, his voice trembling. He

looked down. "My mama's waiting for me at home! Please!"

The boys' laughter was full of scorn.

"Your mama? Aww, poor little Rabbit." Owen rolled up his sleeves. "I've been looking forward to this all year. What do you think if we sent some rabbit stew home for your mama? Would she like that?"

Robbie blinked and felt tears run down his cheeks, while a spreading warmth covered the front of his trousers and coursed its way down his leg. Cheered on by his friends, Owen made short work of the boy, who now lay bruised and moaning near the path through the woods.

Owen sneered. "Thanks a lot, little Rabbit. Because of you I'm going to be late for my lesson."

Robbie looked up at Owen, who'd started to walk away, but then turned back for one more kick in the stomach. One by one the boys cleared away and their jeers and sneers were replaced by the sound of a late spring breeze rustling through the boughs of the great oaks arching overhead. Robbie lay there, his flesh stinging and ribs bruised. His ragged breath stirred up the dust on the ground.

He could be reasonably sure the boys had all left, including the bully, Owen. Robbie wanted to lie there until the worst of the pain passed. He must pull himself up in a few minutes or he might stay there in the forest the rest of the day or even all night. As he contemplated his situation, he heard a familiar voice call to him from further along the path. It was a girl's voice and he was sure he knew who she was.

She hurried toward him and stopped. "Robbie! I was coming to see you – I heard all the noise and – my goodness, get up! We have to get you home now!"

Through a swollen eye, Robbie could only see her feet and ankles. She was wearing black shoes with crisp white socks turned back neatly over top. He could make out only the silhouette of her head, framed by hair hanging loosely about her shoulders. Straining his vision, he could see that she appeared to be wreathed by the towering trees and backlit by splintered sunlight, which lent the girl the aura of an angelic helper. It was exactly what he needed at that moment.

* * *

Having taken a few moments to enjoy his victory, Owen Delmott realized how late it was and hurried back through the woods. He said goodbye to his friends, collected his bicycle and slung his violin case across his back. He felt a chill in his veins as he rode back into the cobbled streets of old Sandwich, knowing full well the professor would be furious if he arrived late again for his music lesson. With renewed energy he pedalled his bicycle as fast as he could.

When Owen arrived at the professor's home, he dropped his bicycle on the steps and rapped impatiently on the side door. When the maid answered, he rushed past her and down the corridor. He stopped in front of the professor's study and tried to catch his breath before he tapped on the door. There was no answer. For a few brief seconds Owen thought the professor himself was late and that this burst of anxiety had all been for nothing.

Alas, the great door did open and the greying professor, dressed smartly in his usual business suit and tie, gazed down his nose at the dishevelled young musician. He looked at his pocket watch and huffed, then snapped its lid shut.

"You're late again, Master Delmott. This makes the tenth time this year. What excuse have you diligently prepared to offer me *this* time?"

"I'm sorry I'm late, professor," Owen said. "I got a flat tire on my bicycle so I had to run with it all the way from school." The lad lowered his head.

"You may enter my study." The professor's voice showed his irritation. He ushered Owen in and closed the door. The air was heavy with stale cigar smoke. The professor walked briskly to the leaded glass windows and an excellent view of his manicured grounds. He twisted several handles and each window swung open in turn.

The professor's study reminded Owen of his father's law office, the main difference being the austere presence of a black Steinway grand piano in the centre of the room and a fieldstone fireplace located on an outer wall. With its oak panelling, supple leather brass-buttoned chairs and fine appointments, it seemed to perfectly mirror the personality of this stodgy, old, cigar smoking musician.

In preparation for his lesson, Owen set about to open his violin case, as usual.

"Master Delmott, pray tell, what on earth do you think you're doing?" Professor Hergicksen asked with one greying eyebrow raised.

"I, uh –"

"Master Delmott! For three years now I have tolerated your tardiness, your lies, your lack of respect and your indifference to your musical studies!"

The boy sensed the change in attitude towards him. Gone was the grandfatherly, nurturing professor who had been his mentor, encouraging him to pursue bigger and better ambitions.

"Young man! You of all people should know who I am and show the respect due me!" boomed the professor's voice. "I have been teaching bright students for many years, and I'm ashamed to admit that at one time I had high hopes for you! Do you even realize how much money your parents have invested into your musical training? Do you understand how important it is for them that you become successful? You're a bitter disappointment, young Delmott – a disappointment to me but more so a disappointment to them. If you respected me, your future, and all the effort that has gone into your training, you would've at least had the courtesy to do whatever was possible to arrive at your lesson *on time*."

Strangely enough, Owen felt relieved. After all, the professor was right in many ways. Despite what others said about his talent, he knew deep down he didn't want to be a musician at all. He could play, yes, but reasoned it was all just a big act. Just then, as expected, the fateful moment arrived.

"Master Delmott," the professor said after he re-composed himself and took another puff of his cigar. "Please gather your things and depart my study. I should not wish to see you again. Your parents shall forthwith be notified."

Owen took his violin, still undisturbed in its case, and proceeded to the door. A plan was already hatching in his head as to what he would tell his parents. He retraced his steps down the corridor and emerged outside into the bright spring sunshine.

Taking a deep breath, he took a few last moments to survey the surrounding landscape from the top step of the professor's porch. He walked past his bicycle, took his violin out of the case and held it on his shoulder in the usual playing position. He paused, thought, and, still holding the violin by the neck, swung it with all his might against one of the pillars of the professor's home. The violin instantly shattered, making one sickening, final note upon its death. He stomped his foot on the broken pieces of the body, further cracking and breaking the parts left over. In his hand he held the scroll with strings still attached, bouncing and dangling grotesquely. He gathered up the splintered remains and arranged them haphazardly into the case. He smirked, thinking that made two things he had finished off in a single day.

Mounting his bicycle, he set off. The jagged pieces of varnished kindling and coiled strings rattled and shook as he rambled down the cobbled road towards home.

Chapter 2

Owen Delmott lived in a well-to-do neighbourhood in nearby Windsor. His stately, white-sided two-storey home was surrounded by an eight-foot wrought iron fence through which one could see the manicured lawn, hedges, and the guest house out back.

Having placed his bicycle in the shed, Owen ran up the steps of the rear veranda. When he entered the kitchen, he found his mother tidying up after her weekly meeting with the ladies from her church. She stopped what she was doing when she saw him.

"Owen! Why, why are you home so early? Don't you have a music lesson now?"

"Mother," he said, frowning, "I got into a fight after school with that horrible Stuart boy, and oh mother, what am I going to do?" he said, pressing himself into her plump, comforting chest.

"Sit down, my son, and tell me what happened."

"That horrible little Robbie Stuart! He had been harassing me since last year when I won the violin competition. Today he challenged me to a fight behind the school!"

"What did you do? Did you fight him?"

"Of course mother, I not only fought him, I beat him real good. He will never bother me again. However –"

"However what?"

"Before leaving, Robbie took my violin and smashed it to bits! He's such a sore loser!"

Restraining a smirk, Owen reached for his violin case and opened the lid. His mother recoiled back in her chair, raising a hand to her mouth.

"My goodness, Owen, look what he did!"

"Mother, the whole thing is completely shattered! I tried to explain what happened to Professor Hergicksen but he wouldn't listen. He gave me a huge lecture about why I don't respect him, and then he threw me out and told me never to come back!"

"Now, now, my son. You needn't be so upset. I will explain everything to your father as soon as he comes home. We'll make sure to get this whole thing sorted out."

* * *

When George Delmott returned home later that evening, he poured himself a stiff brandy. A long, lanky figure with a receding grey hairline and piercing blue eyes, he sat down and listened to the whole story from his wife, Clara. After she finished, there was an awkward silence in the room.

"Don't we pay Hergicksen enough for these lessons? He ought to understand what it's like to be a boy and get into fights. Owen had the clear right to defend himself. Hergicksen could've considered that, don't you think?"

"Yes, dear. Of course."

"So, tomorrow morning that old dog is getting a visit from me. By the time I leave there, this whole situation will be sorted out. After I'm through with him, I'll visit Robbie Stuart's parents. That boy needs to be taught a lesson about picking fights and destroying other peoples' property."

"What should we do about the violin?" asked Clara.

George scowled at her. "Of course I'm going to make them buy him another one of the same quality!"

"But George, dear, the Stuarts are not wealthy people!"

"That's not my concern and neither should it be yours. Life is tough. Their boy would do well to consider his actions beforehand! First, a violin. Next it'll be pick-pocketing, petty theft, then bank robbery and Lord knows what else. I'm actually helping to save the boy!"

Clara massaged her brow as if she had a headache.

George sighed, sipped his brandy and leaned forward. "Clara, look, we've worked very hard to get where we are in life, and we're far from finished. People are jealous of us. They're jealous of our success and won't hesitate to prevent us from reaching our goals. Robbie Stuart smashing Owen's violin is a perfect example of that, don't you see? In that boy's childish mind he thought he could stop Owen from becoming successful as a musician. When Owen gets older, he'll realize that people will use much more clever means to prevent him from doing great things in his life. This sort of behaviour has to be stopped now, and people must realize they can't bully him – or us. We are strong people, Clara, and we need to show that strength. I can also assure you that by the turn of the century we're going to own half this town and every major business in it. You can see the number of properties we've acquired already! These kinds of things only come to people who work hard, are not intimidated by others, and who possess a strong constitution."

"But George –"

"Please, don't interrupt me! Strength breeds strength. When my father was alive he knew the value of hard work and determination. Why do you think he willed the café and the better part of his estate to *me*? Use your head! He did it because he knew I had the business skills to make everything successful. Of course, Joseph is good at the day-to-day operations at the café, but when it comes to anything important, such as dealing with bankers, handling stocks, bonds and securities, my father knew I was the best qualified."

Clara sighed.

"Now what is it?" asked George as he gulped down the last of his brandy.

"Nothing. You know best, dear. Do as you must."

* * *

Early the following morning Delmott was true to his word. He went straight to the professor's home, pushed past the stunned maid who answered the door, and barged into the professor's study. He found Professor Hergicksen gazing out the open window over the grounds, cigar smouldering away, as usual, between his fingers.

"Oh Mr. Delmott, won't you please come in and make yourself at home? I believe we might get a bit of rain today," said the professor, back still turned.

Delmott walked right up to the desk and stopped.

"Hergicksen, you know why I'm here. What is this matter with my son? Why was he expelled from his lessons?"

"I'm sure the boy explained everything to you, didn't he?" said the professor, turning to face Delmott. "If he didn't, perhaps I can fill in the blanks – or add a few more details."

"Details? *Details*? Details such as what?" said Delmott.

"Well now Mr. Delmott, perhaps he mentioned to you that he deliberately – and with full knowledge and foresight – did wilfully commit the act of destroying one fine Sebastian Götz violin."

"How dare you!" the lawyer hissed.

"Mr. Delmott, I dare say I witnessed the whole sorry spectacle myself with these very eyes. Come with me."

The two men walked outside under the slate-grey sky. After a brief search through the grass, the professor picked up some small fragments of the violin, including the soundpost. Presented with this evidence, George Delmott was speechless.

"Hergie," he said in a calmer tone, "there must be something we can do to set this right. My son wants to be a great violinist! He wants to be taught by the best!"

"From what I saw, George, he doesn't want to be a violinist at all. He is an angry young man, very angry," replied the professor, matching Delmott's conciliatory tone and placing the broken pieces in his hand. "I would strongly suggest you have a talk with the boy.

Regardless, my mind is made up. With your son having such an attitude I can no longer accept him as a student. As a matter of fact, I'm not accepting any more new students at all. You know, at my age I should be slowing down, but sometimes that's difficult to do. Now if you'll excuse me, I have a busy day. I've got a train to catch this afternoon for my concert in Toronto tomorrow."

Through years of practice, training, and working with people of all types, Professor Hergicksen deemed himself to be an excellent judge of human character and thus could easily assess peoples' motives and predict their actions. Regrettably though, he lacked the ability to foretell his own future – that by the time this day finished, his life would never again be the same.

Chapter 3

Professor Herbert Hergicksen always preferred to travel first class. By the time he arrived at the train station late that afternoon, the sky had become decidedly more menacing. As was always his practice, he arrived well ahead of his departure time. Normally the train would have been waiting and people already boarding, but not even his first class ticket could save him from the problem then confronting him – there was simply no train to take. People were milling about on the platform, leaning over one another to gaze down the tracks in the hopes of seeing a rising black plume of smoke in the distance. Still, nothing.

At that moment, through a bullhorn, the station master announced that the train would not arrive for another three hours due to a mechanical problem. Angry shouts erupted from the crowd, but no amount of complaining could change their situation. Professor Hergicksen, having only a small overnight bag and his rare, beloved J.B. Vuillaume violin in its case, elbowed his way through the crowd to the station master's office. He entrusted these items to the station master and trotted off, ever-present cigar in hand, to Delmott's Café, located about a block away, to perhaps nibble on a sandwich and sample some of the fine coffee he had heard about but had not had the pleasure of tasting.

The sky was now beginning to darken considerably, even turning an ominous shade of green and black. Professor Hergicksen discarded his cigar and quickened his pace down the sidewalk, his black overcoat pushed up hard behind his legs by the freshening wind.

The professor arrived at the café in the nick of time, entering just as a sharp crack of thunder struck in perfect unison with the small, clattering brass bell mounted on the door. Closing the door against the worsening weather, and with relief, he looked round and saw that the whole café, which consisted of maybe a dozen tables, a large central stove and a serving counter, was completely deserted.

Glancing at the sign hanging in the door, he realized the café had just closed. He knew he ought to leave, but the rain was now driving down in blinding torrents. He stood there and looked around, wondering why the proprietors would leave the place unlocked. He resisted the urge to light another cigar.

Just then, the door to the café burst open; somebody rushed in against the rain and weather and pushed the door shut, nearly knocking the good professor off his feet. A young girl, sopping wet, her dress soaked to her skin; she stood with her back and hands pressed up to the door, holding it firmly shut. She was drawing in huge gulps of air as if she'd been running for her life.

Huff, huff, huff, "Good afternoon, *huff* Maestro!" said the girl, trying to catch her breath. She swallowed hard and continued. "Oh, please, I hope you won't leave! It's pouring rain outside and you'll catch your death!"

The professor burst out laughing. "Me? Catch my death?"

The poor, fair-skinned girl didn't appear to be much more than ten or eleven years old. She looked at him with large, ice-blue eyes highlighting her oval face, and her chestnut coloured hair hung wet and limp about her shoulders. Focusing squarely on him, she gulped and, again catching her breath, managed a smile.

"Please, Maestro, won't you have a seat? Let me make you a cup of our *finest* coffee."

"You work here? Well, all right, you may," said the professor. He looked at the weather again and, sighing, hung his overcoat and hat on the coat rack. He took a chair at a table near the window, viewing the spectacle outside. "Don't you think you should dry yourself off?"

"Oh, it's only water, Maestro! It's nothing to worry about. In fact, my father says that water gives us life! He also says that with enough time, water dries off!"

Not willing to dispute the undeniable validity of this fact, nor contradict the girl's father, the professor nodded. "Well miss, you wouldn't allow me to catch my death by venturing into this deluge!"

"Yes, well Maestro you're an old, wise man and I, well…I, yes, well of course you are old, but you're far more *wise* than you are old – and very learned!" she said as a redness spread across her face.

Professor Hergicksen sat there bemused at her blabbering and makeshift compliments. He chuckled. The girl wiped her feet and squeezed the water from her hair. Then, with drips marking a path across the wooden floor, she made her way past the big stove and around the counter to where the coffee percolator was located.

"My name is Alexandra and my papa runs the café," she said. "And everyone knows who you are, Maestro. My father took me to some of your concerts and I always had a dream that someday I would meet you in person and that you would share with me all your greatest experiences in the best concert halls around the globe and that maybe you'd tell me all the secrets of all the greatest concert violinists of all time!"

"Well now, I –" said the professor. Another blue flash of lightning was soon followed by a great rumble of thunder.

"Oh please Maestro, you *must!* My father told me there's no such thing as a coincidence, that everything in the universe has a purpose! That means our meeting today was written in the stars!" she said as she boiled the water and ground up the coffee beans.

"First, I should desire that you'd stop calling me Maestro," he said as he looked at the waterfall of rain slide off the awning. "Such titles make me very uncomfortable. However, you may call me Professor Hergicksen."

"As you wish, Professor Hergicksen, but Maestro is really such an elegant title. I've read so many books about music and when I was a little girl I had all my dolls arranged in a symphony, the larger dolls playing the big bass instruments, the medium sized dolls in the brass section, and of course my favourite dolls, the small ones, would always play the violin. Don't you think it's great Maestro? Er, I'm so sorry, please I *beg* your pardon, Professor Hergicksen!" she said in one breath just as the coffee percolator finished its job.

The professor rolled his eyes and sighed. "Well, since you seem so insistent on calling me Maestro, you may. You may also bring me some coffee."

"Oh thank you! Right away, Maestro! What do you take in your coffee?"

"I take it black. That way nothing pollutes its true flavour. Milk and sugar are nothing more than noise," he said resolutely. "You see, it's the same with music. Too many distractions take away from the true flavour."

"Oh Maestro, I agree w-w-with you!" said the girl, shivering. She promptly poured two cups and sat with him at his table.

"Do *you* drink coffee, miss? And just how old are you?" he said, squinting.

"I'm t-t-twelve years old," she replied as she handed him his coffee with shaky hands. She then sipped her own coffee, the professor assuming she wanted it more for its heat value than its taste. She recoiled, turning her nose up at the noxious brew.

"Young lady, really now..." He had already forgotten her name. "You're freezing to death. I'll not be party to the demise of a young woman!" He got up, retrieved his coat, and placed it round the girl's shivering shoulders. "That should help."

Returning to his chair, he reached into his pocket and withdrew his cigar case and a small box of matchsticks. Lighting one of his cigars, he gently puffed on it and, as the end of the cigar began glowing red round the edges, curls of white smoke billowed into the café.

The young waitress gazed up at him, placed a handkerchief over her mouth and nose, and coughed lightly.

"Oh dear, how rude of me. This is a terrible habit of mine, but dare I say, it's my only vice." He quickly extinguished the cigar as if it were some cheap stogie.

The girl leaned forward at the table with her fingers interlocked, looking at the great master, eyes fixed on him. The professor sensed she had something urgent to say.

"Maestro, I can play the violin too! I only have a small children's violin though, but I practice very hard. I even used to take lessons with Sister Madeline at school and I was doing really very well. Then one day she told me she'd rather teach my cousin Owen. It was absolutely the worst day of my life! Then Sister Madeline left and now Owen is taking lessons with you. Please Maestro, can I take lessons with you, too? I'd be a good student, I learn very quickly! Please? I've so dreamt of it, I so want it!"

Professor Hergicksen leaned back in his chair. He studied the aspiring musician sitting across from him, all the recent events replaying in his mind: He had just expelled the girl's cousin from his lessons. He had just told the boy's father he wouldn't take him back. Finally, he said he would not be accepting any more students. He sighed. He was a man of honour, a man of his word. He must be firm. He wondered how he could ever justify taking on another student, let alone a girl, let alone this female cousin of the boy he had just expelled.

The girl sat across from him chewing on a strand of her hair, her eyes large and expectant.

Professor Hergicksen sighed again and leaned forward. "Young lady, look. This is not easy for me to say. I'm an old man. I have done so much in my life and I cannot possibly do any more. I'm afraid to say I cannot accept you as my student."

The young girl searched his face, tears welling up in her eyes, her lower lip quivering. She bolted up from her chair, casting his coat from her shoulders and onto the floor. Sobbing, she tore across the café to the small door beyond the counter which led upstairs.

The professor sat there dazed, hearing the sound of the girl's footsteps running up the stairs, followed a moment later by the sound of falling objects from above and the heavy creak of an old bed.

He rubbed his eyes, wiped his face and sighed. He put two coins on the table, collected his coat from the floor and hat from the hat rack and departed the café. The rain had lightened to a drizzle, and he trudged back to the train station along soggy streets.

Throwing herself on the bed, Alexandra deliberately turned to the wall, her whole body heaving in great sobs, her tears soaking into the pillow. She avoided looking at the chaotic mess on the floor after sweeping off the orchestra of dolls neatly arranged on her hope chest.

Chapter 4

The train eventually arrived in Windsor and Professor Hergicksen eventually played his concert in Toronto the following day, but it was the worst performance of his professional career. Billed as the top soloist of the 19th century in all of Canada, he proved to be a big letdown to the audience. The newspapers were merciless in their criticism. "Past his Prime" read one. "Lacklustre" read yet another and, the most stinging of all, "An Amateur Performance." Absent were the crisp accents, bright pizzicatos and towering arpeggios which once adorned his playing.

Professor Hergicksen, the virtuoso who stood on stage in his fine tuxedo, had to endure the sound of dwindling applause and muted silence. In the aftermath, he knew exactly why it was so and no one, save he, could explain the reason for his disastrous exhibition.

* * *

The following day ushered in a new spring freshness. Scattered rays of morning sunshine spread through the windows of Delmott's Café – and also into the upstairs bedroom, into the face of the girl who'd cried herself to sleep the previous night.

"Alexandra! Wake up!" said her father from the café downstairs. "Breakfast will be ready soon!"

The girl moaned and obliged. She got up and changed from her rumpled clothes to something more suitable for a Saturday morning –

a light blue dress with short sleeves. She arranged her hair in a bun and went down the stairs. She could already smell the pancakes cooking; her father made them every Saturday. He stopped what he was doing and greeted her at the bottom of the stairs.

"Good morning, Angel. You refused dinner and spent all evening in your room. You didn't even say goodnight. Are you ill?"

"No, Papa, I'm not ill. I just saw all my hopes and dreams wash away with the rain."

"What do you mean?" Joseph furrowed his brow as he scooped the pancakes onto her plate. He brought their breakfast to one of the tables by the window.

"Not there, please Papa. That table is now forever cursed and I cannot bring myself to sit there ever again," she said with renewed energy.

Her father cocked his head to the side, swept his black hair straight back, and squinted.

"Papa, I must tell you that the Maestro came here yesterday."

"Hergicksen? Really? I never thought I'd live to see the day."

"Yes. This is where we sat when – and I asked him – and he said he wasn't taking any more students."

Still offering her a puzzled look, Joseph moved their breakfast to the next table. Alexandra, whose appetite had always been hearty, now picked at her food with her fork.

"I wish you wouldn't let that upset you so. That man's too big for his britches anyway."

She ignored the remark and talked into her plate, only looking up briefly to see his face. "Papa, I've always wanted to be a musician. You know I love music so much. I can even remember playing some songs with Pépé when I was little. I really miss him."

"So do I. He loved you and loved playing the violin with you. He called you his little protégé."

Alexandra looked up and sighed. "Papa, I know things are hard now, but I'm sure I could still find time to learn and study when we're not busy or when there are no customers in the café. I just need a good teacher."

"I wish I knew somebody," he said. "Anyway, finish your breakfast before it gets cold."

He sat across from her eating as slowly as she. Alexandra knew her father well enough to know he was deep in thought about some matter, yet she dared not ask him; he always had so much on his mind and the business of the café was always so pressing. Since her mother left, her father had to fill the role of both parents while also minding the family business – the latter of which he did mostly by himself, often with Alexandra, and usually with hired help.

He cleared his throat. "Please, hurry up and eat."

Joseph excused himself and, leaving Alexandra at the table, disappeared up the stairs. She could hear him walking around in the spare room. He seldom went there and often told her not to play there because it was a storehouse full of many breakable antiques that had belonged to her grandparents.

After a few moments he returned with an old, oblong wooden box which he placed on the counter. Alexandra rose from her chair.

"What is it, Papa?"

"Alexandra, I've been keeping this safely stored for many years. Honestly, I've really been afraid to even touch it myself because..." he paused, running his fingers over the edges of the box, "because it was my father's – your Pépé's. It was his dearest possession."

"Can we open it, please, Papa?"

"Yes, of course. Let's do it together."

The wooden box may have been a sandy colour at one time, but now its wood had darkened by the passage of time. It even smelled old. It had clearly been built by hands long ago and designed so as to protect its valuable contents. Joseph used a small bottle opener and pried up at the lid. At first it resisted, then it creaked a bit, and finally it relented and Joseph pulled it free.

Alexandra would never forget what she saw inside. "Oh Papa, Papa! Could it really be?" Gazing into the box, she immediately knew what it was by its size, shape and contour. "May I?" she asked. Her father nodded. Alexandra smiled and reached inside the box, lifting out an old, worn, leather-covered violin case. She placed it down on the countertop. Embossed on the lid, just above a small carrying handle, were the initials D.C.D.

"This was your pépé's violin, Alexandra, and now it is yours."

"Oh Papa! This is *the* greatest present I could ever receive!" She threw her arms around his neck, covering his cheek with kisses. "Thank you, thank you, oh a million times thank you!"

"I wanted to give this to you a long time ago, but you were too little. A small child has arms too tiny for a violin of this size, and so you'd have never been able to play it – until now. Go ahead, Angel. Open the case."

Alexandra turned to her father and smiled. She sniffled and, with trembling, curious fingers, opened the clasp which held the case closed. She eased the lid upright, and there inside she beheld all the grandeur of all the greatest symphonies of the world pouring out all their magic, all of history's greatest composers, all the masters, conductors, soloists – all of them, and all of them speaking to her; all of them playing only for *her*.

Through this great musical cacophony, she could hear the quiet, solitary voice of her long-departed grandfather whispering to her.

"Play."

Chapter 5

By the time Delmott's Café opened for business that day, Alexandra had examined every part of her pépé's violin. She compared it, side by side, to her child's violin, and it was indeed much larger. To her dismay, two of the strings were broken as if someone had overtightened them. Regardless, she knew that strings were frequently replaced and she could always get more. As for the instrument itself, not only did she inspect every grain of the chestnut coloured wood, she also saw the imprints of her pépé's fingers on the ebony fingerboard, revealing several of the more commonly played spots. She noticed a small nick, or maybe a notch, on the fingerboard as well, about halfway between the scroll and body of the violin. She looked at the tuning pegs, examined the scroll, even held it up to look at the thickness of the two remaining strings as they crossed over the bridge. She plucked each one lightly with her index finger; listening to the different tone each gave. She decided they were out of tune as well, and feared tightening them lest they too should break.

She allowed her mind to wander freely. *What songs did he play on this instrument? What was the first song he played? What was his last? What was his favourite?* The only person who might be able to help would be her father, so she made up her mind to ask. However, the questions needed to be asked at the right moment – a moment when he could sit, talk, and they would not be interrupted.

* * *

Joseph indeed was a very busy man, especially on Saturdays when the waitress, Marcie, had her day off. Now that summer was here, he was relieved that Alexandra could help him with the customers. He was pleased she worked so willingly and never complained, doing as best as any twelve-year-old could. Despite that, he didn't want his daughter growing up in a restaurant environment, and he certainly didn't want her to be a waitress for the rest of her life. *If you're going to be a career waitress, this is exactly how it all starts,* he thought. The prospect terrified him.

"Oh Alex! Can we have some more coffee?" asked Charlie McKay. A burly, bearded man who frequented the café daily with his friends, he looked too large for the flimsy bentwood chair upon which he sat. Joseph was dreading the day it would collapse, sending the man crashing to the floor.

"Here you go, Mr. McKay!" Alexandra poured him and his friends another cup.

"You're in an extra good mood today," he said, winking. "Why so happy?"

"My papa gave me a present!"

"Oh? What'd he give you? New clothes? New shoes? Or perhaps it's a secret?"

"Why don't you show him?" said Joseph from behind the counter.

Alexandra turned to Charlie McKay and smiled. "I'll show you sometime, I promise! I've got quite a bit of work to do on it before I show it to anybody!" she said as she turned away to serve another customer, leaving the man rubbing his beard.

Towards closing time, business had slowed down and only two customers remained in the café. Joseph decided it would be a good time to do the bookkeeping, so he sat at his usual table by the window, sipping on his coffee and writing. He liked that table because it gave him a good vantage point from which he could see the whole enterprise, as well as what was happening outside on the street.

Alexandra pulled out the chair opposite him, sweeping her dress behind her legs as she sat down. With her elbows on the table she leaned forward, her chin resting on interlocked fingers. "Papa, tell me more about Pépé. What kind of a man was he?"

Joseph could feel the corners of his mouth rising into a smile. "Well first of all, your pépé was a very hard-working, decent man. You know, he taught me so many important lessons, and somehow he did it while running the farm and this café. He enjoyed tinkering with things too, and he always had some kind of project on the go. He hated doing nothing in the winter, so he took a big chance and put his savings into starting this café. It really suited him. People liked him."

"When did he start playing the violin? Who taught him?"

Joseph was pleased his answers seemed to be sparking a flurry of questions in her young mind. He thought a bit first before offering a reply. "Well, I can't honestly answer those questions. He had been playing it as long as I can remember and I really think he taught himself how to do it. Oftentimes he would entertain customers in the café – and he really enjoyed playing those little concerts with you. You and him, you made quite a team."

"Oh Papa, do you think I could teach myself like he did? Do you know any of the songs he played?" She sat across from him, eyes twinkling, a new eagerness rising in her voice.

"Well, he played so many, you know, but I can't remember the names of them all. He played fast and slow ones, happy and sad ones, and he played them all on that same fiddle. He loved it almost as much as he loved his family. Sometimes it really got on your mémé's nerves, but she never complained about it, not even once. 'People could have worse habits,' she'd sometimes tell me. It's a pity I didn't take after him and play the fiddle too."

"Do you know where he got his fiddle from?"

"Well, I don't really know the answer to that, either. He said he bought it from a pedlar who was passing through, but I never did know if he was serious or joking. One thing's for sure though – he bought it secondhand, judging by how old it looks."

"Oh it would be so wonderful to play it like him! Wouldn't it be grand?"

"I'm sure it would, Angel. Anyway, I think you've done enough for today. Why don't you go visit a friend, perhaps Emma? Some fresh air will do you good."

"Thank you, Papa, but I'd really rather not. I would love to sit here and play Pépé's violin!"

"Hmm, well it's rather difficult with only two strings, don't you think? I'll tell you what, while you're away I'll try to get you some strings. You can tell Emma all about your violin."

Alexandra sat a moment, looking out into the sunny street. "Papa, instead of visiting Emma, would you mind if I took the violin and paid a visit to Robbie? He got beat up in a fight with Owen and perhaps a visit might do him some good. I can see Emma another time."

Joseph rolled his eyes. "Owen again, huh? Why doesn't that surprise me?"

"May I, though?"

Joseph studied her face. He knew his daughter. She was a trustworthy person who worked hard, was good at school, and who always took excellent care of her things. "All right. Please give my regards to the Stuarts and wish Robbie well. Oh, and one more thing: Please come home before dark!"

"Yes of course, Papa!" she said with laughter in her voice before standing up.

Alexandra hadn't much reason to laugh in the past while, but whenever she did, it was sincere, honest and contagious. It was also uniquely her own.

She carefully packed the violin in its case and set out for the Stuarts' place about two miles distant. Great oaks, elms and massive, 40-foot-tall Jesuit pear trees lined the road along the great Detroit River leading up to Stuart's lane. She remembered the nuns at school telling her that the trees were planted by Jesuit priests some one hundred and fifty or more years prior, a living reminder of the area's French heritage.

Another common sight along the river were the ferries that took passengers back and forth between Windsor and Detroit. If she were lucky enough, she could even see the great steamships which plied the river with their happy passengers. She faintly remembered going to the river with her mother, and they would sit and watch the steamships, wondering where all those passengers had come from and where they were going.

When Alexandra was about halfway down the Stuart's lane, Nelson, their Rottweiler spotted her. He came bouncing across the field to greet her. Had she been a stranger, Alexandra knew this type of reception would have been very unpleasant. As it was, she was nearly knocked off her feet by the charging, playful beast, but managed to keep him at bay. She stroked his rough coat, and he pranced at her side, proudly escorting her the remaining distance to the house.

The Stuart home had been made from rough-hewn logs nearly one hundred years before. It was a storey and a half tall with a veranda spanning the front. Two windows stood on either side of the front door. Inside was a modest parlour beyond which was the large country kitchen. Behind the house was a small flower garden and sitting area. The farm itself spread out and across the back and sides of the house, and a large, dilapidated barn sat some distance behind. A small woodlot and meadow occupied the edge of the property through which a pleasant, meandering stream flowed.

With the dog at her side, Alexandra marched up the steps and rapped smartly on the door. A few moments later, it swung open and there Robbie stood, eyes wide and mouth open.

"Alexandra!"

"Oh Robbie, I'm glad to see you're all right! I've come to pay you a little visit and to show you my new present!"

"What is it? What have you got there with you?" he said.

Alexandra stepped in the front door and into the parlour. "Oh it's a very special present. My father gave it to me today and I want to show it to you!"

Unfortunately, she would have to wait. Robbie's parents soon joined them and ushered Alexandra to the kitchen where Mrs. Stuart not only served fresh lemonade, pastries and candy, but plied her with endless questions about her life. Alexandra knew the Stuarts enjoyed it whenever she visited, but she hated all the attention they lavished on her, wishing she could visit Robbie without their intrusion.

At long last, Mr. Stuart excused himself and left while Mrs. Stuart set about collecting their dishes and tidying up. Robbie and Alexandra went into the parlour where the cased violin sat on a chair next to the sofa.

"Open it now, please!" said Robbie. "I want to see it!"

Alexandra sat on the sofa, assuming the posture of a proper young Victorian girl. She placed the violin case on her lap and eased the lid open. A wide-eyed Robbie sat next to her. There they both beheld the finely made instrument – clean and well-kept and, with the exception of the two broken strings, looking like it had just been played the previous day.

"Wow!" whispered the boy. "It's *magic!*"

"Shh! I know!" whispered Alexandra in return, glancing towards the kitchen in the hopes Mrs. Stuart had not overhead. She looked again at the violin. She remembered her father saying that everybody views things in different ways. Perhaps some people could look at a violin and see nothing special at all, while to others the magic would be clear as day. Alexandra hoped the magic she had seen when she first opened the case would carry over when she started playing this violin, and wondered if Robbie, or others, would be able to see that magic the same way she did.

"But can you play it?"

"Well now, I certainly aim to! It's bigger than my old violin, but I'll manage. I also have to continue teaching myself, though. The Maestro isn't accepting any more students. He told me so himself."

"You *met* the Maestro?"

"Yes, he actually came into the café when we were closing," she said, an air of resignation in her voice. "I know of no other teachers, either. So, I've watched the street musicians play, I watched the Premier's Competition when it was in Windsor, and I even went to two of the Maestro's concerts. Now it seems I must resign myself to watching others. Robbie, everyone says it's hard to play the violin, probably the hardest instrument to ever learn, but I won't let that stop me. I've watched the violinists all very carefully and it's not impossible to do. Someday I'll be a concert violinist and play in all the great orchestras around the world!"

Alexandra closed the case, stood up and moved towards the door.

"Well, I hope you can do it!" he said as she stepped outside.

Alexandra smiled and turned back to face Robbie, who was waving goodbye in the doorway. "I think having a magic violin will help. Don't you?"

Chapter 6

Alexandra rose early the next day without any prompting from her father. It was Sunday, and time as usual to attend morning mass at the grand St. Alphonsus Church. She enjoyed attending mass – but not because of any religious obligation, though she believed in God. She adored the pageantry of the mass, which she considered much like a performance. She enjoyed the booming organ music, the smell of incense, seeing the priests in their fine vestments, the parade of altar boys, and even the nuns who had completely covered themselves from head to toe, including their hair, with black and white habits. She often wondered if the reason the nuns kept their hair so carefully covered was because they were really bald underneath.

Sunday mass was, by default, the social event of the week. Local Catholics would gather in this ornate, hallowed building and listen to the mass, though few could understand the Latin. Alexandra would amuse herself by looking at all the ladies in their finely decorated Sunday hats. Sitting behind them offered her a splendid view of the wide assortment, and she would pretend the heads which were too plain or boring would be sliced off, leaving only the pretty ones remaining.

In attendance at mass that day was the entire Delmott clan. George and Clara, who had donated a substantial amount of money to the church, had their own pew near the front, a visible marker of their elevated social position.

After the final hymn was sung and mass ended, the congregation filed slowly out the main door and into the spring sunshine. All the Delmotts stood together talking outside the church, an uneasy tension brewing between Alexandra and Owen.

It wasn't always like that. Alexandra remembered when they were small they used to play together like brother and sister instead of cousins. Aunt Clara would often bring Owen to the café, and while their mothers merrily chatted away or busied themselves doing this or that task, the two cousins would sit on the floor and play with wooden hand-painted toys brought by Uncle George or sometimes even with Alexandra's dolls. Often the cousins would chase each other around the café, squealing happily through and around the tables and chairs where the customers sat – sometimes to their bemusement and often to their annoyance. The two cousins grew apart when Alexandra was only four – about the same time her mother left.

As they were standing and chatting about this and that, Clara's latest news caught Alexandra's attention.

"Sometimes good can come out of bad, Joseph. Owen has a new violin teacher!" she said as she ruffled and squeezed the boy's shoulder. "George went to Detroit and hired him. He's a very smart and talented musician. We're going to have him ferried across the river three times a week, and he'll come right to our house. George also bought Owen a new violin while he was there. It's much better than the old one."

"Well now, I do hope he enjoys them both," Joseph said looking at Owen.

George chimed in as well. "Yes, and this new teacher has a much different approach to musical education than Hergicksen, who is clearly past his prime. I think the fresh approach should serve Owen well."

"It might if he can control his temper!" said Alexandra, her gaze focused on Owen.

"Really now, Joseph, you must learn to control your daughter's rude tongue!" said George. "Is she *still* jealous about the lessons with

Sister Madeline? My my. Owen has a fine musical career waiting for him, but with such poor manners like that, your daughter will surely find herself working in a saloon serving drunks."

Alexandra looked round at the people still standing in front of the church. "Papa, excuse me please, Emma is about to leave!"

"Go on," said Joseph.

Alexandra left the small circle of people, not having the spirit to tell them anything about her violin or musical ambitions. Moreover, she had no time for Owen now. She rather enjoyed thinking about how recklessly people used that phrase, "I have no time" and its sister phrase "I'm too busy" because they didn't really mean that at all.

"Hello, Alexandra," said Mrs. Brindle, who taught at St. Alphonsus School where most of the local children attended. Her black-haired, bespectacled and freckle-faced daughter Emma stood next to her.

"Good day Mrs. Brindle," said Alexandra as she smiled at Emma. The two friends walked a short distance and began chatting.

"Alex! Have you heard what Owen did to Robbie? Oh everybody is talking about it!"

"Yes," Alexandra sighed. "I know all about that. He'll be all right though – I know that, too. Now let's talk about something else. What are you doing today? Would you like to come to my place? I have something to show you. I'm sure my father won't mind."

* * *

Joseph Delmott certainly did not mind, especially on a Sunday when the café was closed. He rather enjoyed it when Alexandra entertained her friends there in an otherwise silent café.

As soon as he and the girls arrived, Alexandra darted up the stairs, leaving Joseph to wait next to Emma at the counter.

"She's wasting no time, is she?" he said.

Emma only smiled as she waited on her stool.

Alexandra returned with the black case containing her instrument.

"Oh this is it!" said Emma. "Open it, please!"

Placing the case on the counter, Alexandra opened the lid with care. Emma leaned in closer, eyes wide, gazing at it through her spectacles.

"Wow, it's so *enchanting!*" she exclaimed, face radiant.

"Yes it is! I have every intention of playing it!"

"Before you do that, you'll need these," said Joseph, reaching into his pocket and handing his daughter a small envelope. He knew she would be pleased.

"Strings! Where'd you get them?"

"I have my ways, dear. But why are we talking? Put them on!"

Alexandra set about the task straightaway. Joseph was impressed at how his daughter, with her nimble fingers, wound and strung the new strings onto the ancient instrument with an assurance well beyond her years. Then, while plucking each string, she adjusted each of the four pegs on the violin's scroll this way or that until she seemed satisfied with the sound.

"Sister Madeline called this relative tuning," Alexandra said. "If you don't have a tuning fork or piano, it's the best you can do!"

"I suppose getting you a set of tuning forks is easier than getting a piano, so that will be my next project. For now, are you ready for your world premiere?"

With a smile on her face and eyes brightening, Alexandra lifted the well-played instrument to her shoulder. Before placing it firmly there, she tossed her head back once and nestled the instrument between her chin and shoulder. She placed the bow over the thinnest of the strings and paused. Joseph waited with anticipation while Emma looked on.

Alexandra took a deep breath and pulled the bow across the string. It rang out clear and crisp, filling that old place with a sound not heard from that instrument in ages. She smiled, shuffled herself on the stool, straightened her back, and did it again.

The beaming girl glanced at her father and Emma as she made each open string sing from the movements of the bow. Joseph was pleased at his decision to give her the instrument, and the look of pure delight on his daughter's face was more than enough reward.

"Oh Alex, it sounds great!" said Emma. "Can I try it? Please?"

"Yes, in a minute." Alexandra looked at the position of her bow over the strings before playing a short series of notes.

Joseph remembered his father playing this same instrument, the crispness and clarity of the notes and how the man had often warmed up before playing one of the hundreds of songs he knew by heart. The only regret he had that day was not being able to recall the name of one single song. He saw himself standing between two generations, an unworthy link connecting the past with the future. Now it became his hope that his daughter would find the love in this old instrument that he himself had missed. *Oh, if only my father could see her*, he thought. *If only Helen could see her.* He remembered how proud Helen was of Alexandra and how she had encouraged her musical ambitions. That had all come to end with her sudden departure when Alexandra was little. He wondered if she would ever return – or even if she was still alive.

The music stopped. "You try it now." Alexandra offered the instrument to her bespectacled friend.

Emma tentatively placed the instrument on her shoulder under Alexandra's direction. Then, grasping the bow with her whole fist, Emma awkwardly hacked at the strings and each one squawked under protest. Alexandra giggled. Joseph winced. Emma huffed and, after a few more failed attempts, handed the instrument back to its owner.

"Better to try and fail then never to try at all!" said Joseph, his words unsuccessful in soothing the pouting Emma.

Their moment of levity was spoiled when all eyes turned towards the sound of someone knocking on the café door. Professor Hergicksen had returned.

Joseph motioned towards the professor, who eased the door open so that the brass bell only gently dinged. He had his overcoat folded over his arm and his hat was removed. He bowed slightly after stepping in.

"Thank you for allowing me entry, kind sir. I hope I'm not disturbing you. I know you are closed today, but I was in the area and I wanted to stop by. I have something I'd like to say."

Alexandra had placed her violin behind the counter, an action which struck Joseph as rather strange. She stood pressed to his side, her arms around him and her head nestled against his chest.

Fixing his gaze on Joseph, the professor began. "I have come to apologize to the young lady about the other day, and it is my sincere hope she might forgive me."

Alexandra remained silent. Joseph looked at her face and noticed she was staring at the professor. Emma stood nearby, watching the professor, a quizzical look on her face. The professor cleared his throat. "There is a performance at the Detroit Opera House across the river Friday next. I am not playing, but merely going as a member of the audience. However, if it would please the young lady and you, sir, I would be honoured if you would both accompany me."

Joseph had taken his daughter to several musical performances in Windsor, even to some of the professor's concerts. To take her across the river to hear an orchestra at the world-famous Detroit Opera House would certainly fulfill one of her biggest dreams. Furthermore, they had never been to the U.S.A. even though it was within sight of Windsor. He thought it would be a great opportunity to expose her to professional music. He looked down to the daughter he was protecting and squeezed her shoulder. "Shall we go, Angel?"

From the shelter of her father, Alexandra gazed at the professor. "Thank you sir, but I'm afraid I'm too busy."

Chapter 7

Though other people would have accepted the invitation to the concert, it was not what Alexandra wanted from the professor. She wasn't the vengeful sort, but she believed the pompous old man didn't take her musical ambitions seriously, that she would be content with just going to a concert. She felt he was treating her like a child, trying to buy her off with candy, then patting her on the head and sending her off. Since her mother left a very demanding and stressful life working in the café to "take time to rest," as her father put it, Alexandra had to grow up faster than most children her age and her thinking reflected that – especially when she was challenged by situations like she'd just had with the professor.

Alexandra went up to her room as soon as Emma left for home. She took out every piece of sheet music she had, propping each one up in different spots until her room resembled a miniature practice studio. She wondered which of these fine selections would be the first song she'd play on her pépé's violin.

She raised the violin up to her shoulder, but paused. She wanted her first song to be something that had meaning to her. She sighed, but then something caught her eye. She smiled and placed the violin on her bed and reached up to the shelf. "Perfect," she said aloud. In her hands she held a small, polished, wooden music box which had belonged to her mother. She turned the handle several clicks and raised the lid. Musical excerpts of "Blue Danube" played, and

Alexandra watched the delicate mechanism within, remembering when her mother would hum parts of the song to her. When the cylinder slowed to a stop, Alexandra placed the music box back on the shelf and took her violin in hand. She moved the bow across the strings, and the instrument responded with a sweet, melodic voice – coming alive, rewarding her with a sound even Strauss himself would surely have been pleased to hear.

Following that, she played several pieces, including "The Maple Leaf Forever," "Soldier's Joy," and "The Blue and the Gray," a song popular during the U.S. civil war. She made up her mind to play her violin every day. She often wondered if her pépé had played it in every free moment he had and whether he would be proud of her diverse musical tastes, including her desire to become a concert violinist – the whole idea of which was now taking on a life of its own.

As the days wore on, Alexandra spent much of her waking hours playing, refining, and perfecting her technique. She recalled all the training she had taken under Sister Madeline. She drilled herself on technical exercises and played all the songs she already knew, eventually playing them all by memory. She remembered her father saying that one of the characteristics she inherited from her grandmother was that of being a perfectionist in everything, and so it was only natural that this extended to her music.

She became more and more attached to her instrument and practiced at every opportunity. She often wondered if her music carried into the café, and whether that would be upsetting or pleasing to the customers as they sipped their beverages and chatted.

* * *

Marcie Gionelli was the waitress Joseph hired soon after his wife left. She moved about the café with an easy, effortless grace.

"More coffee, please Marcie!" said a familiar voice.

"Charlie McKay!" said the middle-aged waitress, laughing. "You know the rules! You've been here longer than ten minutes. You're no longer considered a guest. You know where the coffee pot is!"

The big man grinned and winked. He poured another cup for himself and his friends.

As Marcie entered the kitchen, Alexandra joined her. "I think you're hungry, *Vogelein!*" said Marcie, using the German word for little bird that her own grandmother used to call her. "I think even musicians need to eat from time to time! Can I get you something?"

"Oh no, no, Marcie!" said Alexandra as she washed her hands. "I'll just make myself a sandwich. No need to trouble you!"

Alexandra deftly gathered together what she would need – several small strips of pork and vegetables. She started slicing them.

"Well, you're getting pretty good at doing that!" said Marcie.

"You mean I'm getting good at making sandwiches?"

"No, no," she laughed. "I mean you're getting good on the violin!"

"Thank you, Marcie! My biggest dream is to be a concert violinist someday, so I have a lot of practicing to do! I hope I wasn't disturbing anyone."

"Oh, no, no!" Marcie said as she cleaned glasses with lightning speed and set them up to dry. "Some of the customers have remarked that perhaps we've kidnapped a musician and are holding him ransom!"

"Hey, I'm not a he!" Alexandra said, putting her hands on her hips. "But if there's ransom money, maybe you can give it to me and I can use it to buy some music books!"

"You can be sure of that!" Marcie said before going back out into the café, leaving Alexandra behind the counter to eat her sandwich.

As Marcie served one table, from the next she heard Charlie calling towards the counter. "Play us something, Alex!"

Marcie looked as Alexandra, still chewing, got up and walked over to where Charlie sat with his friends. The girl swallowed and cleared her throat. "Well, Mr. McKay," she said, smiling. "I'd be happy to play for you, but – "

"I don't know if this café serves music, Charlie!" said Marcie.

"May I, Marcie, please?" said Alexandra. "Papa says it's always important to please the customers!"

Marcie winked at Alexandra. "Why not? Go ahead."

Charlie laughed and Alexandra scampered up the stairs.

"Sit down, Marcie, for heaven's sake!" said Charlie, motioning towards an empty chair. Seeing no harm in it, Marcie took a seat at Charlie's table.

After a few moments a beaming Alexandra returned and stood near the table. She positioned the instrument in the crook of her neck, her bow ready to strike the strings. "What would you like to hear, Mr. McKay?"

Charlie turned his eyes to the ceiling for a moment and stroked his beard. "Well, you know, back in Nova Scotia they always played fast tunes. Can you play something fast?"

The little girl with the big dreams smiled and played a rapid series of fast notes, notes as clear and crisp as a snowfall in January, followed by a lively Celtic tune. Marcie didn't know the name of that tune, but nonetheless she was delighted to be part of Alexandra's first real audience. Apparently the men did too, as they sat at the table and began to hoot and stomp their feet in rhythm. Marcie settled back in her chair and watched, impressed at the speed with which the fingers on the girl's left hand could easily find their place on the fingerboard, hitting the right spot every time. Moreover, the girl wasn't even looking at where her fingers were going. She played with a mischievous grin on her face, sometimes looking ahead, other times this way or that. More than once she played directly to her and Charlie.

While Alexandra was playing, Marcie noticed Joseph enter the café from the back door. She nodded to Alexandra as if to say *I'll be right back.* She rose from her chair and walked behind the counter. She stood with Joseph and watched Alexandra perform.

"I was out back and heard violin music coming from the café and not from Alex's bedroom window," Joseph said in a voice just loud enough for Marcie to hear.

"Your daughter is really getting good, Joseph," she whispered. "Customers say so. They tell me every day. Then today, Charlie asked her to play a song."

Joseph furrowed his brow. "I don't know that I want her playing for a bunch of ruffians."

"Why not? Look at them, Joseph! They're happy. She's happy. Everybody's happy! You always say you like happy customers, don't you?"

Joseph paused. "Of course I do, Marcie. They pay the bills. All right, well I suppose there's no harm in it – for now."

The two stood and watched Alexandra, with Marcie shifting her gaze between Charlie's glowing face and Alexandra's animated movements on the violin. Just as Marcie was leaving to rejoin Charlie at his table, another movement caught her attention. She glanced down and smiled, catching Joseph tapping his foot.

When Alexandra struck the final note, the sound of clapping hands replaced the violin music.

"Bravo, Alexandra!" Joseph said from behind the counter.

When Charlie finished clapping, he leaned on the table with one elbow, stroking his beard. He stood up and bowed to the fresh-faced musician. Alexandra offered her usual laugh and curtsied. Charlie reached into his pocket and pulled out some coins, sifting through them in his hand.

"This is for you, Marcie, but this one here, this is for Alex."

"Thank you so much, Mr. McKay!" said Alexandra, face aglow. "I really didn't expect anything! I'll be sure to save it in my piggy bank."

**

Alexandra never expected any tips. Any money she did receive she always stored safely in her piggy bank. "Save for a rainy day," her father would always tell her.

Whenever an opportunity to play arose, she treated each occasion as if she were giving a private concert. The Stuarts were one of her favourite audiences. Oftentimes she went there and played some new songs, and if she happened to be playing for them in their back garden, their dog Nelson would lay at her feet, pressed up to her leg. Robbie was insistent on playing the violin too, badgering his parents about taking lessons. "If you get into a fight, a violin is not going to protect you," his father told him right in front of her. So, to her regret, little Robbie Stuart had to set aside any violin ambitions he had – at least for the time being.

As the days turned into weeks, Alexandra learned many new songs and refined the old ones. She also enjoyed playing her violin in the park, sitting on a blanket under a tree overlooking the river.

One Sunday afternoon in late July, she was sitting with Emma under the spreading branches of an old maple tree. Alexandra had just finished playing, and the two friends chatted and watched the ships pass by.

"How old do you think this tree is, Emma?"

"Well, I think it's really, really old. Probably more than a hundred years old, maybe even a hundred and fifty."

"I think so too, because it's so large and round and fat. Can you imagine all the things this old tree has seen? I mean, it's probably seen every ship passing by ever since there were ships! Before that it saw Indians paddling up and downstream in their canoes, even the great chief Tecumseh himself. It probably saw the first Europeans arrive and watched as the British captured Detroit for a time. I wonder how it got here? I hardly think somebody planted it! Maybe it was part of the great forest, and because it was such a majestic and beautiful tree, the axeman took pity on it and spared its life."

"Or maybe the axeman didn't like this kind of tree, so couldn't be bothered with it," said Emma. "Honestly, I never think about such things."

"So what *do* you think about?"

"Well, I think about my homework, doing my chores, helping my mama cook. Things like that," said Emma.

"That's all? But that's so boring! I have chores too! I have a lot of them at the café, especially since it's just Papa and me living there. I never let that stop me, though."

Alexandra sat a moment, looking up into the branches. "Do you see that yellow bird up there?"

Emma looked up, scanning the branches before focusing her vision on something. "Yes, I see it."

"Did you know that Marcie calls me her little bird? It's *'vogelein'* in German or *'petit oiseau'* in French. I like it when she calls me those names. Of all the creatures, a bird is the freest. It can fly anywhere and, since it carries its own instrument, it can sing anytime it wants. It is truly blessed. I would love to be a bird! Would you like to be a bird, Emma?"

Emma sat motionless, eyes fixed and centered behind her thick glasses. "I should go home now," she said. "My mama probably wants me to help her make dinner."

Alexandra smiled, and the two girls gathered their things and set off for home. As usual, they walked together until they passed the train station before parting ways.

The train station was a modest size, yet there were always people coming or going or waiting. As they passed, they saw an old, dark-skinned woman in threadbare clothes sitting near the sidewalk. She held a cup in her hand with a few small coins in the bottom. She looked at up at the girls.

"Help me!" she cried. "My son, my son! My poor son is sick and I must go to him in Toronto! Please!"

Alexandra wondered what tragic situation had led this woman here. Though the odd person dropped a coin or two in the old lady's cup, most people tended to pass by, or look in the other direction.

Alexandra looked at the woman – then at Emma – then back to the woman. "I don't have any money with me, but if you want, I can play a song or two for you. Perhaps people will put money in your cup."

The woman looked up at Alexandra and, after a moment's hesitation, nodded.

"Alex!" Emma said. "You can't do that! You don't know who that is!"

Alexandra dismissed her friend's protests. She had seen other people on the street play for money, so maybe there was some value in that. It was worth a try. Alexandra placed her case on the ground near the woman and prepared to play. She lifted her violin to her shoulder, drew a large breath, and began. The ancient instrument resonated with a soulful, sorrowful melody, with drawn-out notes and lower, dark tones. She closed her eyes as she played, allowing her mind to wander, allowing the music to flow through her, to flow through her mind, her arms, her entire being. She felt quiet and at peace as she played. Emma stood silent. The poor old woman had long ago stopped wailing.

Alexandra's mind lifted, a new sense developing within her which she could not explain. With her eyes still closed, she could see the woman before her in an entirely different place and time.

This woman was now much younger, probably only fifteen. She worked someplace under the scorching sun with many other people, picking white shreds of something from tall plants that grew in vast, open fields. All the workers were watched by a man on horseback equipped with a whip and pistol. Aggressive dogs with big teeth seemed ready to pounce on those who dared escape the man's authority.

"Two-hundred fifty pounds is what they want me to pick today and I know I ain't nowhere near that and the day is wearin' on and my back is killin' me..."

Alexandra continued to play, the soulful melody spreading throughout the environs. With her eyes still closed, she was barely aware that passersby were dropping coins into her open violin case.

In a large home with white pillars, a young man, looking nervous, prepared to play his violin...

The train whistle shrieked. Alexandra, jarred by the combination of the visions and the train whistle, opened her eyes and fixed her gaze on the old woman. She stood in numbed silence, not knowing what to make of what she had just seen, nor how to react to this woman who had had such a difficult life. She certainly didn't want to say anything there and then, especially since a small circle of people had gathered around. They clapped when Alexandra finished playing, and some of them even approached and placed money into her open case, which contained an assortment of coins, and even some dollar bills. Emma stood by, mouth agape.

"Ma'am, I'm so sorry! I don't know what to say, really." She looked down into her violin case. "Oh, here, please, this is for you," Alexandra said to the woman. "I hope it will be enough for you to go to Toronto."

The old woman collected the money with her gnarled fingers and put it into her bag. She nodded at Alexandra and spoke to her in a strange accent. "Thank you ever so much! And what be your name, young lady?"

"My name is Alexandra Delmott, but you can call me Alex."

"Well now, I reckon that's a mighty fine name you have there Miss A.D., but Alex done sounds like a boy's name to me. So, good luck Miss A.D. with your career on the fiddle."

Alexandra, still unsure of what to say, smiled and nodded. "Thank you, ma'am. Good luck to you, too."

Emma, mouth ajar and eyes wide, offered no further protest to her benevolent friend.

Alexandra put her violin away and walked through the modest crowd with Emma until they reached the street.

"A.D.? Really? That's funny!" said Emma. "I've got to remember that. Hey how would you spell that so it sounds like how she said it? Maybe A-Y-D-Y? Well, I should really go home now. My mother's going to be worried."

"Emma, a really strange thing happened while I was playing for that woman!" said Alexandra, ignoring her friend's comments.

"Yes, yes! People gave you a lot of tip money, I saw it!"

"No, that's not what I'm talking about!"

"Alex, or should I call you Aydy? I really must go home now. I'm already late. Let's meet on Wednesday?"

"Yes, of course! We can visit Robbie," said Alexandra after a brief pause. "Come to the café and we'll go there together. Can you bring some of your mother's strawberry preserves? We shouldn't go there empty-handed. I have some things I can bring, too. I also want to tell you what I saw!"

"Very well, tell me then. Now I have to go!"

Emma hugged her and the two friends went their separate ways.

As Alexandra began her own walk home, she heard a familiar voice.

"Ah-hem, Miss Alexandra?" She turned round to find none other than the Maestro himself standing there. She instantly recognized him – not just as the old Maestro, but as the young violin player in her second vision.

*　*　*

Professor Hergicksen would never again forget her name. "Are you going home, Alexandra? May I accompany you?" The professor noticed Alexandra looking him up and down. The girl did not take long to give him the answer he sought.

"I'd like that," she said.

The two began walking towards the café. "I just returned from London and was in the crowd. I heard your wonderful playing and saw what you did for that woman," he said. "This really is what life is all about, you know, using your talent not just for yourself, but for the benefit of others. I wish there were more people like you in the world."

Alexandra blushed and offered him the first glimmer of a smile. This lasted only a moment before her expression returned to neutral.

"I do wish to again offer you my most sincere apologies for not accepting you as my student. Mind you, I still cannot take you as my student, but perhaps you can accept *me* as yours. Even at my age, there are some things I can still learn. There might even be a few things I can share with you. For example, perhaps there are some classical pieces you'd like to play. I do have quite an extensive library."

Alexandra remained silent as they walked together, the professor wondering if this aspiring young musician would be convinced by the depth and sincerity of his proposal.

"Well, I think that's a very good idea, Maestro. All right, I agree," she said. The old professor's heart leapt for joy.

Alexandra grinned, and a small, restrained laugh escaped in her voice. When they arrived at the café, the professor opened the door for his new musical colleague.

"When shall we meet?" he asked as she stepped into the doorway.

"I'm free Wednesday afternoon."

"Perhaps we could meet at 2:00?"

"I'm afraid I'll be busy at that time. However, I should be free at 5:00 p.m. Would that be all right?" asked Alexandra.

"Yes, it would. Do you know where I live?"

Alexandra offered a full smile to the professor as she disappeared into the closing doorway.

"Everyone knows where you live, Maestro."

Chapter 8

"George!" said Clara as she prepared dinner. "What brings you home early?"

"Hello, dear," he said, entering the kitchen from the back veranda and giving Clara a peck on the cheek. "I've decided I should get round to doing some painting in the guest house, and I wanted to buy the paint before the shop closed."

"We could've hired someone to do it!"

"Nonsense! They'd never do the job as well as I can. Besides, it's a simple job and I don't mind doing it. Now that I have the paint, I can do it when I get some free time."

"All right, dear. You know best."

"Where's Owen?" said George, sitting down.

"He's with his friends. I expect he'll return shortly," she said as she placed the ham in the oven.

"He should really be practicing his violin, Clara. Why did you allow him to go out?"

"George, dear, he had been practicing all morning, so I told him he could go."

"All right, then," he said. "Remember, the Premier's Competition is coming up soon, so he'd better be ready. I hear there are going to be many good players there. I've put a lot of faith in Franko to get him ready."

When Owen returned and washed up for dinner, the three took their places at the table.

"How's the practice going on your violin, son?" asked George.

"It's going well, Father."

"That's not what Franko tells me. He says it's slow, difficult and laborious with you."

"I'm trying my best, really I am!" said Owen. "He gives me such difficult pieces to work on!"

"Good. That's all the better. You need a good challenge. By the way, I've heard reports that your cousin is doing very well on the violin. It would be a shame if you were usurped by a girl, Owen."

"What does that mean?"

George rolled his eyes and sighed. "It means if you're not careful and don't work hard enough, she'll take your place and be better than you. Would you like that? Would you like a girl to be better than you? If you don't work hard, that's exactly what's going to happen. I will help you as much as I can, but the rest has to come from you. Remember that, Owen."

The boy pursed his lips. "I understand, Father. I won't let little miss Goody Two Shoes be better than me."

George smiled. "Good. Keep that attitude not just with her, but with everyone else. You see, son, people think that just because we have a bit of money we can buy anything we want. It's not true. Most things are impossible to buy. Honour, respect, and of course talent are not something that can be bought."

"But Father, I'm working hard on the violin!" said Owen. "Mum will tell you that!"

"It's not just about playing the violin," said George, rubbing his eyes and the bridge of his nose. "We have several matters here we need to address. First of all, you need to understand that your mother and I have been working hard these many years to build a good life not just for ourselves, but for you. We've established ourselves, are respected, and are making plans to achieve even more. However, we must be careful. People are watching us, Owen. They're jealous of our success. They'd take away all we've ever worked for the first opportunity they got and think nothing of it. For instance, if you go about telling lies, it can get all of us into a whole lot of trouble. It reflects badly on your mother and me. They'll wonder what kind of a son we're raising. What were you thinking when you lied about your violin? You know, when you get caught in a lie, no one will ever be able to trust you again. They'll say, 'Owen? Oh, yes, we know about him! He's a liar and takes after his father.' I can't have people thinking I'm a liar, Owen, not at all. Do you understand?"

"Yes, Father," Owen said, lowering his head.

Later that evening after Owen had gone to bed, George sat in his favourite chair sipping a brandy. Clara sat near him, knitting. "How are your social groups?" asked George.

"Oh George, everything is going so well! In the church group, Mrs. Bellemore is the new secretary and she's so strict! We need that! Mrs. Barker is organizing a quilting bee and Mrs. Tellier wants me to bake cookies for the church bake sale!"

"I wish you'd stop mentioning that name," said George.

"Which name?"

George sighed. "Barker."

"Oh yes, I forgot. I'm sorry."

"Yes, yes. When you mention that name, it stirs up bad memories."

"Yes, of course dear. We must always avoid situations which stir up bad memories," she said, her tone sarcastic.

"What are you implying, Clara? We've already talked about this. No more mentioning my father's visions or especially the fire. Is that understood? We've kept it secret for how long? Sixteen years? One false step and we could lose everything. Do I need to lecture you as I did Owen?"

"Of course not, dear," she said, returning to her knitting.

* * *

Mornings were the time of day Marcie loved best of all. She enjoyed the cheery customers, the fast pace of her work, the friendly banter. Now that Alexandra was playing her music regularly in the café, it added even more to the merriment. Marcie enjoyed hearing the different melodies Alexandra played – some slow, others fast, even some waltzes and resonating, deep love ballads. She knew that due to these impromptu performances, the café was becoming a much busier place. However, she found it difficult to keep up with so many new customers. Even Emma and her family were coming to the café more often, Emma soon getting into the habit of calling Alexandra by her new nickname, Aydy. Before long everyone was calling her Aydy – everyone, that is, except her closest family members.

"Marcie," Joseph said at the end of another busy day. He was working at his usual table, a mess of papers spread out before him. "Could you come here, please?"

"Of course, Joseph," she said, squinting one eye at him at his strange request. She sat sideways in the chair across from him at his table, ready to jump up. She pushed every scattered thought from her mind.

"Ever since Alexandra started playing her fiddle for the customers, business has increased way beyond what I could have ever imagined," Joseph said, looking at her over his half-moon glasses. "The place has been very busy every day and it seems it's getting busier all the time. I've been going over the numbers, and the workload. I think this work is too much for you to handle, so I've had to make a difficult decision."

Marcie knew she wasn't as spry as she once was, yet she tried to do her best. "You're going to fire me, aren't you, Joseph?" she said, sulking.

"Fire you? My goodness, Marcie, I'm so sorry!" he said, removing his glasses and reaching his hands out to hers. "I didn't mean to make it sound that way! No! In fact, I'm hiring two more people! I want another waitress and a cook. I want you to be the head waitress. Of course, I'll increase your salary. You'll be in charge of these new employees and the daily running of the café. Can you do it?"

Marcie rose from her chair and hugged Joseph, almost spilling his coffee into his lap.

"Mercy sakes woman!" Joseph said. "Sit down, there's more! I'm hiring these new people until such time as business dies down. I don't know that it will die down, of course, but soon Alexandra must return to school and concentrate on her studies. Knowing her, though, I think she won't have a problem spending some of her free time playing for the customers. We could also arrange her own playing schedule instead of these haphazard performances."

"Yes, of course, boss," Marcie said, nodding.

"I also want you to help me hire this new cook and waitress. Since they'll be under your charge, you'll be responsible for them. Naturally, I make the final decision when it comes to hiring."

* * *

Later that night when all the lights were off, Marcie had gone home, and the café was closed and locked, Joseph crept upstairs with his candlestick. Reaching the top of the stairs, he tapped on Alexandra's bedroom door. All was quiet inside.

"Angel, are you awake?"

"Yes, Papa," came the voice from within.

"May I come in?"

"Yes, Papa," she said. "Come in."

Joseph eased the door open, his candle cutting lines through the darkness. He saw all her things neatly placed about the room. Her violin occupied the night table next to her bed. The girl was already under the covers, which she had pulled up to her neck. Joseph put his candle down on the night table and sat sideways on the bed.

"I wanted to wish you a good night and sweet dreams. I also wanted to say how very proud I am of you." The flickering glow of the candle softened her cheeks and twinkled in her eyes.

"Thank you, Papa. I'm proud of you too."

"I'm proud not just because of what you've done with your violin," he said, "but also of the fine lady you're becoming. We have many blessings in this life we can count, but none can be more important than the love we have for each other."

"I know, Papa," she said, her eyes searching his face. "You've taught me so much, and I'm so very grateful." She shuffled herself into a sitting position and smiled. "I'm so happy you gave me Pépé's violin. It will always be the best present I could ever receive and I shall treasure it forever."

"I'm pleased to know that, but remember Angel, it's only a tool. It doesn't define who we are. In fact, all these things we have and we learn in life are just tools. We can do many things, we can speak ten languages, we can have top marks in school, we can have all the money and power and friends in the world, but it's our strength of character, our convictions, our integrity that make us the people we are. That's the real reason I'm so proud of you."

"Papa, do you think Mama would be proud of me? Do you think she still loves me?"

Those words always cut Joseph. He looked down at his daughter, at her searching eyes. Every time she asked that question, he tried to give an honest answer, and each time it became more difficult.

"My dear daughter, sometimes life brings us pain which no words can ever heal. I wish I could say I knew where your mother was, if she'll return or even if she's still alive. I know that she needed a long rest after working so hard. Let's just say this: wherever she is, be it in heaven or on earth, that she still loves you. You see, whether we are here, or whether we are there, we still love. Let's just say that she's loving you from afar."

"I really miss her, Papa. I hope I'll see her again someday," she said, sniffling. "I just hope you don't ever leave me. I don't think I could bear it."

"I'll never leave you, Angel," said Joseph, roughing up her hair. "Someday, though, you'll leave me when you start your own life with your own family."

"That's not going to happen for a long time!"

"That's right. So now, you can do well at school, be with your friends, help in the café from time to time, and play your violin."

Alexandra managed a smile.

"Tell me a story, Papa, please. Tell it to me like you did when I was little."

"All right," said Joseph, repositioning himself. "Once upon a time there was a little bird who lived with her mother and father in the branches of a great tree in the forest. They had a happy life singing songs, watching the other birds in the sky and watching animals pass by on the forest floor. Her parents would bring her many tasty things, such as worms, insects and spiders…"

"Eww!" Alexandra wrinkled her nose.

"Not so to a young bird, Angel! Now let me finish! The young bird grew and grew, getting stronger with each passing day. She longed for the day she could spread her wings and fly. 'How glorious it would be,' she thought, 'to be able to soar across the sky and weave through the tree branches as my parents do! I'll be so free!'

"Then one day, the little bird's wish came true – but not the way she had dreamt of it. While her parents were searching for food, a gust of wind pushed her right out of the nest!"

"Oh my!" said Alexandra, sitting back up again. "But it's so high up! What happened?"

"You see, the little bird, like it or not, had to fly, but not for the reason you might think. Do you know why?"

"So that she wouldn't fall all the way to the ground?" asked Alexandra.

"Yes, that's right! That means to survive. The moral of the story is that life is full of difficult situations, and we can never predict what's going to happen next. We all have to spread our wings and fly – just like our baby bird did. We can allow ourselves to fall all the way down to the forest floor and be eaten, or we can make a decision to spread our wings and not just survive, but to really live. So, you can do the same."

"But that bird had a mother!"

"Yes, and that bird had a father, too. The gust of wind came when neither was there. Of course people don't have wings, but we have minds. We use them when a gust of wind, problems, come into our lives. Now you should get some sleep. Goodnight, Angel. I love you."

"Goodnight, Papa," she whispered. "I love you too."

Joseph stood up and brushed his hand across her cheek. Taking his candlestick, he started towards the door, the glow illuminating his path and making long, dwindling shadows across the floor.

Stepping out of her room, he took one more look back at the girl who was watching him from the safety of her bed.

* * *

Wednesday brought the fulfillment of the promise Alexandra made to Emma – they would pay a visit to Robbie. Afterwards she would attend her first study session with the Maestro. However, for her visit to Robbie, she didn't just want to sit in his house, nor in their back garden. She wanted to go for a picnic on the banks of the little creek which ran through the woods just beyond the old Stuart place. She packed some fresh bread from the nearby bakery, collected some tomatoes, cucumbers and peppers from the café and packed up strips of salted fish. Emma would already be bringing some of her mother's strawberry preserves and perhaps a few other surprises from her mother's pantry. She hoped Robbie could scrounge up a blanket as part of his contribution.

Meanwhile, the "Help Wanted" sign in the café window had attracted a good many people, and there were just as many applicants lined up outside the door as there were customers in the café.

"Don't worry about us, we'll cope," said Joseph. "You go have a good time with your friends and enjoy your lesson with the Maestro."

Emma soon arrived, and the two girls began walking to Robbie's house. Emma carried the wicker picnic basket and Alexandra, of course, carried her violin. It never left her side.

"Oh Alex! You wanted to tell me something, remember?" said Emma as the pair walked.

"Yes, I did, but I changed my mind. It was like some sort of a dream, really. Not important."

Emma shrugged and they continued their walk. As they approached Robbie's place, Nelson, as usual, came galloping across the field to meet them.

"Here he comes! Look out!" Alexandra said upon seeing the happy beast bounding across the field. Like a large, overgrown puppy, he leapt at Emma.

"Eww, get him off me!" she cried, turning her face away and wincing as the great Rottweiler welcomed her with licks to her hands and face.

"I think he likes you!" Alexandra said, laughing.

"He likes me more than I like him!" Emma said, wiping her face on her sleeve.

Their arrival at the Stuart's farm was unannounced and Robbie was nowhere to be seen. The girls walked round to the back garden where they found him building a birdhouse. He stopped when he saw them.

"We've invited ourselves to a picnic at your place today!" Emma said. "Would you like to come? Can you bring a blanket?"

He placed his tools down and grinned. "Let me ask. I'm sure it'll be all right."

A beaming Robbie returned after several minutes with a blanket and even more food for their basket. The trio – plus one happy Rottweiler – marched off towards the stream which meandered its way through the woods near the farm.

"Isn't it a grand day?" Alexandra said. They chose a grassy area along the bank of the creek, a cheery spot in the forest and perfect for a picnic. The sun shone through the trees, forming intermittent patches of sunlight and shadow on the ground. Robbie spread out the blanket and the girls arranged a feast from the basket. Nelson sniffed about as if to ensure the area was safe.

The three sat on the blanket and began eating, Alexandra carefully holding her other hand under the one she ate with to catch any stray bits of food that might drop on her dress.

"I perfectly love summer," said Alexandra. "Except for when the fish flies come."

"Horrible things!" said Emma. "My aunt and uncle have a cottage near the lake and there are *millions* of them there!"

"At least they don't bite – unlike mosquitoes," said Robbie, swatting at an imaginary insect.

As they sat and enjoyed their miniature banquet, they chatted and joked about as good friends do. After a while, Alexandra stood up and got her violin.

"I'd like to play a few songs, would you mind?"

"Oh yes! Please Aydy, could you?" said Emma.

"If Nelson approves, so do I!" said Robbie, just as the dog returned and sprawled out on the blanket in front of them.

Alexandra loved this forest woodlot. It was so refreshing to the mind and spirit, and it was one of the precious few remaining in the area. No other venue could be more perfect than here in this paradise with her two dearest friends. She hoped she could encourage them to take up music so she could have her own little trio of strings to play with anytime she chose.

With violin in hand, she began playing an assortment of melodies, her bow dancing across the strings, the fingers on her left hand darting up and down the neck of her violin. As usual, she couldn't help grinning as she played. She reasoned it was much better to grin like a fool than to be like those sour-faced, stuffy old violinists who cared nothing of their facial expressions.

As Alexandra played, Robbie sat and swept his arms through the air as if he were a conductor, and Emma sat sideways, propping herself on one arm and watching, as always. After a few moments Alexandra closed her eyes, imagining that the trunks of the elms were really the grand colonnades in a great European cathedral. The forest canopy also formed a magnificent, vaulted ceiling – one worthy of all the artistic grandeur of Michelangelo. She imagined her friends with her in this cathedral, with Robbie playing the cello and Emma the viola. Together, their music would conquer the world, granting them the privilege of escaping to any time, any place, whenever and however they wanted. Such wonderful power music has, she thought, such majesty. Pure magic can be the only outcome.

In her mind, she could see Robbie in a small gymnasium with an older man who was calling out instructions. "Remember your stance, boy! Keep your left foot forward! Your left hand should be there to defend your face, your right hand ready to deliver a crushing blow to your opponent!"

Next, she could see Emma's mother. She was busy cooking and Emma was helping. "Why don't you take up something like Alex? You're such a lazy girl! All you do is eat eat eat!"

"But Mama, I tried, I can't do it!" said Emma.

Alexandra opened her eyes and looked at her little audience. Though the visions were interesting, and even a bit entertaining, they did not disrupt her playing. After a few minutes, Alexandra finished her song. Robbie and Emma clapped their approval.

"My goodness!" said Alexandra, holding her violin in one hand. "I could see you! Both of you!"

"What? Why not? We're right here!" said Emma.

"Robbie, I should have asked you about the boxing lessons, and Emma, I had no idea —"

At that moment, Nelson's ears pricked up and he looked towards the woods. In an instant, he bolted from the ground and charged. Alexandra placed her violin on the blanket.

"Where's he going?" said Emma.

"I don't know, but I don't want him rambling around in there," said Robbie. "He's going to get all covered with burrs and brambles and I'm the one who's going to have to clean him! C'mon, let's go get him."

Alexandra and her would-be musical colleagues waded into the dense underbrush.

"Nelson! Nelson! Come here boy! Get back here!" Robbie led the girls through the thickening woods, branch by branch. Alexandra guarded each step, pushing aside the thorny branches of the wild rose bushes and hawthorn saplings. Despite her best efforts to stay clean, she noticed her dress had picked up some burrs. She reasoned it was a small problem she could deal with before setting out to the Maestro's.

"Nelson!" she cried once more. A small distance ahead she heard some rustling in the leaves as the dog was pawing at something. "Nelson! There you are! Come here, boy!"

Robbie and Emma saw the dog and approached him. Alexandra noticed it was trying to get at a small, black animal with two white stripes down its back.

Then, it happened. The skunk reared itself and sprayed the three friends, but hit Nelson directly in the face. The dog yelped.

Emma looked at the front of her dress. "Alex! My mama's gonna kill me!"

Robbie appeared more collected. "C'mon, we have to wash Nelson's face!"

Meanwhile the dog, using its paws, was trying to rub its eyes. Robbie led him out of the thicket and down to the water's edge.

He scooped some water in his hands and tried washing Nelson's face. The girls tried helping, but the dog would have none of it. He tried to run, but with the size of the beast it took all three friends to restrain him – and all three ended up falling into the shallow, muddy water.

When they finally managed to wash the dog's face and had him under control, they collected their things and hurried along the pathway towards Robbie's house.

"What are you going to do about your visit with the Maestro today, Aydy?" said Emma.

"Oh Emma! It's absolutely the worst day of my life! No lesson today. I'm going straight home!"

"But you can't just *not* go to your lesson! The Maestro is expecting you!"

"She's right, Alex," said Robbie. "If you don't go, or if you're late, you'd be no better than Owen. The Maestro will think so, too."

No words from anyone could have helped Alexandra make up her mind more than those. She bid goodbye to her friends and trotted off to the Maestro's well-kept manor.

When she arrived, she stood in his yard, crying out at the top of her lungs. "Maestro! Maestro!" She saw several open windows and wondered if her voice would carry far enough inside. "Maestro! Are you there!? Could you please come outside?"

Before her voice became hoarse, the side door opened and the Maestro emerged, a puzzled expression crossing his face. "What on earth happened to you?"

Alexandra could feel her face becoming hot. She wondered what she must look like as she stood half wet, covered in partly dried mud and dirt; the smell of skunk radiating from her clothes.

The Maestro stood on the stoop, hands on his hips as if he were studying her. "Haven't we met each other like this before?" he said, laughing.

"Maestro, that's not funny! I've just had a rather unpleasant encounter with a skunk, a dog and a creek. I've had quite enough for today, thank you, and I think we should cancel our session. I'm really sorry."

The professor chuckled. "I think it's not your best fragrance, either! I don't know what you've been doing, but I think you're right. Off you go home now!"

Chapter 9

It didn't take long for Alexandra to get herself cleaned up after her encounter with the skunk, and in a couple days she couldn't detect any trace of the odour. She played her violin in the café every day, soon endearing herself to the new cook, Bill, and new waitress, Sophie. She enjoyed the compliments from the locals, and also those who had travelled from nearby towns specifically to hear her. Sometimes even famous and wealthy people would come by. One such celebrity was the whiskey magnate and area's largest landowner, Hiram Walker. On a cheerful day in late July, Mr. Walker and a small group of men arrived and sat at one of the tables near the wall. Alexandra watched them as she sat behind the counter sipping on a bowl of soup.

Alexandra found it curious that the men would glance in her direction as they spoke. Finally, one of Walker's men rose from his chair and approached her.

"Excuse me young lady, my apologies for disturbing you, but I understand that you play the violin here. Would you mind playing a song for Mr. Walker?"

"Mr. Walker? Mr. Hiram Walker?" she said, placing her spoon down. "Yes, of course. I'd be pleased to."

The man nodded, giving her a half-smile before returning to his table.

Alexandra pushed her soup aside, wiped her hands and picked up her violin, which she kept safely tucked behind the counter during the day when she wasn't playing.

To her, Mr. Walker looked every bit as much the rich man she'd heard about. He had a high forehead, grey hair, close-set dark eyes, a full moustache, and a narrow beard which covered his chin but didn't quite cover his cheeks. He was wearing a business suit, and Alexandra thought he was just a bit overdressed for this modest café.

"What songs can you play?" he asked in a clear Boston accent.

"What songs would you like to hear, Mr. Walker?"

"Well, I'm known as a whiskeyman, but most folks don't know I'm also a church goer. I'd be pleased if you could play both kinds of songs."

Alexandra fought to restrain a laugh, yet nevertheless smiled at the gentleman. She glanced towards Marcie, who was standing behind the counter, watching. Turning back to Walker, she raised her violin to her shoulder, took a deep breath, and began playing "Amazing Grace." She started the song with a series of introductory notes, and began playing the main melody with reverent feeling and emotion. The whole café was hushed as the music from her violin rang out and filled the room. She closed her eyes and continued playing.

A man, who appeared to be in his mid-20s, sat at a desk entering numbers into a ledger as the light from an oil lamp cut through the darkness. He looked to be studying these numbers without rest, and many papers were spread out across his desk.

"You know, we could buy that land across the river," he said to a young woman as she entered the room. "Our finances are quite good, Mary. I think we should take the chance. This seems to be the perfect time."

Alexandra opened her eyes just as she finished the song. Despite the number of people in the café, all was hushed. She squinted a bit a Mr. Walker, wondering for a brief moment about him and the man in the vision. Raising the corner of her mouth into a half smile, she dove headlong into the next song, a Celtic jig, playing it with lightning speed and rhythm.

After she finished, the whole café erupted in applause. Alexandra curtsied and Walker smiled and clapped with delight. He leaned forward in his chair and motioned with his finger for Alexandra to come over. She handed her violin to Marcie and bent down towards Mr. Walker. Placing his aging hands in hers, he put some kind of rolled-up paper in her palm. Alexandra took a quick glance at it and gasped.

He whispered in her ear. "This is your tip – and our little secret."

* * *

George Delmott continued to be troubled all summer by the professor's cutting, yet truthful words about Owen. Moreover, he was disturbed that Owen's progress on the violin wasn't going as fast as he'd hoped, while Alexandra was accelerating so quickly that her fame was spreading across the town, countryside, and probably beyond. He had often seen such determination to succeed in some of his clients and even in some of his adversaries. Those people would stop at nothing to get to the top, and he sensed the same thing in Alexandra. As the girl's popularity spread, he felt that sort of thing was outshining his own family's status and that, of course, would never do.

Late one night, when he was sure Alexandra would be sleeping, he dropped in to the café to talk to Joseph. They sat at the corner of the counter.

"Joseph, I've heard all about Alexandra's great progress with the violin. I want to offer you my congratulations. I hope she'll be successful with it in the future."

"Thank you," said Joseph. "She works at it everyday and really enjoys it. I wish you'd drop by sometime so you can hear for yourself. Bring Clara and Owen, too. She'd really like that."

George almost choked. "Well, you know things are very hectic at the office these days and every minute counts," he said in a quiet voice.

"But George, there's got to be a free minute or two when you can drop in! Things can't be that busy! Besides, you're the only person in Windsor who hasn't heard her play."

Nothing could move George Delmott from his position. He fixed his gaze on Joseph. "By the way, don't forget that the violin your daughter is playing belonged to our father."

"I'm well aware of that," said Joseph. "She's taking very good care of it."

"When Father died we decided his business should continue, and you should stay on as the manager. Thus far everything has been going well. Since you and I had no interest in playing his violin, you agreed I should sell it. So, I paid you your half of it and packed the violin in a crate with the intention of selling it later. I never did get round to doing that and in the end, put it in the spare room. Don't you remember?"

"Yes, I remember. If I hadn't been so pressed for every last dime, I would have kept it!"

"Not my problem. You actually thought you'd get away with giving it to Alexandra? Do you think I'm stupid? I wonder how many other things from our parents' estate you've pilfered because you 'needed the money!' Anyway, the fact remains that you gave the violin to Alexandra without my knowledge or permission."

"She's taking very good care of it, George. She knows how valuable it is. I'm sure she'd never let any harm come to it. Besides, she's inseparable from that instrument!"

"That's not the point, Joseph. It was not yours to give. You shouldn't have done it."

Joseph sighed. "Look, perhaps we can come to an agreement. What if I just buy it from you? How much would you like for it?" he said as he reached into his pocket.

George laughed under his breath. "No, *you* look, Joseph. You don't seem to understand something here. Whether I sell that violin or not is really none of your business. Of course I'm no longer interested in selling it. My son is making fine progress and I've decided I want him to play our father's violin."

Joseph glared at him, pursing his lips. "You'll actually take my daughter's prize possession away from her?"

"No, you'll do that," said George, his voice immovable.

"There's no way on God's good earth I could ever pry her fingers from that instrument! Besides, Owen already has another violin! Why does he need two? You can go to hell."

"No need for such harsh language, Joseph, but as you wish," said George. "I'm closing the café."

"*What?* You can't be serious!" said Joseph, lowering his voice after glancing towards the stairs. Leaning forward, he growled deep and low. "You haven't cared about that violin in years! You've never talked about it, and now you want it back and threaten me with the closure of the café, of our livelihood!"

"The choice is yours, Joseph Delmott," said the lawyer. "I've closed other businesses, sold the assets and re-developed the property. I would not hesitate to do the same here."

Joseph sat on his stool, eyes focused, lips still pursed. "I can't understand how you can be so pigheaded over a violin. Very well. You've pushed me into a corner and left me no choice. At least grant me this: give me some time to get Alexandra another violin."

George thought about it a moment and nodded. "Agreed," he said, smirking. "You have until the end of the month."

On his walk home, George felt relieved at having avoided another major catastrophe, believing he had done the right thing by forcing Joseph to hand over the violin. He knew the instrument had little monetary value, yet there was something strange about it. He remembered how his father acted every time he played it, the little, annoying comments he made each time he finished a song. On more than one occasion, George didn't even have to see his father play. It was enough just to hear part of the song from another room or even out in the yard.

It all culminated that day when he visited his father at the farmhouse to help with the spring planting. His father had greeted him at the door and finally told him, in detail, about the visions he got whenever he played that particular violin. He told George that he'd had a vision of him setting fire to a little shop, which later spread to half the town. George couldn't take a chance that Alexandra, who by all accounts was excellent on the violin, might be able to see into other peoples' memories as well with that instrument. He couldn't take a chance that at some point she might learn the truth about him and try to expose him for this crime – and, perhaps, other crimes he'd committed.

* * *

The next day, Alexandra rose early. Though it was only 7 a.m., the temperature was already soaring and she could tell, by the buzzing sound of insects in the trees that it was going to be a hot, sticky summer day. For her venture outdoors, she chose her light blue dress with small white polka dots. She would be more or less comfortable in that.

She gathered her violin and set off in the thick morning air to meet the professor at his study, singing along the whole way.

This time she walked right up the steps and to the side door of the professor's home. With a bit of trepidation, she knocked twice with the brass knocker. The door was answered by a middle-aged maid in uniform – a handsome, rather plump woman with greying hair.

"You must be Alexandra Delmott. Please, won't you come in? The professor is expecting you."

"Thank you ma'am," replied Alexandra, stepping inside. If it hadn't been for the maid, Alexandra felt sure she would have got lost in the house.

"Come with me. I'll show you to the professor's study."

Cradling her violin case protectively, she started down the black and white tiled corridor. As she walked, she drank in the sights of the professor's home. She marvelled at the polished oak panelling which extended half way up the walls, the old portraits, and the fine corridor tables adorned with fresh roses. The place felt like a combination of a home and museum. However, she could see no trace of a wife anywhere, nor could she see any portrait of the grand master posing with a woman. Alexandra wondered if he had even been married at all. If not, it wouldn't have surprised her. After all, she reasoned, a man with such a demanding career wouldn't have been able to devote the necessary time to raising a family. The thought made her a bit sad.

The maid rapped on a big oak door. "Miss Alexandra Delmott is here to see you."

The professor answered straightaway. "Thank you, Cora. Oh wait, Cora, could you bring us some lemonade, please?"

"Yes professor, right away."

Turning to Alexandra he said, "Good morning. Won't you please come in?"

"Good morning to you too, Maestro – and thank you. You have a lovely home. It's every bit as charming as I could have imagined." Despite the fact every possible window in the study was open, she could still detect the faint odour of cigar smoke.

"Thank you Alexandra, please, sit down!" he said with enthusiasm. "Make yourself comfortable."

"Thank you Maestro." She sat on the sofa and looked around at all the plaques he had from around the world, the shelves along the walls filled with books of music, and of course the grand Steinway piano in the centre of the room.

"I didn't know you played the piano, Maestro!"

"Yes I do. However, the violin is my first love. I find the piano a bit awkward to take anywhere on the train," he said, chuckling.

Alexandra laughed as she spoke. "Well, I suppose you're right, Maestro! I love my violin, I can take it anywhere and everywhere – and I do."

The stone fireplace, complete with a fine mantle, did not escape her attention.

"We won't be needing that today," said the professor.

"Yes it is warm today, Maestro, but autumn will soon be here. My papa likes autumn. It's his favourite season and it's mine too. What's your favourite season, Maestro?"

"Mine is spring. I find it rejuvenating after a long, dreary winter."

The door soon opened and Cora entered carrying a tray with two glasses of lemonade. She placed the tray down on the polished surface of the coffee table. With steady hands, Alexandra reached for a glass.

"Will there be anything else, sir?"

"Thank you, Cora, no."

She left the two musicians alone with their music and conversation.

"I have no money to pay you, Maestro," she said, sipping her drink. "My papa told me I have to save all my tip money."

"Remember, these are not music lessons in the strictest sense of the word, so no money shall change hands. As I said earlier, I hope we can learn together. We can meet three days a week."

"Shall we start?" she said, placing her glass down.

The professor nodded.

Alexandra smiled and set about to open her violin case. The professor watched. He took his own violin in hand.

"Let's start with an interesting technique," he said, looking quite pleased.

Chapter 10

Professor Hergicksen enjoyed his musical sessions with Alexandra. As the days passed, an idea occurred to him. Early one morning he stepped into the café, the brass bell clanging brightly. He saw Alexandra right away.

"Good morning, Maestro! Won't you have a seat?" she said, interrupting her work with the morning diners.

"Thank you, my dear!" He took a seat near the window. "I wouldn't mind –"

"A cup of coffee?" Alexandra said, smiling. "I know – black."

"Very good! You might now call me a regular! By the way, would your father be in? I should like to speak with him."

Alexandra turned and skipped off to the kitchen. A few moments later Joseph emerged, removed his cook's apron and sat across the table from the professor.

"Good morning, Joseph," the professor said amidst the chatter and clatter in the café.

"The same to you, Professor Hergicksen."

"Please, Joseph, call me Hergie."

"Very well, Hergie, what brings you here today? Did Alexandra have a good lesson?"

"Yes, yes, very good, but I'm not here about that. I came here because I wanted to speak with you."

"Is everything all right?"

"Yes, yes! I have not mentioned anything to Alexandra, but there is a new conservatory of music opening in Toronto. I am well familiar with the people who will run it, and I think it would be splendid, and serve Alexandra's musical ambitions, if we were all to pay them a visit. Perhaps we could call it a little musical holiday. It would also be a good opportunity to meet other musicians and to see what music is like in the big city."

Joseph rubbed his forehead. He turned his head towards the kitchen as if he was looking to see where Alexandra was. He rubbed his chin once and leaned forward.

"Hergie, your timing couldn't be more perfect. I was meaning to ask you something, too. Before Alexandra returns, I want to say it's a splendid idea you have. In fact, not only that, it's a marvellous idea. She doesn't know it yet, but I want to get her a new violin, so I would like to, if you don't mind, impose on your kindness by seeking your expert advice in getting her this new instrument. I can think of no one better. I believe there must be several shops in Toronto."

"It's no imposition whatsoever, Joseph. Nothing would please me more."

"Good. There's one more thing, Hergie," Joseph added. "Please do not mention a word about this new violin to Alexandra. Not a word."

The professor thought it was strange of Joseph to make such a request, but perhaps he wanted to surprise her. "Very well then."

At that moment, a smiling Alexandra came with two cups of coffee and sat next to her father. The two men were silent.

"What's wrong?" she asked, eyes darting between each man. "Did I interrupt your conversation?"

The professor remained silent.

"I have some news for you, Angel," said Joseph. "What would you say if I told you that the three of us are going to Toronto to visit the new conservatory?"

"Really, Papa?" she said before turning to the professor. "I've always dreamt of going to the big city! What's it like at the conservatory? Wouldn't it be wonderful to see how all the musicians work together? We could hear so many different kinds of instruments, maybe we could even meet some of the musicians? Oh it's like a dream come true!"

"You truly are a musician, Alexandra," the professor said, chuckling. "You're a born musician through and through."

"Of course I'd love to go, Maestro! Papa, may I ask Emma to join us?"

Joseph looked at the girl, pausing a moment as if he were giving her request fair and full consideration. "All right, you may," replied Joseph. "That is, of course, if Mrs. Brindle will allow her daughter to travel that far away from home in the company of yourself and two men."

"Very good now," said the professor, not caring how the situation with Emma would turn out. "Alexandra, your coffee is delicious, as always. If it's convenient for you both, I'll make the arrangements and we'll leave on Tuesday."

* * *

When the day arrived for the trip to Toronto, Marcie was already at work. She'd arrived well before opening time to prepare for the extra workload which would befall her, Bill, and Sophie.

As she arranged the usual fresh-cut flowers on each table, she heard the sound of light footsteps descending the stairs. She glanced once in the direction of the sound and, turning a second time, fixed her gaze on the young woman there. Alexandra was clutching her violin case in one arm and holding the front of her dress slightly up with the other. She was wearing an apricot-pink dress, and a matching bonnet was tied neatly under her chin.

"*Bonjour, mademoiselle!*" said Marcie, "You look *fantastique* today for your very big trip to Toronto! When do you leave?"

"*Merci* Marcie!" said Alexandra, all smiles. "The Maestro is coming here first in his carriage and then we will all go together to the train station. But first I'll prepare myself something to eat. I'm so hungry!"

"Oh you just sit right down!" said Marcie. "I've made French toast for you! I'll bring it right out."

It was a rare day Marcie served anything to Alexandra, but this time she not only served her French toast with syrup, but also sat down next to her at the counter and sipped on a cup of tea.

"Where's your father?"

"He had some errands to do. He'll return soon."

"All right," said Marcie. "By the way, where will you stay in Toronto?"

"The Maestro has reserved rooms for us at the Queen's Hotel. Papa says it's a very luxurious hotel, one of the best. I've never stayed in a hotel, Marcie, and I can just imagine what it would be like. Maybe there are servants, doormen, a waiter for every table? Wouldn't it be grand! Oh, I wish you could come with us! We'd have such a wonderful time!"

Marcie took another sip of her tea and placed her hand on Alexandra's shoulder.

"Now you go there and have a good time! Don't think about me; I'll get there yet!"

Alexandra frowned. "Wouldn't you like to travel, Marcie? Go on a bit of a holiday and leave Windsor and Essex County – at least for a while? I mean, the world is really such a big place and it's getting bigger all the time. Don't you have any dreams? I think everyone should have a dream, everyone should create..." She paused. "Create something in their lives."

"Well now, my dear, I have six children at home, no, seven! I forgot my husband, so it's hard to dream of anything beyond what I should make them for dinner the next day!"

Alexandra lowered her head for a few moments, raised it back up and sighed. "Can I play a song for you, Marcie?"

"Of course you can! But isn't the Maestro coming soon?"

"I have time."

When Alexandra finished her breakfast, she opened her violin case, removed the instrument, and turned a small knob on the end of her bow and perched the violin on her shoulder. "What would you like to hear, Marcie?"

"I'm not sure! I usually don't get asked this question everyday!" she said, laughing. "Maybe you can play 'Au Clair de la Lune?' It's always been one of my favourites."

"I like that one, too," said Alexandra, smiling. Marcie watched and listened as Alexandra gracefully wove her way through the tune. Marcie thought about her time in Berlin, how her mother and grandmother sang the song to her and, of course, of how she used to run and play with her little brother. Before Alexandra finished the song, Marcie noticed that the girl's smile had faded and she appeared noticeably somber.

"Bravo!" Marcie said. "You played it exactly as I remember it."

"Thank you." Alexandra placed the violin down on her lap and loosened the knob on her bow.

"Is something wrong?" asked Marcie.

"Yes. No. I don't know. I don't know what to think or what to say. I – I don't want you to think I'm crazy!"

Out of the corner of her eye, Marcie caught the sight of a horse and carriage stopping in front of the café.

"I think the Maestro is here!" said Marcie. The coach carrying Prof. Hergicksen had indeed arrived. A few moments later, Joseph returned.

"Are you ready, Angel?" he asked.

"Yes, Papa."

"I thought you'd be happier than that to go to the big city! All right then, let's be on our way."

He and Alexandra stepped outside. Marcie, wiping at wet eyes, smiled and thought about the private musical performance her boss's daughter had given her. She leaned in the doorway, watching them disappear down the road.

* * *

Despite her experience in the café with Marcie, Alexandra was pleased that her trip was beginning in such style. She viewed this as a taste of wonderful things to come. The professor, wearing a top hat and dark suit, swung the door of the coach open. The pair entered with Joseph taking Alexandra by the hand, helping her navigate the little step going into the carriage. He tossed their bags up to the coachman, climbed inside and closed the door. They were off.

They didn't have far to go. The train station was busy as usual as the threesome arrived. They saw a beaming Emma and her mother there along with several bags deposited near their feet.

"Good morning, Mrs. Brindle!" Alexandra said as she stepped off the carriage. Emma was equally well dressed for her trip to the big city, wearing an olive colour dress and matching hat.

"You all have a wonderful time in Toronto!" Mrs. Brindle said as she handed Emma a carpet bag containing what Alexandra thought Emma would need for an entire fortnight – even though they would only be away three days.

After collecting their belongings from the coach, they set off towards the waiting train. The big, hulking train stood next to the platform, and Alexandra could see the enormous black engine at the front. As the mechanical beast sat idling, she could see small puffs of white steam rising and evaporating from near its wheels, while lazy wisps of black smoke rose into the air from its main smokestack. The whole engine looked rather impatient, she thought. It seemed unnatural just sitting there, as if it would be more comfortable hurtling down the tracks at speed.

"Come on, Alexandra dear!" said the professor, who had just boarded the train, "Don't dawdle!"

The first class cabin was indeed everything she thought it might be. It featured plush upholstery, the finest patterned carpeting, sconces on each panelled wall, luxurious drapery and even tables between the fore and rear-facing seats. As the gentlemen in their suits and ladies in their fine dresses boarded, Prof. Hergicksen motioned to Alexandra and Emma.

"You two may sit here."

They were delighted. Alexandra sat near the window on the left side of the train, hoping to get a good view of Lake St. Clair as they passed. Emma seemed happy with the aisle seat. The two men sat in rear facing seats directly opposite the two friends, a table between the men and girls.

The conductor called out the traditional "All aboard!" and closed the door. A clanging bell seemed to wake the big steam engine from its slumber. It huffed and chugged, and Alexandra could imagine that engine coming to life, spewing a towering black plume of soot high into the air. Smoothly, the train began to move and the landscape started sliding past their window.

Alexandra watched as the town of Windsor gave way to the lush green fields and woodlots of Essex County. As she sat mesmerized by the passing scenery which flashed by her window, she imagined all this land as a massive forest – untouched by Europeans eager to clear away the land and establish homesteads. Now most of the forest was gone, replaced by vast farm fields, though every once in a while she could see the wounded land where part of a forest once stood, with hacked, splintered tree stumps protruding from the ground, logs and branches swept up into windrows to be burnt. Oftentimes she could see the orange glow of these fires all the way from the café and, if the wind was right, she could even smell the smoke.

Since it was August, everything was at its prime – especially the corn. From her window on the train, Alexandra could see ripples of wind fanning across the great expanses of those fields which had, years ago, surrendered their forest majesty to the advancement of humanity. Occasionally, she could see a small flock of passenger pigeons flying from one woodlot to another. She remembered her father telling her there used to be many more of these birds, millions upon millions in fact, so many they could blacken the sky at noon as they flew overhead. He concluded by telling her that the few which remained were an easy target for hunters and a cheap source of food.

She glanced at the two men sitting opposite. They were engaged in an animated, lively discussion about some topic, using hand gestures to reinforce whatever points they were making.

"Aydy?" asked Emma, "Are you going to play your violin in Toronto?"

Alexandra blinked. She turned to Emma and smiled. "What? Well, I brought it with me so I think yes – but only if the Maestro wants me to."

The train chugged steadily along, the steam whistle blowing at every crossing.

"I really hope he does ask you. But I have a question. How can you play it with your eyes closed? I can't even play it with my eyes open!"

"Oh that's because it's really a *magic* violin!" Alexandra said, winking. "That's why I can play it with my eyes closed."

"But I can't play it at all! Is it only magic for you?" Emma asked, her eyes amplified and made more inquisitive by her glasses.

"Oh, Emma!" Alexandra said, folding her arms in her lap and sulking. "You're making me feel so very low!" She turned sideways in her seat, facing Emma, and continued. "Wouldn't it just be perfectly dreadful if, after all this time, the whole thing turned out to be a cruel joke? If the violin were really magic, and it worked only for me, that means I don't have any talent at all!" She crossed her arms again and pouted.

Her father, appearing distracted, cast a wary glance across the table before resuming his conversation with the professor.

"I'm sure you can play it even if it's not a magic violin!"

"But Emma, I really do think it's a magic violin! How could I possibly learn so many songs so fast? People tell me I'm really talented, but even talented people have to work long and hard to play these songs!"

"But Aydy, you do work long and hard! You also have a special gift for music!"

"I don't know that I do. Also, strange things have been happening. I was going to tell you…"

"Strange things? Strange things what?" said Emma, getting her words mixed up.

Alexandra leaned in, cupping her hand around Emma's ear.

"Promise me you'll keep this a secret! Promise!"

"All right," whispered a hushed Emma, "I will."

"Lately, when I play the violin, I get very strange visions. Even today, I was playing a song for Marcie and I had a vision of when she was just a young girl. She was playing with her little brother in the yard at their house in Berlin. She was so happy."

"Alexandra, you're scaring me," said Emma.

"That's not all, either. I had a strange experience when I played for the lady near the train station and also when I played for Mr. Walker in the café."

"Did you have a vision about me?" asked Emma.

"Yes."

"What was it?"

Alexandra sighed. "That your mother thinks you eat too much and she wants you to take up a hobby like me. I had that one the day we got sprayed by the skunk."

"Oh my goodness!" said Emma. "I just can't believe it! How could you know that?"

"I don't know! I have no control over it!" Alexandra glanced towards her father to make sure he wasn't listening.

"What about the other visions?" asked Emma. "Were they bad? I mean, what were they about?"

"I'd rather not say, but they weren't bad visions. I wasn't scared and I didn't mind having those visions at all. They were real life-like. Did you think I looked scared when I played for the poor lady?"

"Well, no you didn't. You looked all right to me, just like you were concentrating on your playing."

"It's true, I was concentrating but at the same time I allowed myself to be taken up by the music. It really takes you into a different world, and Papa says I have a very active imagination. He also says that an imagination is like a brain – everyone has one but not everyone uses it. Right, Papa?" She snapped her head to the side, finally catching her father trying to listen in on their conversation.

"What's that, Angel?" he said, raising his eyebrows.

"I was just telling Emma what you said about people having an imagination but not using it," she said, her mood brightening.

"Ah yes, of course. Then again, some people have overly vivid imaginations, don't they, Alexandra?" He winked as he spoke. Professor Hergicksen appeared puzzled, and Emma just smiled.

At that moment, the steward arrived with their lunches.

Chapter 11

When the train arrived at Toronto's Union Station, the four descended the steps onto the platform. Professor Hergicksen was comfortable with these surroundings, but the other three behaved as if they were in a foreign country.

"Come on, this way! Our hotel is just a short walk from here."

The three followed obediently, with the professor leading, elbowing their way across the busy platform and through the train station. Alexandra carried her violin but the professor had chosen to leave his at home. He believed he had good reasons for that. He didn't want anyone to think he was trying to re-establish himself as a virtuoso, and certainly didn't want anyone to think he had reduced himself to busking on the street.

With their bags in hand, the four strolled leisurely along Front Street. As they walked, the professor acted as their tour guide, ever sure to point out some interesting and notable sights. When they arrived at the hotel, the two girls were rapturous with delight.

"Oh Alexandra, just look!" said Emma. "Isn't it lovely? We're royalty!"

"Yes, it's true," remarked the professor. "Did you know that your name, Alexandra, is a very royal and regal name? In fact, famous queens in Eastern Europe and England had that same name."

"I wish my name were regal," said Emma.

"As a matter of fact, it is," the professor said. "As we speak, there's a Dutch queen on the throne with your name!" Emma smiled in reply, and the four continued their walk.

Professor Hergicksen always enjoyed staying at the Queen's Hotel as he secretly enjoyed feeling like royalty himself. With its huge cupola its most notable feature, the hotel's massive façade spanned nearly an entire city block – and the hotel was nearly as deep. Rows of stately windows were neatly spaced along its width, culminating in the central focal point, the grand front entrance. Conveniently located on Front Street near the provincial parliament buildings, it fulfilled every expectation a traveler could have.

"Good afternoon, Professor Hergicksen and welcome back!" said the check-in clerk.

The professor acknowledged the greeting and turned his attention to Joseph. "I always stay at the Queen's Hotel when I'm in Toronto."

"I trust your good judgment, professor, and I see the ladies here do as well," Joseph remarked.

The clerk gave them their room keys. Alexandra and Emma would stay in a room adjoining Joseph's while the professor would have his own private room. All of them would stay on the fourth floor, the top.

While walking through the drawing room, the professor noticed Alexandra slowing down as she looked about here and there. "Don't dawdle, dear!"

"But Maestro! This room is so lovely and elegant! What is it for?"

"This is called a drawing room. It's not for art, though. It's from the word 'withdrawing,' and this is where ladies and gentlemen of the higher social classes can withdraw in order to relax."

"I'm not from a high social class, Maestro, but I can just imagine myself here sitting on that sofa and playing my music to entertain royalty whilst sipping tea."

"I'm quite sure you'd be welcome here, my dear," he said, just as a bellhop entered.

"May I carry that for you, miss?"

Alexandra clutched her violin case close to her chest with both arms. "Thank you, no. I prefer to carry it myself."

"We're grateful for your assistance, sir, but I think we can manage," added the professor.

"Very good, sir, ma'am. Enjoy your stay at the Queen's."

The four guests made their way up the stairs to their rooms.

* * *

The hotel rooms were just as luxurious and well-appointed as the rest of the hotel. By this time, Alexandra and Emma were fully engaged in their royalty fantasy and Joseph did nothing to dissuade them. "Young ladies, I do believe it is time for you to dress for dinner."

The two friends went to their part of the room and closed the door.

Joseph believed that everyone was having a marvellous time living and basking in this temporary nobility. That is, everyone except him. He knew the time was coming when he had to speak the horrible words to his daughter which would, in all likelihood, tarnish her holiday.

Emma and Alexandra emerged from their room, both dressed in elegant dinner gowns and appearing even more regal than when they were travelling on the first-class train. They had also taken meticulous care to do each other's hair up, too, swirled upwards at the back and presented nicely towards the front in the latest fashion.

Joseph had likewise taken the time to change into his dinner clothes, but unlike the young women, his merriment was decidedly muted. At that moment he heard a knock on the door.

"Excuse me, Joseph, are you ready?" came the professor's voice through the wood.

Joseph swung the door open. "I am almost ready sir. However, would you mind escorting young Emma to the dining room please? Alexandra and I will follow shortly."

The professor squinted at Joseph. "Of course, if you like. I would be pleased to escort the young Miss Emma to dinner."

Emma joined the professor and the two set off towards the hotel's main dining room. "Don't be long!" said Emma, turning back as she walked down the corridor.

Joseph wanted to get this unpleasant task finished as quickly as possible. Even still, he felt like he was about to slaughter some innocent creature, to betray his daughter and dash her hopes. His heart was pounding and he began to sweat.

"Papa, what's wrong?" asked Alexandra. "Are you all right? Are you ill?"

"Please sit down. I must talk to you about something."

"About what, Papa?" said Alexandra as she sat ladylike in one of the upholstered armchairs. Joseph sat in the one next to her.

"Angel, I'm afraid I've made a terrible mistake."

"What is it, Papa? Please tell me! What happened? Is there a problem with the café? You're not going to give me up for adoption, are you? Oh I couldn't bear losing you like I lost Mama!"

Joseph sat leaning forward in his chair, hands clasped together over his knees. His desire to reduce the drama of the news had met with complete and absolute failure. Alexandra began caressing the back of his head, and he turned to look at her, noticing that her eyes were beginning to moisten.

"Whatever it is we can manage it, Papa, but *please* tell me."

Joseph drew a ragged breath and sat up. "Angel, I gave you my father's violin because I knew you would cherish it, play it and love it every bit as much as he did. The problem…" he sighed. "The problem is that it belongs to your Uncle George. He wants it back in order to give it to Owen. He's quite insistent on this point and nothing I say or do can change his mind. I have no choice. I must return the violin. I am so sorry."

"No," said Alexandra. By her tone of voice, Joseph could tell that her resolve seemed to be cast in iron, unshakable as a mountain. "You're not going to give it back to him. I will."

Joseph looked up. Alexandra's face was flushed and the tears that had welled up in her eyes had already run down her cheeks, yet she looked so brave and beautiful. She sniffled and wiped her cheeks with the backs of her hands.

With a voice sounding like it could break any moment, she continued. "Papa, I remember you told me the violin was only a tool. I can get another violin someday. Owen can play Pépé's."

"I promise, Angel, we will get you another violin before we leave Toronto," he said, taking her hand in his. "I've already asked the professor to help us buy one, and he agreed. He knows some excellent luthiers in the city."

"Are you sure, Papa? I can wait, it's all right."

"I am going to get you a fine violin my dear, and no one can ever have any rights to it except you." He was as firm in his resolve as she was in hers.

"Whatever violin you get me, Papa, I promise I'll cherish it always."

Joseph and Alexandra stood up together and embraced. They left the hotel room, making their way to the dining room to join the professor and Emma.

"Welcome, you two," said Professor Hergicksen, smiling and rising from his chair while Emma sat and watched. "I trust everything is all right?"

"It is, Hergie," said Joseph. "We just had a little father-daughter conversation, and all is well." He pulled a chair out for Alexandra and she took her place at the table.

Dinner at the Queen's Hotel in Toronto was truly a culinary experience. They had the best of everything – triple-plated cutlery, crystal water pitchers, glasses for cold and hot water, English bone china and fresh-cut flowers on every table. All of it was carefully set out on the finest linen tablecloth with embroidered serviettes. It was difficult for Joseph to imagine that there were people who ate like this every day. He assumed the professor had long ago taken such luxury for granted.

After they examined their menus, the maître d' arrived and took everyone's order, but didn't write a single thing down. "Yes sir," and "Yes ma'am," and "Will there by anything else?" were all he seemed to say.

After the maître d' left, Joseph turned his attention to the professor. "Hergie, I understand that you had a long career in music. If I may ask, is it possible for other people to be as successful as you've been?"

"Good question, Joseph," replied the professor. "Normally, no. However, with me, all is not as it appears to be. I come from a family of investors, and my father had business interests in companies around the world. He also bought and sold stocks and bonds – something which I continue to do to this day. However, these activities never did occupy all my time, so I was able pursue what I really love – music. When I retired, I returned to Canada and bought my house in Sandwich."

"Interesting story, Hergie. Thank you."

The professor smiled.

"I have a question, too, Maestro!" said Alexandra.

"You may ask," said the professor.

"Could you please tell me where you got your violin? What's the story behind it? I think everyone has a story to tell about how they got anything, and I would really like to hear yours. Would you mind?"

"Well," said the professor, "I'd be happy to tell you if you'd really like to hear."

"Oh, yes, please!" said Alexandra, sitting upright in her seat. Emma raised her eyebrow sceptically.

"As you may well know, I was born and raised in Toronto and received my musical education here as well. After graduation I went overseas to England and joined an orchestra where I played and taught for many years. I already had a violin by then, but it's not the same one I use now. I played in France, Germany, and Hungary. I eventually went to Kiev and played there with their best orchestras. For Christmas one year I was given this fine instrument by one of the young musicians, and I still have it to this very day. I treasure it as you treasure yours."

Alexandra squinted at him. "Oh that's marvellous, thank you so very much Maestro! But –"

"You're welcome!" he said. "Now that's enough about my violin. What about yours?" he asked, leaning forward on one elbow. "What's the story of *your* violin?"

"The story of my violin really begins tomorrow, Maestro. I'm giving my present one to Owen." She glanced at her father and smiled.

"Aydy! No!" said Emma.

Professor Hergicksen sat back in his chair. "You're giving your violin to Owen? Do you happen to know what he did to the last one?"

"He won't destroy this one, Maestro. Frankly speaking, I hope he comes to love it. He was a good player at one time and I'm sure he can be again."

"I don't understand why you'd ever do such a thing!" He turned to Joseph. "Never mind. You have your reasons, whatever they are, and I won't meddle in your affairs by pressing the issue. However, before we leave this subject I would like to go on record as saying this is not a good idea, not at all, Joseph. In any event, it's your choice. I do hope everything will be just as you say."

Emma stared at her friend and did not speak. When they finished their meal, the professor motioned for the maître d'. "One bill, right here," he said. After thanking the professor, they all stood up and left the hotel, putting aside this conversation. Following an evening stroll along the Toronto waterfront, the four returned to their rooms for the evening.

Alexandra and Emma went to their room to ready themselves for bed while Joseph scanned the local newspaper from his room. After a short time, the door adjoining the two rooms opened and Alexandra emerged.

"Goodnight, Papa, and thank you for such a splendid day! Please don't fret over the violin. Everything will be all right."

"Angel, why don't you allow me to bring the violin to Owen? You've been through so much already and remember, the mistake was all mine."

"No, Papa," she sweetly insisted as she kissed him goodnight on the cheek. "I'll bring it myself." She started back to her room, but suddenly stopped. She turned back to her father and smiled. "I want to play a song for Owen."

Chapter 12

The next morning found Alexandra rising early. Emma had started kicking her in her sleep, so she felt it just as well to get up and start the day. Besides, she wanted to go down to that drawing room and perhaps play some songs quietly before breakfast.

She donned her blue dress with white polka dots, adding a white sash around her waist. After writing a note to Emma, she took her violin and went down to the drawing room. Nobody was there except for a hotel worker arranging flowers in the lobby. She positioned herself on the divan, back straight, pretending she was a princess. Taking her violin in hand, she drank in the atmosphere of that ornate little room.

She closed her eyes and played the first song that came to her mind. Her bow barely touched the strings as she played an assortment of melodies, some longer than others. She allowed her mind to wander away with the highs and lows of the music, imagining the others who had sat on this very same divan and dreamed.

The sun shone in a cloudless sky as a young man strolled down a cobbled street, arm in arm with a young, blond-haired woman. They walked past many ornate buildings, even a great cathedral with golden domes that shimmered and sparkled in the sunshine. The couple looked so happy together. They were chatting and laughing, and she spoke with a strange, foreign accent. They were in the company of friends, most of whom were speaking a different language. However, this did not appear to bother the man. He was glowing; he looked so full of energy, so full of life.

Upon finishing her song, Alexandra opened her eyes to find the Maestro listening from a chair opposite her divan.

"Good morning, my dear. Please don't mind me. I was just enjoying your music."

"Oh Maestro! I'm so embarrassed!" she said, trying to push the vision from her mind. "I hope I wasn't making too many mistakes!"

"Nonsense!" he said, chuckling. "I'm astonished at this gift you have for playing the violin. I wish I could have done that at your age. You know, I started when I was five, and even with all the dogged practice I had, when I was twelve I was nowhere near as good as you are now."

Alexandra could feel her face warming at the compliment. "Thank you, Maestro. I don't know that I deserve all the credit, though."

The professor leaned forward, elbows on his knees. He looked plainly at her. She recognized that look in him; he always sat like that whenever he had something serious to say.

"When I first met you on that rainy day in the café, I knew you were different. When you asked, no, *pleaded* with me to teach you, I really wanted to do it, you know. I really did. I wanted you for a student. You were so enthusiastic, so eager to learn, so unlike your cousin, so unlike anyone else I've ever met. I'm such a stubborn old fool!"

Alexandra smiled politely. "All is forgotten, Maestro. Do you know if the restaurant is open? I'd not mind some breakfast. Would you care to join me?"

Joseph and Emma soon joined Alexandra and the professor for breakfast, and afterwards it was time to visit the conservatory. Alexandra hoped that after their visit they could go shopping and perhaps visit the luthier as her father had promised. This was one of the rare times she let her violin out of her sight. However, it was safely locked in their hotel room so she didn't need to worry. After all, she reasoned there'd be no point carrying two violins.

On their way to the conservatory they walked past many interesting buildings, some with large canvass awnings, as Delmott's Café had, while other shops and homes were clad with white-painted siding and elegant verandas. When they walked past one particular home, Alexandra noticed a group of girls, poorly dressed, lined up outside the front door as if they were waiting to enter.

"What's that place, Maestro?" Alexandra asked.

"That, my dear, is a residential school for girls," he replied.

"What does that mean?"

"It's a special place for girls – there's a different one for boys – who have no parents or whose parents are no longer able to care for them. They come from all different parts of the province to live and study here until they're old enough to make their own way in this world."

"Can they study music there?"

"No, I'm afraid not. It's just a place to learn the basic fundamentals of life, and nothing more," he said.

"It's so tragic, Maestro, to think of girls my age living in that horrible place and not being able to do anything creative!"

The professor nodded his agreement as they walked past the residential school and around the corner. At last they arrived at their destination – the conservatory.

The conservatory was located on the corner of Dundas and Yonge Streets in a rather plain-looking building. The professor had said that it wouldn't be officially open until September, but he was well acquainted with the people who would run it, and thus could take his guests for a tour. Even before reaching the building, Alexandra could already hear the sound of cellos, basses and all manner of screeching from the string section, occasionally punctuated by the blast from a brass instrument. They climbed the steps and went inside.

"Welcome Professor!" said the attendant, "What brings you into town?" Alexandra was pleased that everyone knew the professor, even in a giant city like Toronto.

"Well, well, it looks great! I'm really impressed!" said the professor. "I've come to visit your great Conservatory with my friends and perhaps see a few familiar faces!"

"Very well, sir. Make yourselves at home."

Alexandra browsed around while the professor chatted with different people. She strolled about with Emma, eyes glowing and mind wandering.

"Do you play anything?" asked a young musician from behind her back.

She turned around to find a young man of about sixteen or so. He had reddish brown hair and an eastern Canadian accent.

"I beg your pardon, sir?" she said.

"Hello, my name is Alfred and I play the cello. I'm from New Brunswick."

"Alexandra Delmott. I play the violin. Some people call me Alex and others call me Aydy. This is my friend Emma. Someday she'll play the violin, too."

"Oh, I've heard about you," said Alfred, smiling and shaking his finger. "You're getting quite a reputation, you know. What brings you to Toronto? Are you going to study music here?"

"No, I'm just here with my father, Professor Hergicksen and Emma to visit the conservatory – and to get a new violin."

"Maybe you'd like to play something? I'm sure you can borrow somebody's violin. There are plenty of them here."

For the first time, Alexandra felt compelled to turn down an opportunity to play. This was not because she didn't want to, but because she wasn't sure she could do it at all. She needn't have worried, though. She was rescued by yet another stranger.

"Alfred! Come here! We're getting ready to start!" shouted a woman from across the room.

"Excuse me, I'm so sorry," said Alfred. "I'm afraid I'm needed in the quartet. You're welcome to listen if you like."

The professor and Joseph soon arrived and they all took a seat. The quartet played Boccherini's "La Musica Notturna delle Strade di Madrid." Alexandra, as always, studied their fingering movements, concentrating her attention on the violists and violinists. Occasionally she would glance at the professor if she heard a mistake and he, in turn, would look at her. Joseph and Emma seemed oblivious.

After visiting the Conservatory, they went shopping at some of the local clothiers. Alexandra remembered her father saying that no trip to the big city would be complete without a shopping trip, and so she relished the opportunity to do so with Emma. The two friends tried on a variety of different dresses, mostly practical ones they could wear for the upcoming school year. Alexandra also bought, and even wore out of the store, a mustard-yellow cardigan sweater which complemented her dress well. Finally it was time to visit the luthier.

"You know, my dear, there are many luthiers in Toronto," said the professor as they meandered their way along the crowded sidewalks. "Each one of these luthiers plies his trade; I dare say they're all trying to establish themselves as North America's answer to Antonio Stradivari! Try as they might, not all of them are good. However, you needn't worry. I know who the good and bad ones are. We're going to one on Adelaide Street, not far from here."

"I trust your good judgment, Maestro." Alexandra thought him to be the perfect man for the job.

"You know, Hergie," said Joseph, "I don't think I can afford a Stradivarius violin!"

"Well my good sir, it should give you some level of comfort to know I can't afford one, either. I dare say that a Strad in good condition is worth a king's ransom!"

"Very good then! Thank you, Hergie. Value versus price it will be. We shall nonetheless choose a fine instrument. I'm quite certain that this violin will not be her last." Joseph turned to Alexandra. "Right, Angel?"

"Well yes of course Papa, that's right," she said, a glimmer of hope boosting her spirits.

The luthier's shop smelled of freshly cut wood punctuated by the faintest hint of varnish. There was a small work bench in the centre of the room with violins and violas in various stages of construction, some of which appeared to be held together with many small clamps. An assortment of strange tools was spread out on the workbench while finished violins hung on pegs affixed to the walls.

"Perhaps this one will suit you?" offered the luthier, an older man near the professor's age.

Alexandra tried to look enthusiastic about this new violin, believing that if she looked enthusiastic enough then maybe she might become so. She put the violin on her shoulder with deft familiarity. Looking straight down the strings to the scroll, it looked almost exactly like her grandfather's violin, except there was no notch in the fingerboard and the whole violin was somewhat lighter in colour. Also no finger marks were present on the fingerboard at all. Any marks made would now be her own.

"Do you like it, Angel?" asked Joseph. "Why don't you try it?"

It was certainly a fine instrument crafted by a professional luthier, and it was really quite beautiful. It fit well on her shoulder and she felt strangely comfortable with it.

Alexandra smiled, sighed, and took the bow. She decided to play "The Kesh Jig," a lively Celtic dance tune.

She held the bow in the usual way, striking a series of notes. It was not what she expected, not as she remembered.

"Is everything all right?" asked Joseph. As usual, Emma sat and stared and the professor watched.

"One minute, please," said Alexandra. She took a deep breath and tried calming herself.

When she played again, the violin resonated sweetly in the luthier's shop. Her fingers seemed to remember where to go, and they matched perfectly with the particular string she was bowing at the time. She even managed that trademark smile everyone knew so well. She hadn't lost a thing. Everything she learned on her grandfather's violin she could now play on this one, and she was delighted, except for one thing – she felt a bit sad at the thought that maybe her grandfather's violin had no magic in it after all.

Alexandra tried several violins, but returned to the first. "I like this one best of all," she said.

"Well, I think we've settled that!" said the professor. "Shall we be on our way?"

* * *

Before long, they found themselves spending their last night in the hotel. After the lights had gone out, the two girls lay awake in bed, talking. Emma thought this to be the perfect time to ask her questions.

"Why are you giving your grandfather's violin to Owen? It doesn't make any sense to me."

"Papa told me I ought to give it to him because he made a mistake giving it to me in the first place," whispered Alexandra. "It really belonged to Uncle George, but Emma, I've been thinking about it. I really know that violin has special powers. I mean, think of it! Do you remember what I told you on the train? How could I learn all those songs in such a short space of time if magic wasn't involved somehow? Most of those songs I heard only once in my life. It's really impossible; no one has ever done that! Sure I can play another violin now, but so what? Maybe it will happen to Owen too?"

"But, Alex," said Emma, purposely using Alexandra's short name and not her nickname. "What if Owen *is* able to play it? What happens if he learns all the songs with that violin helping him the same way it did you and what if... what if...."

"Then maybe he can regain his love for music!" Alexandra said, sitting upright in bed and turning to face Emma. "Don't you think that would be grand! I hold out hope for him Emma, I even pray for him every night, though I don't know that it'll do much good. He's really such a stubborn boy!"

"What if he gets mad and smashes it, too? Really, Alex, it could happen!"

"He won't do it. He would have to answer to his father, and he can't lie his way out of this one. But I have a strong feeling he's going to give it back to me."

"What happens if he gets those visions?"

"He can't get them. I know it. Don't ask me how, but I just know."

Chapter 13

The train pulled into Windsor at precisely 3:00 p.m. the next day, Friday, with the foursome aboard including their luggage, purchases – and two violins. Emma's parents were there to welcome her back, and soon everyone set off for their homes. Joseph and Alexandra walked back to the café with Joseph carrying their bags and Alexandra carrying the violins.

After greeting Marcie, Alexandra brought both violins up to her room, removed them from their cases and placed them on her bed. She positioned them up side by side and inspected them, comparing any differences in colour, texture, even the arc of the bridge. She would have to learn this new violin as intimately as she knew the old.

* * *

Before he prepared breakfast on Saturday morning, Joseph sat at his table drinking his usual cup of coffee and thinking about the few days that had just passed. He always enjoyed the peace and quiet of early mornings; it was his favourite time of day. It afforded him the opportunity to unwind, to think about life and to mentally prepare for the day ahead.

Just then, the morning quiet was shattered when Alexandra began shrieking from up in her bedroom as if she were being murdered. Dropping his coffee onto the floor, Joseph sped across the café and bounded up the stairs, taking them three at a time. He threw the door to her room open wide, and rushed in.

"Get it off! Get it off!" she screamed, sitting up in bed, arms wrapped around her legs. Tears rolled down her face and she bit her bottom lip.

Joseph saw the problem immediately. He reached down and plucked a big, black spider from her bedsheets. He carried the leggy creature to the open window and threw it outside.

She was still shaking after that encounter with the arachnid, so Joseph sat on the bed and hugged her.

"Everything's all right, Angel. Calm down, I've gotten rid of it."

"Thank you, Papa," she said, snivelling, "but how could you touch that thing?"

"Well, Angel, I didn't like touching it. It was very unpleasant for me, but I did it because it was necessary. Sometimes we need to do unpleasant things."

Her eyes searched his face.

"I have to give Pépé's violin to Owen today," she said, still sniffling. "That's going to be unpleasant, too."

"Well, true, what you're doing today is unpleasant as well, but it's also a very brave thing to do. It shows you have a strong character."

Alexandra frowned.

"What's wrong, Angel?"

"Papa, I don't understand something. You know so many things and you're so brave and wise. I just can't understand why Mama left."

"It's not easy for me to understand, either. That'll have to be a topic for another day. All right, why don't you get up and get dressed? I'll start making breakfast."

*   *   *

Following their usual Saturday morning meal, Alexandra walked up the stairs one methodical, deliberate step at a time. When she entered her room, the morning sunshine spread a false cheeriness through the place. Despite that, everything in her room was in order. Her sheet music was still placed round the room and her pépé's violin was on the bedside table, as always. She'd liked it there as the last thing she saw when she fell asleep and the first thing she'd seen when she woke up. For one last time, she put both violins on the bed and compared them. One was new and the other, though well-kept, was visibly older. She took a 'mind photo' of the two instruments, as she liked to call it. She believed that mind photos were even better than real photos, because the former you could bring anywhere and look at anytime, while the latter was dependent on photographic equipment.

After a few moments, she placed her pépé's violin in its case. Before closing the lid, she draped a small white cloth over the violin, folding its corners and tucking them around the edges of the instrument to protect it.

When all was ready, she walked downstairs to meet her father, who was sitting at his table.

"When you come back, I want to be your first audience on your new violin, agreed?" said Joseph.

"Very good, Papa, I agree. I'll be all right. I can do it."

"One more thing before you go. Have you thought of a name for your new violin?"

Alexandra smiled. "Yes, her name is Nellie. I've named it after Mémé."

"Really?" he said, raising his eyebrows. "You remember I told you that she wasn't all that fond of violin music."

"I know, Papa. I hope that's all right. The Maestro said if we dedicate a song to someone and play it as best we can, then that person will at least be charmed by the thought. I wanted to do that for Mémé with the whole violin."

"Well that's very thoughtful of you," he said as he escorted her outside the café.

Waving goodbye, Alexandra set off for her uncle's house with her beloved grandfather's violin in hand. As she walked, she turned round and saw her father standing in the doorway of the café looking in her direction.

It was about a two-mile walk to her uncle and aunt's place and Alexandra went along at her usual pace, trying not to get sentimental.

When she arrived, she went to the back door, which was the door always used by family and friends. Clara met her there.

"Please come in, dear," she said. "Won't you sit down? Can I get you anything?"

"Thank you, Aunt Clara, I've already eaten. Are Owen and Uncle George at home?"

"Your Uncle George had to work today, but Owen is home. Would you like me to call him down?"

"Please. I'd like to see him."

Owen came into the kitchen. He smirked.

"Hello, Alex. I see you have something that belongs to me."

"This was our grandfather's violin," said Alexandra. "Before I give it to you, I want to play a song."

Owen and his mother looked at each other.

"I've heard you've been making some great progress on the violin, Alexandra!" said Clara. "Please, go ahead and play a song for us. We'd like that, wouldn't we, Owen?"

Owen scowled. Alexandra knew he didn't like being outdone by her, but reasoned he had little choice now. She opened the case, placed the violin on her shoulder and began playing the first song that came to her mind – a simple, beginner-level rendition of "The Blue and the Gray." She played it twice through from beginning to end. The music resonated through the house and environs.

Clara squinted and wrinkled her nose.

Owen burst out laughing, his voice full of mockery. "That's all? That's it?"

"Owen! How can you say that?" said Clara. "Alexandra tried her best!"

"Mum, can't you see how amateur she is? Ha! And you thought I was fooling *you!* She's had all summer to play, and that's all she's done!"

Alexandra put her grandfather's violin in its case, replaced the white cloth over the instrument and folded its corners in exactly as she had done earlier. She closed the lid and handed it all over to Owen. "I'd best be going home now." She spun around, walked out of their kitchen, down the steps and to the sidewalk. She did not look back.

* * *

George Delmott had, in fact, been home the whole time. He changed his mind about going to the office on Saturday and, without telling his wife, took the time to do much needed painting in the guest house. When he heard the simple song being played, he thought Joseph had delivered the instrument and that Owen was playing it. He was pleased and smug that his plan had worked, and he continued happily at his tasks. After he finished, he returned to the main house where he found his wife and son already eating supper. He took his place at the head of the table.

"How was your day, dear?" asked Clara.

George ignored her question and started eating. "Did Uncle Joseph bring grandfather's violin?" Owen produced the instrument, still in its case.

"Here it is, Father," said the boy, beaming. "But Uncle Joseph didn't deliver it. Alexandra did. It's mine now and she'll never touch it again."

"Owen!" said his mother. "I've had quite enough! What's wrong with you? It must have been very difficult for Alex to give it over. You know, she really liked that instrument."

George was pleased that Owen was enjoying the moment and did not chastise him for his remarks. "Well, no matter. The instrument is in its rightful place and we needn't worry any longer."

"She was very polite, George," said Clara. "Before she left, she even played us a cute little song. Wasn't that nice of her?"

George Delmott stopped eating and glared at her. Then, bursting into a rage, he slammed his fist down hard on a bread plate, shattering it. Clara and Owen jumped in their seats.

"She did *what?*"

A look of terror spread across Clara's face. Owen sat solidly in his chair.

"Can't you see what she's done?" he raged, face burning, droplets of spit shooting from his mouth. "She's played us all for fools!"

"But George, really, it was just a simple song! What could be wrong with that?"

"Everything is wrong with that! How could you let her play? You have no idea what that violin can do in the right hands! You've no idea the kind of power it has and the kind trouble it can stir up for us!"

"You didn't say there was any power in the violin, George! I thought it was only with –"

"We're finished!" George cried. "We're all finished!" He put his head down on the table and sobbed.

Chapter 14

Delphis Delmott's violin sat unopened in its case, secure in the custody of George and Clara and safely stored in their wardrobe. George believed he had succeeded in achieving two of his three goals: First, to pry the family heirloom out of his brother and niece's hands and second to stop Alexandra from directing attention away from his own family. The third and most important goal, to protect the secret he had carefully guarded these many years, still eluded and frustrated him.

George Delmott was a firm believer in the old saying – the end justifies the means. He could also see that his son was growing up to be just as conniving as he was. Perhaps that wasn't such a bad thing after all he thought; the world is fiercely competitive, people have to be tough in this life and one must do anything possible, legal or not, in order to survive. George hated to be outdone in his professional or personal life, and he believed this little twelve-year-old niece of his had blindsided him in the most serious way possible: through her graces and charms, thereby making her not only the greatest con artist of them all, but the greatest threat to him personally.

* * *

Remarkably, Alexandra had quite a pleasant walk home and even felt a bit of relief after giving her pépé's violin to Owen, and pushed all negative thoughts from her mind. She liked strolling by herself as it gave her time alone to think without being distracted by the chatter of other people. On this particular walk she fixed her mind on being strong, being brave. She decided this was the perfect time to make a new start, and now she even had a lovely new violin to make that start with.

When she approached the café, she saw it was busy as usual. On nice days like these, little tables were set out under the sprawling canvass awning so that customers could sit outside. Since it was Saturday, Marcie had her day off and the new waitress, Sophie, was working while Bill was busy cooking. Joseph was running around filling in all the gaps.

"Hey where were you?" Charlie asked Alexandra from one of those tables. "We've missed Aydy and her fiddle! Won't you play us a song?"

Alexandra remembered telling her father he would be her first audience on her new instrument, but of course this man seemed so insistent. "Hi, Mr. McKay!" she said, "I was in Toronto the last few days and now I've just returned from my aunt and uncle's house. I'd love to play you a song, but I'm afraid there's a name ahead of you on my dance card! Give me a minute?"

"Sure! But don't keep us waiting!"

Alexandra entered the café and saw her father clearing a table. He saw her and spoke first. "Hi, Angel! How'd it go today?"

"Oh, Papa! It went really well! It wasn't nearly as hard as I thought!" She sprang up and down on the balls of her feet several times, hands clasped behind her back. "I gave the violin to Owen! I did it!" she said, switching to twisting back and forth on her feet, her dress swirling around her legs in response to her movements.

"I'm so very proud of you, Angel!"

"Aunt Clara was there and she was really so nice to me! She's such a sweet aunt! Papa, I only realized now how much I really miss her! But Owen, oh, he's so sad and hurt and lonely. And Uncle George…" She stopped moving and stood still, looking down at the floor, her voice trailing off.

"What about Uncle George?"

"Oh I didn't see Uncle George there, Papa," she said matter-of-factly. "Aunt Clara said he was working, but I –"

"Well I see who she's saved her best dance for! Hey boss, can we be next?" said Charlie, walking in and roughing up Joseph on the shoulder.

Joseph looked at Alexandra and winked, but spoke to Charlie. "Sure, if it's fine by her, it's fine by me." He turned to face Charlie. "May I join you, though?"

Alexandra smiled and dashed off upstairs to get her new violin.

When she returned, she found her father sitting outside at one of the tables talking to Charlie. Both men sat straight up in their chairs when the young musician presented herself and, smiling, she curtsied before she began.

She played some of her lively melodies, her bow dancing and twisting gracefully across the strings while the fingers on her left hand obeyed her commands like good little soldiers. All the patrons of the café wandered outside, and they clapped and stomped to her rhythm. Alexandra roamed through the crowd, to each person and played gaily for them. She played to a young couple, to somebody's old mémé and pépé, to the young family with a baby, even to Sophie and Bill who had interrupted their work for a few moments. She even played to café regulars Mrs. Tellier and Mrs. Labonte. It was a miracle her right arm hadn't banged into anyone, and she felt like her old self again. She always tried to do her best whenever she played, remembering the wise proverb the Maestro once told her: "You're only as good as your last performance."

* * *

As the late day sun dipped below the horizon, magnificent shades of pink and red emblazoned the clouds and scattered these colours across the wide dome of the twilight sky. Joseph remembered when this time of day belonged to the lamplighters, who until the previous year set about their work diligently going up and down the streets lighting each gas lamp, in turn, with remarkable speed and efficiency. Now the streets near the café were lit using electric lamps suspended on wires over the middle of the streets. Though many houses and businesses were using electricity, it was a rather unreliable commodity at best and subject to frequent outages. Joseph preferred the stability of gas lighting, though the long summer days hardly brought about such a need.

When the café closed for the day, Joseph went outside to join his daughter at one of the little round tables and enjoy the evening twilight. She was playing a series of slow songs which echoed into the nearly empty streets. During the middle of a particularly sad song, she stopped and turned a worried face to her father.

"What's wrong, Angel? I like your songs; they're such a nice, peaceful close to the day."

"No, that's all right, Papa. I've quite finished for today."

Alexandra held her Nellie violin in her lap, scroll straight up, cradling it like a child. Still looking at her father, she drew in then released a deep breath.

"Papa, please tell me how Pépé died."

He studied her face, wondering why she would ask such a question. Then again, they talked about the man and his life so much that it seemed reasonable now they could talk about his death.

"All right. As you know, he died of a heart attack when you were only four. Your mémé had already passed on by then but I still helped on the farm from time to time. Your Uncle George was already practicing law in those days."

"Where was Pépé when he had his heart attack?"

"Well, he was home and your Uncle George had just arrived when it happened."

"Where were you?"

"I was out buying farm supplies. Uncle George met me at the door when I returned. He simply told me that me that our father had died."

Alexandra frowned. "Papa, did Pépé always have a weak heart?"

"Well, as a matter of fact, he did. He had problems with his heart his whole life." Joseph thought it strange she would ask such a question.

"Did Uncle George do anything to help Pépé when he had his heart attack?"

"Why of course he did everything possible to help him, my dear!"

"Papa, I have a feeling Uncle George didn't do anything at all to help Pépé," she said plainly.

"Why would you say so?"

She looked at him with big, unsure eyes, stroking the strings and bridge of her instrument with her fingertips. She sighed. "Papa, when I was playing Pépé's violin I would get strange visions of the people who were listening to me. It didn't happen with everyone though, and I can't explain why," she said in a voice barely above a whisper. "I could see things they were doing in their past, maybe some experiences they had. Sometimes the visions came to me when I was playing, and sometimes they'd come later.

"The first happened when I was playing for a beggar woman near the train station. Papa, I could see things that happened to her in her past. It felt so real. Then I had a vision about Mr. Walker's past when I played for him, and then it happened with Marcie ... and with Robbie and Emma ... and even with the Maestro."

She adjusted her violin in her lap, clearly so her tears wouldn't drip on it and risk marring the auburn finish.

Joseph listened, bewildered. He knew his daughter well enough. He knew she wouldn't fabricate such stories, but at the same time she did have a very vivid imagination. "Why didn't you tell me sooner?"

"Papa, I'm so sorry I didn't tell you! I was having fun playing the violin, really I was, and I didn't want to stop. I didn't want you to think I was crazy and I also didn't know if Pépé's violin was really magic or not. Most of all, I didn't want you to take it away."

By now the girl had tears trailing down her cheeks. Joseph reached across the table to dab them with a serviette. She had always been such an emotional creature. "Why did you ask me how Pépé died?"

"Because, Papa, I had a vision about that too. But it can't have been a vision like the others because I would only get a vision when somebody was there while I was playing. Uncle George wasn't even home."

The vision was still interesting to Joseph, and though he could see his daughter was distraught over it, he had to hear. "Tell me about the vision you had of your Uncle George." Joseph reached across the table and held Alexandra's free hand. "It's all right, you can tell me."

The girl glanced up at him with teary eyes. She sniffled. "I was in their house and I really wanted to play a song for Owen. I don't know why I wanted to play a song and I didn't even know which one I wanted to play until I got there. I had a vision about Owen first," she said, her voice trembling.

"Go on Angel, I'm listening."

"It's that Uncle George speaks so cruelly to him all the time. He's always telling Owen how stupid he is, that he shames the family and that he's never going to be anything good in his life. Also, Aunt Clara is always so busy; she never spends any time with Owen. He hasn't got a friend in the world and I think that's one of the reasons he's such a bully," she sniffed, gasping and choking back tears.

"But then Uncle George, oh, it's really so awful, Papa! I had a vision that Uncle George had a very bad quarrel with Pépé in the kitchen of the farmhouse. Pépé fell to the floor and was turning blue. He was trying so hard to breathe; he was reaching his arm out to Uncle George for help, but Uncle George did nothing at all to help him. He just stood there – watching."

Alexandra began crying uncontrollably and almost dropped her violin. The revelation of her vision froze Joseph fast in his chair. He could not question the validity of his daughter's vision as he clearly remembered the day he found his father on the floor of the kitchen as well as the dazed, stupefied look on his brother's face.

"My goodness," he said in a low voice. "Have you told anyone else about these visions?"

"Yes, Papa. I told Emma. That's all. I swear it. I've told no one else and I made Emma promise not to tell anyone."

Joseph rose from his chair and walked around to his daughter. He carefully took the violin from her weak hands and placed it on the table. He bent down to her level, and she instinctively put her arms around his neck and placed her head on his shoulder. She began sobbing anew, her tears soaking through the fabric of his shirt.

After a few minutes, he backed off and cupped her tear-stained face in his hands.

"Don't worry about those visions, Angel. Just please promise me you won't discuss them with Emma, and that you won't talk to anyone else about them ever again except me. Promise? Please Angel, you must promise me this."

The teary-eyed girl looked at him and nodded twice.

"All right, Pépé's violin is gone and everything will be fine," he said in a comforting voice. "You have your very own violin now."

The girl continued crying. "But Papa, I get visions with the new one, too."

Chapter 15

The annual Premier's Competition was truly a grand event in which aspiring musicians could showcase their talents. It was also the last big musical event to take place before the school year started in September. This year the competition would take place at the country estate of Sir Charles Stanley near London, Ontario, some 100 miles distant. It was a major event which attracted people from all over southwestern Ontario, including the social elite from Toronto, London, and Berlin. This year even the Premier of Ontario himself, Oliver Mowat, would be in attendance along with several other politicians and dignitaries. The prerequisites for participating in the competition were either five years of intensive music study in an accredited musical academy, or a letter of reference from a recognized musical scholar.

Joseph and Professor Hergicksen were intent on Alexandra going to this event. They both agreed, one with the other, to encourage her to pursue her musical ambitions as far as she wanted or was able. Professor Hergicksen was all too pleased to sign a letter for Alexandra so she could compete. However, she had her own reasons for going. Among them was that she would be able to meet other musicians and get to know her craft better. She loved playing in public and wanted to see if she could play with other musicians. *Wouldn't it be grand,* she thought, *to be part of a musical ensemble?*

Alexandra was, meanwhile, learning how to tell which visions were important and which ones she could dismiss. The visions about George, Clara and Owen were important, of course, while visions she had of Charlie McKay hauling logs from his farm or Mrs. Labonte singing as she peeled potatoes were easily dismissed. Other visions were even amusing, such as the one she had of Mrs. Tellier as a young girl getting into a fight with a boy, grabbing him by his shirt and pulling off all his buttons.

She and Joseph reasoned that the visions were only a byproduct of her playing and the music was the only reason she played. Now she had gotten into the habit of making light of any unimportant visions until they became like a dream to her and, as such, were almost always forgotten.

* * *

On the day of the competition, Alexandra rose before dawn and went downstairs in a groggy state, rubbing her eyes. She was still dressed in her nightgown and hadn't even brushed her hair. Her father was sitting at his usual table enjoying the morning quiet.

"Good morning, Angel, what's wrong? Are you all right?"

"I slept badly last night," she said, "I don't know, but I think maybe I'm real nervous about the competition."

"Just remember that the main point in going is to have fun. If you move your musical career forward then that's so much the better. Besides, your fans are all going to be there!"

"My fans? Who are they?"

"Naturally that would be myself, the Maestro and Emma. A new fan joining us today is Robbie. I presume you know him?" he said, laughing. "Since it's just a day trip, his parents thought it would do him good. Now let's have some breakfast."

Following breakfast, Joseph excused himself to do some errands and Alexandra went up to her room and began dressing. Then, she sneezed. Then she sneezed again. And again. Hoping her father wouldn't hear, she tried muffling her sneezes. She knew he would insist she stay home if she wasn't feeling well, so she tried her best to conceal her illness. For the time being, she was successful.

Meanwhile, Marcie arrived at work and was busy, as usual, preparing everything in the café.

Alexandra descended the stairs, violin case in hand. She had chosen to wear a light blue dress with white ruffles around her long sleeves, hem and neckline. She caught sight of Marcie, who stopped in her tracks.

"Good morning, *Vogelein*!" Why are you so dressed up?"

A sneeze was Alexandra's answer.

"Oh no! Are you feeling under the weather?"

"I'll be right as a trivet, Marcie. We're all going to London for a music competition. It's my first," she sniffled.

"Are you sure you can go? Maybe you should stay home and get some rest? I'm going to be making my famous pork soup with vegetables today and I can bring some up to you!"

"Oh, no thanks Marcie. Everything will be fine. I feel ... *sniff* ... Better ... *sniff* ... Already." She sneezed again.

"Alexandra, you can't fool a woman with six kids!"

No matter what arguments Marcie could put forward, Alexandra was determined to get to London. Besides, the train tickets had been bought, the letter of reference signed, and everyone was looking forward to going. She couldn't disappoint them now.

At that moment the brass bell on the door clanged brightly. Marcie and Alexandra turned to see who it was.

"Oh, I see you're ready!" said Emma, wearing her olive dress. "I can't wait! Can we walk to the train station together?"

Alexandra looked at Marcie, speaking through sniffles. "Can you tell Papa we'll meet him at the train station?"

"I will, though it's against my better judgment," said Marcie.

Alexandra took her violin and set off with Emma.

Upon their arrival they found Robbie waiting with his father. "Good morning!" said Robbie, looking down at the violin case in Alexandra's hand. "Did you get a new case for your pépé's violin?"

"Not just a new case, but a new violin too," she said, sniffling. "I gave the other one to Owen."

The boy frowned. "But why? Why would you give *him* your magic violin?"

"It's a long story Robbie and maybe I'll tell you sometime. Anyway, here comes my papa and the Maestro!"

With all the greetings and goodbyes said, the five boarded the train and took their seats, waiting to depart. Robbie took his seat between the two girls, looking rather dapper with his new haircut and smart looking suit.

Alexandra sat in her usual place at the window, looking at the goings-on outside; always interested in observing the people milling about and maybe even seeing a ship pass by on the Detroit River. She knew her interest in things beyond the window wouldn't seem strange to her father, who again was sitting opposite them chatting away with the professor. She was sure he wouldn't have a clear view of her face.

"All aboard!" cried the conductor. Alexandra glanced towards the aisle as the final few passengers boarded the train.

"Good morning, brother," said a familiar, passing voice. Alexandra diverted her attention again, seeing George, Clara, Owen, and a smartly dressed young man she didn't know. They were amongst the last passengers to board the train.

"Morning," said Joseph.

"We're taking Owen to compete again at the Premier's Competition in London today," said George, beaming. He scanned the five in their seats, shifting his gaze between the professor and Alexandra. "I heard you're going there to watch. There'll be a lot of good talent there, you might even enjoy it."

Joseph opened his mouth as if to speak, but the words came from an ill Alexandra. She coughed and sneezed, speaking in a muffled voice.

"I'm going there to compete, Uncle George, not just to watch. I know I'm very new at this, but I have lots of help and support here with me," she said as the train started moving.

"Well! I see the kind of support you have here, Alexandra. You've got yesterday's man here helping you and even the schoolboy weakling. I'm sure you'll do quite well." Turning his attention to Joseph, he continued. "Well, brother, you'll obviously stop at nothing to show off your snotty-nosed little star, won't you? After all, why let a little cold ruin your plans? However, all is not lost. Perhaps one of her men can wipe her nose while she plays."

Owen burst out laughing. He looked scornfully at Robbie, who sat there, his vision locked on Owen while nearby passengers turned their heads towards this strange exchange.

Clara remained silent, though her face was unusually rosy. This time the professor stood up as if he wanted to say something. He sat back down when Alexandra spoke up.

"It was my choice to go on this trip, Uncle George. If my father knew I was ill he would not have allowed me to come. I know this. He has helped me through a great many things and he'll help me through this too." She dabbed her nose with a handkerchief. "Uncle George, don't you think it's important to help a member of your family when they need it most? I mean, could you just stand there watching one of them suffer? Could you stand there coldly while they pleaded and begged you for help and not do anything at all? Could you? *Did you?*"

"Alexandra!" said Joseph. "What did we talk about the other day?"

"I'm sorry, Papa."

George stood a moment; an angry redness rising up across his face. He pursed his lips and narrowed his eyes, his vision cutting an unbroken line directly to Alexandra. He stood like that a few moments more before appearing to relax, the redness draining from his face. "Very well," said George, "I apologize to you all for my rude remarks. They were completely uncalled for. Good luck Alexandra in the competition and I hope you feel better soon. Good day to you all."

Alexandra watched her Uncle George and his family take their seats several rows ahead.

The professor turned to Joseph, commenting to him in a low, gruff voice, yet loud enough for Alexandra to hear. "That man's audacity and rudeness knows no depth Joseph. I've never seen a more disgusting exhibition in all my life!"

As it was, Alexandra spent the whole train ride nursing her cold, the symptoms of which had now fully developed. She wondered how she could play her violin like that, especially if she had to sneeze.

"I'm sure the judges and organizers will understand if you withdraw from the competition, Aydy," said Emma.

"I think she's right," said Joseph. "There's no shame in withdrawing because of illness, and everyone will understand. We can take the next train home."

Alexandra dabbed at her nose with her handkerchief. "Papa, do you remember what I told you not long ago? Believe me; it's very important that I play. I know you understand what I mean."

Joseph looked at her as she blew her nose and slouched in her seat. A look of deep concern crossed his face.

"Tea with lemon, please," ordered Joseph when the steward came round. "Actually, make it two teas with lemon."

When the train arrived in London some two hours later, the passengers began to disembark. The elder Delmott clan exited first and politely nodded to Joseph et al as they passed down the aisle. All, that is, except Owen. When he walked down the aisle past Alexandra, he tried smirking at her, but she turned her head to look out the window. After a few moments she sensed him still standing there. Eventually prodded by other passengers to move on, Owen continued down the aisle and exited the train.

Alexandra, sneezing and wheezing, boarded a waiting coach with her travelling companions. The carriage started off, the horses' hooves clopping along the old cobblestone street, bound for the estate home of Sir Charles Stanley.

* * *

A wealthy businessman who made his fortune in the pharmaceutical industry, Sir Charles was about as distinguished as a gentleman could get. Born and raised in Cornwall, England, he had a distinctive accent as well as a pleasant demeanour. He stood almost six feet tall, had a large frame which he filled well, and black hair which was longer on the top of his head and closely cropped on the sides and back. On this day he greeted his guests in his top hat and tails.

Sir Charles' mansion stood on the banks of the Thames River near London. He often entertained guests in the Great Room of the house. In this large, elegant room the music competition itself would take place. Scattered about on the expansive grounds of the estate were several marquees, their sprawling canvas covers providing shelter for the many guests, as well as places for string quartets to practice and perhaps offer impromptu performances. Waiters roamed about the house and garden offering hors d'oeuvres to the guests.

As was his custom, Sir Charles Stanley and his wife welcomed each dignitary and performer upon their arrival. George Delmott's carriage was the first to pull up to the grand estate.

"Good morning, Mr. and Mrs. Delmott," said Stanley. "Good morning to you too, Owen. I trust you all had a good journey. Your guest?"

"May I present Franko Bortellini? Franko, this is Sir Charles Stanley. Franko is Owen's new personal violin tutor and musical mentor," said George.

"I'm pleased to meet you Mr. Bortellini, and welcome."

"Likewise," said Bortellini.

"McLean here will show you all to your places in the Great Room."

Everyone followed Stanley's assistant – except George, who lingered behind. "Stanley, it's time to collect a favour." George's voice was low and businesslike.

"You've been good to me, George and helped me a lot. Of course, just name your favour and it's as good as done."

"Do you remember that concoction you made for me a number of years ago?"

"Of course."

"Good. I brought the rest of it with me today. I need you to administer it to someone," he said as he produced a small vial and handed it to Stanley.

"To whom?" said Stanley, accepting the vial and placing it discreetly in his pocket.

"To that little witch of a niece I have. She's coming here today to perform."

"Little witch?"

George appeared irritated. "Don't be so stupid, Stanley. I meant Alexandra. You know – my brother's daughter. I think she's twelve. Good fortune has made my task a lot easier because she's not feeling well and has some sort of cold. I want you to be the gentleman you are and give her that concoction. Tell her it'll alleviate her suffering. After she takes it, it'll surely put her out of commission for at least several days."

"But George, why? She's just a child! You know how powerful that is and what it can do! What on earth could she have done to deserve that!"

"That matter doesn't concern you."

"I'm not going to be party to this, George. Whatever you have against the girl is your own business, but don't bring me into it. I'll not be the devil's hand – favour or not." Stanley tried returning the vial, but George took a step back.

"This is no time to be a coward, Stanley," said George, hardening his tone. "I'd do the deed myself but she'd likely not accept it from me. But from you – the druggist, the healer – it would be perfect. You could get away with it by saying the medication didn't agree with her system. No one would suspect it. I need you to do this for me, Stanley. Don't disappoint me. You're well aware of all the connections I have. Remember, I've been working on your legal contracts. I've seen your financial statements. I know about your imports and exports and I know you've been cheating the government on tax money. You do know that if you get audited they'll close you down, take everything you've got, throw you in prison. So the choice is yours. I'm not asking you to kill the girl, Stanley, just knock her down for a few days. That's all!"

Stanley looked at George and nodded, then watched as he walked away.

Soon another coach pulled up to the grand estate with familiar people aboard. Its occupants soon exited and Stanley, still shaken by his conversation with George, recomposed himself in order to greet his guests in a welcoming and friendly manner.

"Welcome to the Premier's Competition," he said, forcing a smile. "You must be Alexandra Delmott."

Alexandra curtsied. "I am, and I'm thrilled to be here," she said, sniffling. "You have such a lovely, charming home, Mr. Stanley. It must be very inspiring for artists, musicians, writers, poets or anyone who wishes to have a place in which they can allow their creative minds to wander. This is my first competition and I'm so sorry to attend it with a cold."

"Nothing to forgive!" he said before turning to Joseph. "That one's a charmer. You must be Alexandra's father."

"Yes sir, I am. My name is Joseph, and these are Alexandra's friends Emma Brindle and Robert Stuart. I'm sure you already know Professor Hergicksen."

"Of course! Good day, professor – and welcome."

The professor acknowledged Stanley with a nod.

"McLean will show you all to your places," said Stanley.

***

The grounds of Stanley's estate occupied a picturesque stretch of property along the Thames River in London. Unlike its English namesake, this Thames River was small and many parts of it were not navigable. London itself was named after the capital city in England and strategically located a good distance up the Thames, which some believed would offer a measure of protection against the Americans. Now people made their homes there and the community was thriving. Alexandra wondered how different 'The Big London' would be.

"Aydy! Hello!" came a young man's voice from the crowd.

"Alfred!" Alexandra recognized the cellist immediately and he walked right up to her. She spoke to him through sniffles. "How nice to see you! Are you here with your quartet?"

"Yes, we're playing tomorrow. Will you be staying 'til then?"

"No, I'm afraid not. I'm returning home tonight."

"Well then, I'll come and listen to your performance! Good luck to you, and I do hope you'll get well soon!" he said before going off in the direction of his fellow musicians.

"Everybody knows I'm ill," she mumbled to herself.

At that moment Alexandra noticed the Maestro motioning to her from a distance across a number of people. She went to him straightaway.

"We need to review a few things before you perform. There are twenty-four other violinists registered and so we must ensure your performance is technically flawless. If you can make it past the first part of the competition, you'll have a real chance. Remember that with so many contestants, the first round is limited to only an excerpt of several minutes. The judges are looking for technical proficiency, musicality and presentation. If they interrupt you during your performance, it doesn't mean you've failed; it simply means they've heard enough to assess you. Do you understand?"

"Yes I do, Maestro. I just hope I can make it through without sneezing."

"Well, that's something we best leave to God. All right then, there's a place over there," said the professor, pointing to a garden bench. "Let's sit and review."

While they were discussing things on the bench, Sir Charles approached. "So, this is your first competition, Miss Delmott?"

"Yes it is, Sir Charles. I hope I won't make a mess of it, honestly," she said, sniffling. "It's my biggest dream to be a concert violinist someday and my papa and the Maestro wanted me to come. I can meet other musicians here."

"Have you taken anything for your cold?" he said.

"Oh, excuse me, sir! I must be a dreadful, sorry sight. I've only had tea with lemon."

Stanley stood with his hand in his jacket pocket. He withdrew it, holding a small vial. He looked at it, then at her. He closed his hand around the vial and placed it back in his pocket.

"Tea with lemon is the best natural remedy, Miss Delmott. Allow yourself a few days' rest and the cold will run its course. Good luck with the competition."

"Thank you, Sir Charles," said Alexandra.

After about a half hour, a trumpet blast rang out to call everyone to the Great Room for the competition. In the audience, the premier of Ontario sat in the front row accompanied by his wife and their entourage. Stanley sat with them. A panel of five judges sat off to the side. Alexandra wondered if the professor felt a bit strange being there in his new role.

Following a few welcoming words from Stanley, the competition officially began and the first performer took the stage. Alexandra marvelled at the quality of the music from each one and was saddened when the judges cut many off after only a few minutes. She wondered if it would happen to her. Still, sitting with her father and friends seemed to soothe her nerves, but not her cold. She had to muffle her sneezes so as to not disturb the performers.

"Owen Delmott, please step forward," said the announcer.

Owen promptly took the stage. He bowed politely to the dignitaries, judges, his parents and his tutor, and began playing his excerpt from Bruch's Violin Concerto No 1 in G minor. He played the song with energy and vigour, and the judges let him play his full time allotment. When he stepped down, he cast a superior look at his cousin and took his seat. His parents hugged him and his tutor shook his hand.

"Alexandra Delmott," came the call.

"You'll do fine, Alex! Play well, Aydy! Relax!" her companions assured her. Alexandra, with a clean red and white handkerchief ready, took her violin and proceeded up to the stage. She curtsied, tucked her handkerchief between her chin and the violin and waited for the start signal from the judges. She caught sight of her Uncle George sitting in his place, arms folded across his chest, smirking.

Alexandra, poised and elegant as she could be, sniffled once before plunging straight into Brahms' Violin Concerto in D major, a piece she had learned and practiced with the Maestro every time they had a session together. They chose it because the beginning of the piece could give a good demonstration of her playing ability. She played it forcefully yet gracefully, trying to imitate the technical precision of those masters whom she adored. She closed her eyes and, as she played, she could feel the music, but also felt the magic, which swirled and swept around and through her, causing her skin to tingle. Each plunge of her bow only served to increase the power of this magic, and she became lost in it, swept away to another world, to another place and time.

Alexandra was hoping no one in the audience could detect anything strange about her. However, she hoped they might experience something special, or at least different, in the way she played. After a while she felt the music taking on a life of its own, breathing, brimming with colours, vibrant with sights, energized with sounds – the very fragrance and essence of life itself.

When her performance time was nearing an end, she improvised a melodic finale so that the piece wouldn't sound halted. She held her violin and bow in her left hand and, smiling radiantly, curtsied to the audience. To her horror, not a single person clapped. Her smile quickly faded as she stood motionless in front of a muted audience. She scanned over the people, looking for at least one person who approved her performance.

At that moment, the entire house erupted into applause, everyone rising to give this newcomer a thunderous standing ovation.

"Bravo! Bravo!" shouted the professor, looking happy as a schoolboy, while Emma was jumping up and down and clapping. The atmosphere in the Great Room was truly electric.

* * *

George Delmott, meanwhile, felt as though he were getting heatstroke. His wife and son were tending to him, fanning him with their programmes. When he felt he had recovered enough, he stepped outside to get some fresh air. Stanley met him there.

"George, I wanted to talk to you. I couldn't do it. Maybe you can extort and manipulate other people, but that's not going to work with me. Besides, that girl's got talent, honestly; I've got to hand it to her. Mind you, Owen is a good player too, and in time I'm sure he'll be one of the best, but I've got to sleep with myself at night, George, and if I ever wanted to know another peaceful night's sleep for the rest of my life, I could not bring myself to do what you asked. As for your words, well, you'll just do as you want, anyway."

George hadn't the strength to offer a lengthy counter argument. "Very good then," he said. "You'll sleep well with your conscience at night, but you'll do so on the street – or in prison."

* * *

Following the first set of performances, Alexandra stepped outside with her father. They were sipping tea when Alfred approached.

"Well done, Aydy! I'd have never imagined someone could do that well in so short a time! Please, won't you come play with us? We'd love to have you!"

She considered his offer, but then sneezed. This cold of hers was frustrating beyond belief, but at least she hadn't sneezed during the performance. Now her cold had returned with full force and she felt, for the second time in her life, she'd have to turn down an opportunity to play. Unfortunately the refusal would be to the same person.

"I'm so sorry Alfred, I'd like to, but I'm really not feeling my usual self today. I hope you'll forgive me."

Just then, the professor walked up, interrupting their conversation. "Good news my dear! You're moving up to the next level!"

"More congratulations!" Alfred said. "Well done!"

For this final round Alexandra would play the full length of Mozart's Violin Concerto No. 3. When she took the stage again, she even managed to eclipse her first performance.

When the day's final tally had been drawn up, the judges' decision was unanimous. Alexandra Delmott was awarded First Prize by none other than the premier of Ontario himself.

George Delmott, frustrated at his son's inferior performance and unwilling to bear the sight of Alexandra awarded first prize, departed quickly with his family on an earlier train to Windsor. As for Franko, he was fired on the spot. Through great personal inconvenience and expense, he had to find his own way home.

Chapter 16

Alexandra slept fitfully sitting up in her seat on the train ride back to Windsor, her head resting on a pillow next to the window. Aggravating her sleep were several factors – her sitting position, her cold, and of course the visions she had of her uncle, Aunt Clara, Owen, and others. She knew that being in a train, with other people nearby and listening, wasn't the proper place to reveal the visions to her father. With this settled in her mind, she tried to sleep through the remainder of the train ride. No one dared disturb her.

* * *

"We're home, Angel. We have to get up and walk home now. Can you manage?"

Alexandra rubbed her eyes and yawned. "Yes, Papa, I can do it."

Joseph helped her off the train while Emma and Robbie watched. Their parents waited for them on the platform and, due to the lateness of the hour, they all said their goodbyes and left.

Still standing outside the train station, however, was a worried-looking Professor Hergicksen.

"Well Joseph, what a remarkable day it's been. I do hope the young lady gets well soon. Would you like a ride home?"

"Thank you, professor, but no. I think the fresh air and short walk will do Alexandra good."

"Well, if you need anything, I'd be more than pleased to help. By the way, I've just had a telephone installed in my home, so you can ring me if you need anything." He handed a slip of paper to Joseph, tipped his hat, and was off.

Alexandra recuperated after a few days, but until then Joseph thought it wise not to ask her questions about any visions she may have had. He decided that in due course the opportunity would present itself and they could discuss any visions. He also had one more reason: even he himself was not sure he'd be ready to hear what she might reveal.

* * *

The first school day of September dawned bright and warm, bringing with it not only a new month, but a fresh start. Alexandra donned one of the new dresses she bought in Toronto and her new mustard yellow sweater, which was now her favourite. Making a single braid in her hair, she bid her father goodbye and left.

When she arrived at the school grounds, Robbie saw her first and went straight over to greet her. She hadn't seen him in such a buoyant mood in ages.

"Good morning, Robbie!" she said. "Why so happy? Did your father allow you to take violin lessons?"

"Haven't you heard the news? Owen challenged me to a fight!"

Alexandra scrutinized the boy. There were no bruises on his face. He was smiling. He appeared to have all his teeth and he even walked straight.

"What happened?" she asked.

"I was walking home after my boxing lesson and I happened to see Owen with two of his friends!"

"Really? Go on, what did you do?"

"Well, he challenged me to a fight. I just said no, not interested. He started calling me names, then he took a swing at me but I blocked it. He lost his balance and fell to the ground. I was over him in a second, but before I could hit him he covered his head and face and started crying, 'No! Don't! Please!' " said Robbie, laughing. "His friends both laughed at him and I let him go. You should've seen the look on his face!"

"Wow, Robbie! That's really great! I'm so proud of you!" said Alexandra. She was glad the boxing lessons had proven worthwhile, but was also glad the boy had the sense of knowing when to stop. "You knew two wrongs don't make a right! That's what my papa always says. So, go on, tell me! What did Owen do?"

"I stood back as he got up, but he didn't try to hit me again. I think he was scared! Then he left with his friends. They started walking away and were joking, but I couldn't hear what they were saying."

At that moment, Mrs. Brindle rang the school bell and the students entered the building. They were directed to their classrooms and took their places.

St. Alphonsus was a modest school which served the Catholic community of downtown Windsor. The school was run by a mixture of nuns and highly qualified lay teachers such as Mrs. Brindle.

That familiar school smell of books, chalk, and paper permeated the entire building. Each classroom contained aging double wooden desks made for students to sit in pairs. In the centre of each room was a rather large, ornate wood-burning stove which now sat unused.

Alexandra went to her new classroom and took a seat near the window as directed by the old nun, Sister Rose. After the pupils had taken their places, Sister Rose welcomed them. Well into her fifties and with many years of teaching experience, Sister Rose's face was creased with fine wrinkles, especially around her mouth and the outside corners of her deep-set, blue eyes. Her lips were thin and the same pallid colour as her face. She wore the habit of the Jesuit nuns, with a long dark robe, a white collar which resembled a giant bib, and her hair was completely covered. A large cross on a chain was the only piece of jewellery to adorn her.

All the nuns were strict, including Sister Rose, but others added an extra measure of cruelty. Alexandra tried to be a good student and avoided being disciplined, but she had to be careful. Being naturally left-handed and having to live in a world of right-handed people, she could use both hands equally well – a skill she developed by being forced to write with her right hand. "The left hand is evil, you must not use it," she remembered the nuns saying. She always felt they were wrong but dared not contradict them. She reasoned that God doesn't create anything evil and therefore evil was a choice people made, and that people could do bad things with either hand. In any event, she had to be careful because if the nuns caught a student writing with the left hand, that hand would receive an instant whack across the knuckles from a pointing stick. That wouldn't be especially pleasant for a violin player.

While Alexandra was pondering this concept of evil, Owen arrived at school – late as always.

"Good morning, Master Delmott," Sister Rose said with a trace of annoyance in her voice. "Your place is next to your cousin." She spoke with a dry, parched voice that sounded like she hadn't drunk any liquid for centuries.

Alexandra cringed. Seating arrangements were made on the first day of school, and each pupil wondered who they'd get to share their desk and be partners with for the whole year. She couldn't imagine herself sitting next to her cousin all day, every day, all year through. These seating arrangements were permanent and immoveable like a mountain. They could never be changed unless someone moved, died, or the whole schoolhouse got burnt to the ground. She wondered if the nun had heard about the tension between her and Owen and whether she was doing this to heal or to hurt.

"Perhaps you can tell us what's wrong, Alexandra?" the nun asked.

Accepting the old nun's invitation to speak, Alexandra rose from her place and cleared her throat.

"Sister Rose, I realized only now it has been a secret hope of mine that I should be reconciled with my dear cousin. We can use this as an opportunity to heal our differences and work together the whole year through – happily, merrily in all the tasks you give us to do. I can even see now how happy we will be, just as happy, playful and chatty as we were when we were little!" Her voice began to rise, gathering energy. She bounced lightly on her feet.

"Owen and I share so much together, our common musical abilities, our family history and so much more! Thank you, Sister, this is an arrangement made in heaven!" she said as she smiled at Owen and took his hands, hoping he would join this temporary alliance.

"Yes, Sister, she's right!" he said, hugging Alexandra. "We're going to have a grand time being partners this year!"

Sister Rose stood like a statue at the front of the class. She examined them both with emotionless expression.

"Owen, you should take Kathleen's place next to Pierre. Kathleen, take your place next to Alexandra. Now, please," said the old nun.

Alexandra tried with her all her might to restrain her delight as Owen took all his things and moved next to Pierre.

"We must all make sacrifices in our lives," said the nun. "Now let us review our arithmetic. Look at the board."

When the students were dismissed after that first day of school, they all ran out of the building and to their homes. However, Alexandra was surprised that none of Owen's friends had stopped to greet him, in fact they didn't they pay him any mind at all. Perhaps they heard about the latest incident with Robbie, or maybe something had changed over the summer and they'd become weary of him and his ways.

As for Robbie, he glowed with a new sense of self-confidence. He had a good summer, yes, having spent much of it with Alexandra and Emma, and the boxing lessons surely had helped. More than that, they didn't appear to have made him an egoist. For this alone Alexandra was most grateful as she could barely abide another egoist in her life.

Chapter 17

Business at the little café was doing quite well, and of course Joseph could properly assign much of the credit for this success to his daughter and her music. Some of the real old-timers could even remember when Delphis himself used to entertain the customers. "He'd come right on up to the table and play us a song!" remembered one. "She's just like her pépé," laughed another. "She's petite Delphis!" exclaimed yet another grizzled old man. They'd all stop by to hear the young girl play her fiddle, to remember days past, to meet their old friends and enjoy a tasty cup of tea or coffee. What a happy and lively place the old café had become again!

Due to the success of the business, Joseph decided that the hours should be extended to 8:00 p.m., new staff hired and the menu extended to serve dinner. This was a big risk for him because those customers who came to the café to hear Alexandra playing could never be sure she'd actually be there. Besides, he wanted the café to flourish by virtue of its own merits – excellent service and quality food. Hearing Alexandra play could be considered a bonus.

One September night after the café had closed, Joseph was sitting at his usual table going over the day's receipts and setting his mind on the following day's activities. Alexandra came up to the table with her fiddle.

"Papa," she said, "Look at this!"

Joseph stopped what he was doing.

Alexandra pointed to her violin. "Look at Nellie! Do you see the neck here? It's got *my* finger marks on it now!"

Joseph studied the neck of the instrument through his half-moon glasses. He could see the shiny spots on the wood under the strings, and they reached across nearly the entire length of the ebony surface.

"Well, Angel, you've certainly made this instrument your own, now haven't you?"

The girl beamed and her eyes glowed. "Papa, I want to play a song for you. I want to play it only for you."

Joseph put his pen down, capped the ink jar, and turned his chair towards her.

Alexandra played a lively French folk song and Joseph listened attentively, as he always did. When she finished, he leaned back in his chair and clapped slowly and thoughtfully.

"Well done, Angel! I haven't heard that song for many years. Your pépé used to play it often in the café and as a matter of fact, it was the last song he played for me. I haven't heard it since. Where'd you learn it?"

"Well, Papa, you know I get visions sometimes. I was playing for some of the old men and this song was in their memory. I hope it's not stealing if I got it from there."

Joseph needn't have been surprised at this newest revelation, yet the realness of what he'd just heard only reinforced his belief that his daughter's ability was, in fact, real. Furthermore, it was one thing to get little tidbits from somebody's life, but to get a whole musical composition and learn something was quite another thing altogether. He felt this would also be the right time to ask about any visions she may have had at the competition.

"Sit down, please," he said.

Alexandra placed her violin on top of the papers Joseph had spread out on the table. She sat down on the bentwood chair opposite him.

"Papa, I should tell you about the vision I had of Uncle George," she said, looking straight at her father, her arms folded flat across the table and her fingers interlocked. She seemed to be all business.

"I was waiting for you to say that, Angel! Please go ahead. By the way, you've been keeping these visions a secret, like we agreed?"

"Yes, of course I have, Papa. Don't you trust me?" she asked, puzzled.

"Of course I trust you, Angel! I'd trust you with my life. We also need to remember that there might be people out there who could abuse this gift you have. So far, people think your gift is only about music, and that's great. There's nothing wrong with talented people. They come in all shapes, sizes, and colours. But if certain people, for example, the police, knew about your visions and how accurate they were, they'd take you to every grimy jail to play music in order to find out the details of many horrible crimes. Other people would surely abuse your gift, for example, those shady circus proprietors. They'd have you performing in sideshows, collecting the money for themselves, making you work long hours and reducing you to nothing more than a curiosity! It's bad enough you play your fiddle for some of the characters we have around here. I've allowed it because I didn't see any harm in it. You like playing, they like the music and everything seems good. So as I said, we must keep the visions an absolute secret and guard them as best we can."

Alexandra sat still, nodding in agreement. She drew in a ragged sigh and began speaking in a quiet voice. "I must tell you about the vision I had at the competition, Papa. In my vision I saw Uncle George, who had gone to the farm to visit Pépé. I could see the kitchen of the old farmhouse and Pépé and Uncle George were quarrelling. Pépé was mad that Uncle George had cheated so many good people in some business dealings and taken their money from them. He even said that Uncle George had started the great fire. Pépé knew this because, Papa, Pépé had visions too, just like I do."

Joseph felt a new, icy chill trying to lock itself round him. He looked at Alexandra, nodding for her to continue.

"Uncle George got really angry after Pépé told him some of the visions. He also told Uncle George he was going to visit his lawyer and cut him off from his will the next day and that everything was going to pass to you. Then Uncle George started calling Pépé all kinds of horrible names. He said that the visions were lies, that he didn't know what he was talking about. He called Pépé a poor, uneducated farmer who would rather believe a fantasy than him. He ended by saying that no matter how long he lived, he would always be ashamed to be his son." She sniffled and lowered her head.

"This is when Pépé had his heart attack, Papa. I saw the whole thing. It was just really so awful. Also, I believe that Uncle George did nothing to help because he *wanted* Pépé to die," she said, raising her teary eyes to Joseph.

"Thank you, Angel," said Joseph, feeling drained by this latest revelation. "I can't imagine how difficult it was for you to tell me that."

"Papa, can Uncle George do anything to hurt us?"

"Be sure I would never allow that to happen." He meant the words as surely as he meant anything in his life.

"I understand, Papa. You promise you won't let anything happen to us?"

"I promise. You and I – we always keep our promises. Come, it's late now and you should get some sleep. I'll close things up here."

"Papa, why can't I play the violin without having any visions? I can't even play it in my room with the door closed! I'm sure the music carries down the stairs because I get visions of different people in the café. I can even tell who's here without coming down! I wonder if it happened like that with Pépé?"

Joseph rubbed his face and eyes. He sighed. "I remember your pépé seldom came to the café during the last months of his life. He liked to stay home and play his violin. 'I have peace and quiet here,' he'd say. 'No distractions on the farm.' I always thought it was because he missed your mémé. I tried getting him to come out, even to play his violin with you here, but he seldom did. It would make sense that if no people were around, he couldn't possibly get any visions."

"Do you think I should stop playing the violin when people are around, Papa?"

"What?" said Joseph. "God has given you a special gift, I mean, a special talent, Angel. Besides, everybody loves your music! On the one hand it would be a shame to stop, but on the other hand you need to have a clear mind and enjoy your music. Perhaps you could change instruments – I don't mean getting another violin – but perhaps you could take up the piano, harp, flute or something else. You could even try singing. Maybe the visions will stop."

"No. I want to be a concert violinist, Papa. If I can't play the violin, I don't want to play anything at all."

"You're so stubborn! All right. I just pray that God gives you the strength and courage to deal with any more visions. Just remember you can change instruments any time you want," said Joseph.

"Papa?" she said, getting up from her chair.

"Yes, Angel?"

"Thank you for making me feel better. I'm sure everything will be all right. I do love the violin and could never imagine myself playing anything else. I could never love another instrument as much." She walked around to his side of the table, bent down and kissed his cheek. "Good night, my wise, dear, Papa."

Joseph smiled. "Good night to you, too, Angel."

Chapter 18

When Alexandra and Robbie arrived at school, the other pupils had just entered the building. Sister Rose stood at the door of the classroom, as was her practice, and visually inspected each pupil as they filed orderly inside as if determining whether or not they were worthy to enter her classroom. Everyone was always fearful of the dreaded arm which could go up at any moment, blocking their entrance. If they could make it past that arm, they stood a good chance of making it through the rest of the day.

As she waited her turn to enter the classroom, Alexandra noticed that the nun had an unusually pleasant look on her face. She wondered if the old woman's face would crack if she tried broadening her mouth into a full smile.

When it came time for Alexandra to enter the classroom, the arm shot up across the doorway. "Not you!" said the nun. "You wait out here in the corridor."

Alexandra stood puzzled. She hadn't been late for school, all her homework was done, and all her things were in order. There could be no possible reason on God's good earth why the nun would single her out for any disciplinary action. After a few moments, the nun returned and closed the classroom door, thus shutting herself and Alexandra in the empty corridor.

"Do you know what I want to talk to you about?" said the nun.

Alexandra then realized that she hadn't done her hair in a braid that morning. She remembered the old nun hated loose-hanging hair because it appeared unkempt, much like how a beggar would keep it. "I can't be sure, Sister Rose," she said, palms beginning to sweat.

"Well! You know it's not polite to keep secrets, and that's exactly what you've been doing ever since school started, haven't you?" said the nun in a low voice, her stark eyes clear and cutting.

At that moment Alexandra realized that the nun must somehow know about the visions. After all, nuns are connected to God on a higher level and probably know things most people don't. Perhaps even this nun got visions of her own, too.

"I'm so sorry, Sister! My papa told me to keep this a secret and not tell anyone."

"Well, your father is certainly right most of the time. He's a very modest man and is teaching you the virtues of modesty, too. This is what Christ teaches us. However, winning the Premier's Competition in the very sight of the premier of Ontario himself is certainly something to be proud of. I am amazed, and perhaps even a bit insulted, that I had to find this out secondhand and not from you directly."

Alexandra felt all her anxiety instantly being released. "Sister Rose, yes, that's true. I'm so very sorry for not having told you. I can only imagine how upset you must've been upon hearing the news and how disappointed you were in me for not telling you. I'm sure people tell you all the time about their great accomplishments. Perhaps I didn't think it anything special to brag about. Besides, there were so many talented musicians there at the competition and frankly speaking I was quite humbled and surprised to have been chosen as the winner amongst them."

The old nun listened with unusual patience. "God gives gifts to different people for different reasons. I do hope you will use your gift well and not become self-absorbed in it."

"I would never do that, Sister! I would just like to improve my playing ability and perhaps in the distant future I might even become part of an ensemble or maybe even a quartet or, Good Lord willing, an orchestra," she said, not wanting to reveal too much to the nun.

"Very well, then, I can see how important your music is to you. I hope you will not let it interfere with your studies. Furthermore, it would please me if you could play a song for the class. I have yet to hear you play your violin. Perhaps a duet with Owen would be nice."

Alexandra was always eager to play her violin, but dreaded getting any more visions. Besides, she believed that playing for the class would put her in an awkward social position – especially with Owen. However, she felt the onus to play a duet would rest with him, and was sure he would refuse.

"Yes, of course. I'd be pleased to play for you."

"Good then. It's settled. You'll bring your violin tomorrow and play a song for us," said the nun, opening the door of the classroom and gesturing with a welcoming arm for the girl to enter. "Oh yes, Alexandra, one more thing," she added. "Next time, please do something with your hair."

Alexandra smiled and entered the classroom.

* * *

On the way home that day, Alexandra decided on a whim to drop in to the professor's house. She hadn't seen him since they returned from the Premier's Competition, and now that had school started, she wanted to arrange a new schedule for her practice sessions.

When she arrived at his home, she walked down the sidewalk, past the gardener who was tending the rose bushes, and knocked at the side door, as usual.

Cora answered.

"Is the Maestro home?" Alexandra asked.

"Is he expecting you today?"

"No, but I wanted to see him in order to revise our playing schedule."

The gardener noticed the two talking and turned towards them. "Alexandra! What are you doing here?"

Alexandra looked at the gardener and realized it was the Maestro. He was wearing coveralls, gardening gloves, and a straw hat. He certainly didn't look at all like a professor of music or master concert violinist. "Maestro?" she said. "I am so sorry for intruding, but I was hoping we could review our practice schedule. I didn't know you don't have any gardeners working for you!"

"Yes, actually I do," he said. "They do most of the heavy work, but I take care of the roses myself. I really enjoy this part of gardening, and I especially enjoy roses. I like nurturing them and I've got many varieties here, including some very rare ones. It's my dream that someday this whole town, and probably future city, will be covered with roses from one end to the other. Come, let me show you some of my best."

The great Maestro, in his gardening coveralls, strolled the grounds with Alexandra. He explained all the different types and cultivars in his garden. The roses were made up of many different colours, from pure white to deep crimson reds. They were also in many different sizes, with some growing on long stems while others grew in great thorny bushes. The air was filled with the scent of these blooms, and Alexandra bent down to savour some of them, being careful not to prick her fingers.

The professor clipped some of the more exquisite ones, arranging them in a bouquet which he presented to her.

"Oh thank you Maestro! I love flowers and roses are the best of all!"

"You're welcome, my dear. Consider it a belated gift after a fine performance." Alexandra felt her face warming at the Maestro's words. "I brought some of these cultivars back from Europe," said the professor. "These ones are truly prized. They'll continue blooming right up until the first frost."

"I think we should put them in water, Maestro. Do you have a vase?"

"Yes, let's step inside. I've done enough for today and I'll ask Cora to put these in a vase so that you can take them home. Now, you wanted to revise your playing schedule?"

"I do, Maestro, and I would really like to visit you three times a week if that's possible, if that's not too much trouble," she enquired as they stepped in the side door.

Without saying a word, the professor handed the bouquet to Cora, who promptly disappeared with it to another room. Alexandra imagined this situation had repeated itself many times in the past. She also pondered again why the professor had never married. How wonderful it would be, she thought, to have such a man who'd be in a position to give flowers to his wife every day! She also wondered how he could live in such a magnificent home and on such lovely property yet have no one to share it with. Again, the thought of that made her rather sad.

"Miss Alexandra, did you hear me?"

Alexandra blinked her eyes. "Yes, Maestro?"

"Well my dear, I just said that we can meet Mondays, Wednesdays and Fridays right after you finish school. Also, you needn't bring your violin because I have several here and you can choose one of them to play."

"Thank you ever so much, Maestro!" she said, resisting the urge to kiss him on the cheek.

"Let's not waste an opportunity," said the professor. "We can play something together now."

* * *

Early the following morning Joseph was sitting at his usual table sipping coffee when Alexandra came trundling down the stairs.

"Good morning, Papa! I'm bringing Nellie to school today because I'm going to play a song for the class. Sister Rose found out about the competition, and so she wants me to play."

"Oh it's today that she wants you to play, is it? Sit down, please, and tell me more."

Alexandra took a seat opposite him at the table. She leaned forward, pressing her chest against the table, hands in her lap.

"Yes, Papa, Sister Rose seemed quite insistent. She wanted me to play a duet with Owen, but I'm not sure he will do it. I saw her talking to him during lunch, but that's all."

"Well, perhaps that's all the better and divine intervention will prevent him from going to school today. We do remember what happened at the competition, right?"

"Of course, Papa, but I also think Uncle George left the competition early because he didn't want to be involved in any more visions I had. Maybe it was too much for him."

"Or maybe he has difficulty in accepting a loss at a competition," Joseph said. "Anyway, you should eat your breakfast. Marcie is going to be here soon."

Joseph went to the kitchen and after several minutes returned with a plate of pancakes. Alexandra began gobbling them down as if she hadn't eaten in days.

"I've also revised my music schedule with the Maestro," she said between bites. "I'll be going three days a week after school. By the way, do you like my bouquet?"

"Those are yours?" he asked, leaning over to sniff them. "They're really pretty. I thought Marcie brought them. I didn't know you have a suitor! Am I going to lose you already?"

"Well, Papa, I don't think you'd approve of the Maestro being my suitor," she said, laughing. "He's so old and gnarly. He's also a gardener!"

Joseph burst out laughing and Alexandra smiled impishly as she finished her breakfast. Just before going out the door, she turned back as if she had forgotten something.

"Papa, can you make a braid in my hair? You do such a good job! I dare not try Sister Rose's patience!"

"Certainly I can."

Alexandra retrieved the necessary brushes and combs for the task and sat down on a chair with her back toward her father. He brushed her hair straight back, making strands on each side and weaving them this way and that. He did this many times before and had become quite good at it. People often wondered if he hired a hairdresser, as certainly a man would not know the first thing about styling a girl's hair. On the whole, he felt an overall level of pride in raising a daughter alone. He had already spoken with her about the changes she could expect with her body, such matters as what happens to a woman every month. Most Catholic parents did not discuss such topics with their children, thus leaving them to discover these things on their own. Since Helen had left, the responsibility fell to him. He addressed the topic of reproduction one day after church when Alexandra was asking questions about a pregnant woman.

"There you go my dear, all done!"

"Thank you, Papa!" Promptly standing up, she turned round, kissed him on the cheek, gathered her books and violin and was gone, leaving the little brass bell on the door clattering and echoing through the empty café.

Joseph returned to his favourite table and sat down, his legs crossed. The whole café seemed drained of life after the girl left. He looked down at Alexandra's brush and comb lying on the table. Taking a sip of his coffee, he absorbed the silence of his surroundings. He again looked at the finely decorated hairbrush, the pearly handle, the bristles with stray hairs wound and caught through them. He remembered his wife using this same brush eight, almost nine, years before. He himself had no use for such things and wondered how much longer such feminine objects would remain in his life. Such items were also a painful reminder of Helen and her departure – and his failure. He thought about how busy he always was, how he hadn't spent enough time with his wife, his two-week absence while he worked on the farm struggling against the weather to collect the last harvest. Most of all, he remembered the fateful words of her goodbye note which still continued to torment him.

Life was passing by each day at a time and he wondered what it would be like in the future, in the distant future when Alexandra either moved away to attend some distant music school, or got married and started a family of her own. In either case, the result would be the same – he would be alone. He would be alone even if the café were full of noisy people and he was doing any sort of busywork. No matter what, each morning would find him here, at this table, drinking his coffee, missing his wife, missing his daughter, pondering the future and regretting the past.

At that moment, the brass bell announced the entrance of Marcie and the end of the day's silence. She wasted no time in setting about getting things ready.

"Good morning, Joseph!" she said as she disappeared into the kitchen.

"Hello, Marcie. I didn't get a chance to talk to you yesterday. How was everything?" He had to project his voice so she could hear him.

Marcie emerged from the kitchen. "Well, Joseph, there was a man here to see you yesterday. I told him to come back in the morning, so I expect he'll be here soon."

"Oh really? Did he leave his name?"

"As a matter of fact, he did. He said his name was Sir Charles Stanley."

Chapter 19

While Joseph was helping with the rush of morning customers, he spotted a familiar figure walking in the door. He washed his hands and greeted the new guest, who had taken a seat at the counter.

"Welcome, Sir Charles!" said Joseph, reaching out a damp hand. "What brings you into town?"

"Good to be here, Joseph," Stanley said. "I do hope you and young Alexandra have been well. How is the dear young lady?"

"She's been quite well, thank you. She suffered a couple more days with her cold, but she's been fit as her fiddle ever since," he laughed. "She really had a wonderful time in London and regrets not being able to stay longer. She does hope the competition will be held at your estate next year, too."

"Well, I would love to have her, of course, but unfortunately that won't happen. Joseph, I've come to Windsor to say goodbye as circumstances have dictated my return to England. Before I leave, though, I have some things I want to tell you which are of an extremely urgent nature. I also need to pay a visit to your brother."

Joseph looked at him in alarm.

"I hope I will not offend you with my words, Joseph, because that's not my intention. Nevertheless, I feel compelled to tell you in person and to make a confession as well. I was involved in some business dealings in which your brother did the legal work. He helped me through a great many things, Joseph, pulled lots of strings for me, got me on my feet and helped me to become quite wealthy. I really owed him a favour, and on the day of the competition, he wanted to collect."

Joseph focused his gaze suspiciously at Stanley.

"Look, Joseph, your brother George has some serious personal matters which are deeply troubling to him. I don't know how to tell you this other than to say it bluntly: he wants to harm your daughter. He wanted me to do it during the competition by giving her a rare, highly potent formulation from my pharmaceutical company. He said we could easily get away with it because she was already ill and so any deterioration in her condition could be blamed on her system reacting adversely to it. However, Joseph, I'm convinced that what he wanted me to give her would've been nearly fatal, or at least severely debilitating. I couldn't do such a horrific thing, Joseph. I couldn't do it for any price or under any threat."

Joseph continued to stand motionless, his eyes fixed on Stanley's moving mouth.

"Mr. Delmott, are you all right?"

"I need some air. Let's sit outside," said Joseph.

The two stepped out into the crisp October morning and sat at a table under the awning. The fresh air had an immediate and positive impact on Joseph. He raised his hands to his face, rubbed his eyes, and swept his hair straight back. He now realized that his brother would no longer be satisfied with taking the violin; that he was now threatening Alexandra's life – or at least trying to harm her so she could no longer pose any threat to him.

Marcie stepped outside. She ignored Stanley and spoke to Joseph.

"Joseph, you don't look so well. Can I get you something?"

"I'll be fine, but could you bring me a glass of water, please?"

In a few moments she returned with the requested glass of water, complete with a slice of lemon.

"Let me know if you need anything else, Joseph," she said as she handed him the glass and returned inside.

Joseph took a sip and looked out at the sidewalk and street. Gentlemen walked arm-in-arm with their ladies in the autumn sunshine. He heard the metallic sounds of the streetcars, saw the horses and carriages, and even the street cleaners. The world carried on as usual, but to him it would never be the same again.

"Stanley, there's a question that nags me. Why does my brother want to harm, or even kill, my daughter? Why did you agree, at first, to help him?"

Stanley focused squarely on him. "Joseph, honestly now, your brother didn't tell me why he wanted to hurt her. 'None of your concern,' he said – or something like that. He was very angry. He even called Alexandra a witch! Has Alexandra said anything to you about her uncle?"

"Yes, but I don't want to discuss that with you."

"Very well."

"Now, please answer my other question," said Joseph. "Why did you agree to harm her?"

"Your brother threatened to report me to the tax department, get me audited, and told me I'd lose everything. However, I never had any intention of doing as he bid, and realized full well what the personal ramifications would be. In the days following the competition, I decided to sell my stake in the company and put my house on the market. It's time to retire anyway, Joseph, and to return home. I suppose you could say this whole ordeal was my impetus. In any event, believe me when I tell you I could never harm anyone, especially an innocent child. But be careful, Joseph, your brother is a very dangerous man."

"Thank you, Stanley, for this information," said Joseph, standing up. "My brother is going to get a little visit – from me." He left Stanley alone at his table and set out for the law offices of Delmott, Cord & Brewster.

***

Alexandra took her place in Sister Rose's classroom, where the desks were filled with well-disciplined little students immaculately dressed for school. They were about as well disciplined as they could be, for everyone knew the old nun would have it no other way. However, there was an air of anxiety that day as Alexandra brought her violin. Obviously a performance was in the offing, a rare musical treat from Aydy and her fiddle, officially requested and sanctioned by none other than the good sister herself.

For her part, Alexandra did not want to be in a position where the other students would think she was better than they were, thus making them envious or jealous. The whole thought made her uneasy. She thought she had come up with the perfect idea – perfect until she noticed Owen with their pépé's violin.

The first part of the morning was dedicated to their catechism lesson, but after the morning recess Sister Rose took Alexandra and Owen aside and spoke to them in the corridor.

"I would like you two to play the duet for the class when we go inside," she insisted in her parched voice.

"We could try," said Alexandra, "though we've never practiced together and I can't be sure how it will all come out."

"Well!" huffed the nun. "We shall soon see."

"Sister Rose, perhaps we could have a few minutes to tune our instruments and warm up?" said Owen.

The nun paused, examining the boy as if she were actually considering his request.

"Very well then," she said, begrudgingly. "Take a few minutes at the back of the classroom to get ready."

Alexandra watched as Owen opened the case with D.C.D. embossed on the lid. Inside, she saw the small cloth, still folded over the instrument exactly as it was when she gave it to Owen. The thought crossed her mind that perhaps this was the first time he had opened the case at all.

Naturally, heads turned towards the back of the room to see what the two were doing. Alexandra picked and plucked at the strings of her instrument. Owen took their pépé's violin from its case and did likewise.

Alexandra played a short excerpt from one of her many classical pieces as the old nun looked on.

Owen put their pépé's violin on his shoulder. But when he tried pulling the bow across the strings, there was nothing more than a leaden, hollow sound. Alexandra looked at him and he glared at her before trying again. The result was no better.

"Is something the matter, Owen?" The old nun appeared irritated.

"I'm not sure, Sister Rose. There seems to be something wrong with my violin," he said before trying again. His efforts were rewarded with nothing more than dry, shapeless sounds and ghostly whispers. The students snickered.

Alexandra could see Owen becoming visibly upset and worried he would smash this violin like the previous one. She knew there was nothing wrong with the instrument. The thought dawned on her that if it were a magic violin, maybe it refused to play for Owen and would only play for her. She briefly entertained the idea of taking it from the boy's hands and playing it herself, but if it played for her and not him, it would humiliate the boy and goodness knows what he'd do then.

"Sister Rose, I think something really is wrong with Owen's violin. Perhaps he can return another day with his other violin and we can play our duet then. I can play a solo now if it pleases you."

"Very well. Master Delmott, please take your seat." Owen took his seat next to Pierre amid the muffled snickers of his classmates.

Alexandra, instrument in hand, walked to the front of the class. She stood straight and tall, positioning herself to play her song.

"Sister Rose, I wish to dedicate this song to you, to Owen, and to my classmates."

The old nun nodded from behind her desk.

Alexandra played a fine rendition of "Ave Maria," a song she thought the old nun would like, and not too long. She played it with feeling and reverence, moving her body in small, graceful motions with the highs and lows of the music.

When she sounded the final note, she looked at the nun and was startled to see her face with some real human colour to it, and even more than that, she was dabbing at her eyes with a handkerchief. The students clapped their hands – all of them except Owen. He sat slouched in his seat, arms crossed.

"Thank you very much Alexandra for that enlightening and moving performance," said the nun. She rose from her desk and stood next to Alexandra.

"You're welcome, Sister Rose, and thank you for letting me play for you and my classmates."

Everything was going as planned until Sister Rose spoke again. "Owen, wasn't that a wonderful performance? Don't you wish you could play as well as your cousin?" Turning to the rest of the class the nun smiled. "Don't you all wish you were good at something like our dear talented soloist Alexandra?"

Listening to the nun's words, Alexandra was mortified. Here she was – placed on a pedestal by the starchy old nun, on exhibit for all to see, an unwilling prima donna and worst of all, a teacher's pet. All her hard work at navigating her way around and through the classroom politics while dealing with Owen had been ruined by the nun, spiralling round and vanishing down the drain forever.

Chapter 20

"Where's George?" Joseph demanded to the stunned secretary at the law firm.

"He's in a meeting, Mr. Delmott," she said, clasping her hands together at her chest. "He'll be finished in a few minutes."

"Really? He's finished now!" said Joseph, walking straight to George's office and throwing the door open. He found George there with his partners and two other men. "Get out! Now!" Joseph told the men and pointing at the doorway.

"Gentlemen, please excuse us," said George, his voice laced with irritation.

After the men left, George closed the door. He turned to face Joseph. "How dare you come here and interrupt me like that!"

"'How dare I' you ask? How dare I? How dare *you*, brother! What do you want with my daughter?" Joseph shouted. "I heard you wanted to kill her!"

"Lower your voice! I have no idea what you're talking about," said George.

Joseph walked straight up to George, grabbing a fistful of his shirt and twisting it around his hand. He spoke directly into George's face, enunciating each word through his teeth. "You leave my daughter alone, or so help me God, I'll ensure you never draw another breath."

"Threatening me, are you Joseph?" said George. "That's never a good idea. I've got the law on my side, remember that. What do *you* have?"

"You tried to get Stanley to poison her at the competition!" said Joseph, releasing his grip on George as he pushed him backwards. George stumbled but did not fall. "Stanley came to Windsor today and told me so himself!"

"That weasel!" said George. He straightened his shirt and brushed himself off. "You have no proof. It's his word against mine."

"But why do you want to kill my daughter? What have you got against her that is so serious you'd actually want to kill her? Is it because she knows you caused the fire? Is it because you wouldn't help Papa after his heart attack?"

"Joseph, if you ever come here again, I swear I'll have you arrested. There are witnesses. However, I have no grudges against your daughter. Nobody knows how that fire started and what caused Papa's sudden death. You're insane. Please leave."

"Very well, but remember this: I will stop at nothing to protect my daughter – especially from the likes of you. Keep away from her. If you harm a single hair on her head, I'll make sure that that day is your last."

Joseph turned round and left the office, slamming the door shut behind him. He returned to the café where he found Stanley still sitting outside.

"Were you able to find out anything from your brother?" asked Stanley.

"No, he didn't tell me anything."

"Pity," said Stanley.

"As I understand it," said Joseph, "you're a druggist yourself, not just a drug company owner. Is that correct?"

"Yes."

"Very good. Now listen carefully. I have an idea and I need your help," said Joseph.

***

Joseph knew Alexandra would be pleased to learn about their visitor from London, and his prediction was confirmed the following morning after she came down the stairs.

"Sir Charles is in town!" Alexandra exclaimed upon hearing the happy news.

"Yes, Angel, and I expect him to be here directly. Marcie is coming in today and you, I, and Sir Charles are going on a little shopping trip to Walkerville. He'll be here only a few days, and I know he wants to get a few things for his wife."

"How wonderful! Do you think he has any more concerts? Oh I'd love to play again!"

"What about shopping? Aren't you excited about that, too?"

"Well yes, Papa, of course I'm excited about shopping, I like shopping!" she said as she chased the blueberries around her plate and jabbed at them with her fork.

"Don't play with your food. Eat it up and get dressed. We've got a big day ahead. Sir Charles will be here soon and we mustn't keep him waiting."

Sir Charles arrived a few minutes past 8:00, followed almost immediately by Marcie.

"Morning!" Joseph said to them both. "Thank you for coming in on a Saturday, Marcie. I appreciate that."

"You're welcome!" she said as she disappeared into the kitchen. "Don't mind me! Lots to do! The Saturday regulars will be here soon!"

Turning to Stanley, Joseph offered him a chair at one of the tables near the window.

"Alexandra is getting dressed. I expect she'll be down in a few minutes," Joseph said. "Where are you staying?"

"I've taken a room at the British American hotel and have decided to stay in Windsor for a week. I've never visited this part of the country and there are a few things I'd like to do, and some places I'd like to visit, before I leave for good. I should also pay that visit to your brother."

Joseph sighed. "Alexandra is really looking forward to seeing you. She lit right up when I told her you were coming today. I'm sure she'll be very disappointed when you tell her you're leaving Canada permanently."

Stanley sat forward in his chair. "On the one hand it pains me to have to leave at all, but on the other hand it's good to know I'll be missed by someone!" said Stanley, laughing.

"I understand perfectly. Wait here, Stanley, and I'll go upstairs to see what's keeping her."

"No, please Joseph, sit. She's getting ready and if you go up you'll spoil her entrance. I do happen to know a thing or two about women, you know!" Both men chuckled.

Marcie, rushing around as always, walked past them. Joseph was surprised that Stanley saw fit to interrupt her. "Excuse me ma'am, could I trouble you for another cup of coffee?" Stanley said, gazing into his empty cup.

The busy waitress stopped in her tracks, turned around, and laughed. "Sir Charles, really now! You've been here longer than ten minutes. You're no longer considered a guest. You can get your English backside out of that chair and get it yourself!"

Joseph burst out laughing. "Don't even think you can try winning an argument with Marcie, 'cause you'll lose every time –" He diverted his attention towards the stairs. "Unless you want to try arguing with that one. She'll give you a good run for your money, too!"

Alexandra came down the stairs wearing her pink Sunday dress with pleats adorned with lace.

"Hello, Miss Alexandra," said Stanley. He rose from his chair at the same time as Alexandra curtsied to him. "It's a pleasure to see you again. How are you?"

"Angel, really now," said Joseph. "Aren't you just a bit –"

Stanley placed his hand on Joseph's shoulder. "Shh, Joseph, let her."

Joseph nodded.

Just before the café officially opened, the trio stepped out into the frost-draped morning and boarded a streetcar for Walkerville. The seats were all full, so they stood together grasping hand rails, swaying like reeds in the wind with the movements of the streetcar.

"Do you like travelling by train and streetcar, Sir Charles?" Alexandra enquired with one curious eyebrow raised.

"Well now, I –"

"I perfectly love it – especially trains. I can even imagine what it would be like to travel around the whole country, looking out the window at the passing scenery, feeling the movement of the train below my feet, the happy passengers admiring the view. You do like seeing happy passengers, don't you, Sir Charles?"

"Naturally, my dear, as a matter of fact I –"

"I like seeing happy people too because when they're on the train, I figure they're almost always on holidays and, therefore, are probably always happy. Not so much with people on streetcars, though. I could never abide people with long, sour faces. Don't you agree, Sir Charles?"

"Certainly, I can't see any other way," he said, chuckling.

As the streetcar rattled along, Joseph watched as Alexandra needled poor Stanley with ever more questions.

"Do you like autumn, Sir Charles? I love this time of year and all the scents and freshness of autumn – especially October. It's like a second spring. However, once November arrives things will be different. That month has only cold, rain and skeletonised trees. It seems so barren and forlorn."

"Well, it's certainly different than in England," said Stanley.

"Maybe," came the response from Joseph. "By the way, I hear that England is quite rainy at this time of year. Is it true?"

Stanley laughed. "It's absolutely not true at all, sir! In fact, it's rainy the whole year through!" Both men chuckled while Alexandra, not understanding the joke, wrinkled her nose.

Upon their arrival in Walkerville, the three stepped off the streetcar.

"I won't be a moment," said Stanley. "I've got some business to tend to in the pharmacy here."

"Very well," said Joseph, "Alexandra and I will just be in the shop across the street. There are a few things we need to get, so come join us when you're finished."

* * *

Indeed, Alexandra did need to buy some things – especially shoes. She set out across the street with her father as Sir Charles disappeared into the pharmacy.

After Alexandra tried on several pairs, they were ready to leave. Still, Stanley had not yet joined them. "What could possibly be keeping him so long?" Alexandra wondered aloud. "He said he'd join us directly!"

"Well, it's not our business, Angel. I'm sure whatever he's doing is important and he'll be along – well, look who's here!"

"So sorry!" said Stanley. "I was engaged in conversation and couldn't very well break away! In any event, I have what I need. Shall we go?"

When they returned to the café later that day, Stanley stood beside Alexandra but kept a strange silence. Finally, he took a deep breath and addressed the girl directly. "My dear young lady, I had a wonderful time with you today. However, I'm afraid I must tell you that my wife and I are returning to London, England permanently. I wanted to come here to bid you farewell as I shall be taking my retirement in my home country and won't be doing any more travelling."

"I know," sighed Alexandra, pouting.

"How did you know?"

Alexandra searched for the right words. She glanced at her father, to the ceiling, and then to some distant object in the room before her gaze came back to rest on Stanley.

"Why else would you come all the way to Windsor if it wasn't to say goodbye?" she said, cocking her head to the side. "Windsor is going in the wrong direction if you wanted to take a ship across the ocean! But oh, how I wish I could join you in England! It would be so wonderful, wouldn't it? Much better than taking a train somewhere! You could take me to all the famous opera houses in London! I could visit St. Paul's Cathedral, the Tower of London, Loch Ness!"

"Loch Ness is in Scotland," Stanley said, chortling.

"Oh that's right! I was never good at geography!" she said with a bounce in her voice. "I have a question, though. Where will the Premier's Competition be held next year? I had such a wonderful time there, despite my illness, and I'd love to do it all again!"

Stanley paused. "As for the competition, I'm not sure when or where it will be held. That information won't be known until spring. However, there is a music festival in Ottawa in late May. It's just as big as the Premier's Competition and it attracts people from all over the country. It's also a place where fresh, new talent like yours can be seen by a large audience and many influential people. I highly encourage you to go, if you can."

"Oh Papa, please, can I go?"

"It's a long way off, Angel, both in time and distance. We shall see."

"All right," said Alexandra. "I wish you could be involved in that one, Sir Charles. We'll miss you in any case."

"I'll write regularly," said Stanley.

"When I grow up maybe I can even come and visit you and your wife someday, Sir Charles Stanley," she said, straightening herself up and saying his name in a correct and proper British accent. "That is, provided you have an extra bedchamber in your house for me!"

"Well, my dear, if I don't have an extra room then I'll just build one. So, you needn't worry!"

"That's really wonderful! Can my papa come too? Could you build a room for him as well?"

Stanley looked at Joseph and winked. "Of course. Why not? I'll spare no expense in seeking the comfort of my houseguests."

"Oh, Sir Charles! I'd love to play a song for you, please!" she said, bouncing up and down and clapping her hands. "I've been waiting all day!"

"Well now m'dear, there'll be plenty of time for that! I really should get back to the hotel. It's getting rather late."

"It won't take long, I promise!"

"Alexandra! Please give our guest some peace! He's had a long trip and busy day!" said Joseph before turning his attention to Stanley. "How much longer will you be in Windsor?"

"I'll be here another four days. After that, I'm catching a train back to London. I'll be here to visit you both every day until then. We've got most of our belongings packed and my wife is spending these last days visiting her social circle. I'll stay in Canada another week, then off we go to England. So, I'm moving from London to London. That's rather remarkable, isn't it, Alex?"

"Indeed it is sir!" Alexandra said. "But let's agree that before you go I'll play a special concert just for you."

"I promise you, Miss Alexandra, you will most certainly play another concert for me."

Chapter 21

George Delmott decided that Monday morning was the perfect time to pay a visit to the café with three of his clients. He planned his arrival about an hour after it opened to ensure Alexandra would be in school and there'd be no chance he could hear her play her violin. When they arrived at the café, they did not remove their hats or overcoats. George stood a moment with the men just inside the front entrance. He pointed to various things before walking amongst the tables, noting the fixtures and gazing at the floor and walls. They looked this way and that, surveying the entire establishment.

Soon George noticed that horrible waitress Marcie scowling at him as she served one of the tables. He never did like her and was quite sure the feeling was mutual. She glanced at him once more before disappearing into the back room, only to reappear moments later with Joseph.

"What are you doing here?" said Joseph.

"Why shouldn't I be here? Must I remind you that this café, nay, the whole cussed building is my legal property and I have every right to be here and you, of course, have every right not to like it."

He turned his attention back to the three men. "My apologies, gentlemen. This way, please."

The four proceeded up the stairs, sparing no time for pleasantries. Some of them tapped their walking sticks on the wooden steps and plaster walls to sound out the structure of the place.

"Why are you going up there? That's where we live!" said Joseph.

George had quite enough. He stopped in his tracks halfway up the stairs and turned back to look down at Joseph. "Let me tell you a second time in case you've forgotten: this is my business and I've got a right to be here."

George and the men entered Alexandra's room. They looked about the whole place, past the fine, dainty decorations Alexandra had placed on the walls, her collection of dolls, and her music propped up in various places.

"What is the meaning of this!" Joseph said, following them up the stairs. The four stood together and spoke in low voices, ignoring Joseph and his protests. "Yes, I'm sure it won't be a problem," one of the men said to George in a hushed voice. George nodded before walking with the men into Joseph's room to inspect it as well.

Finally, George turned to Joseph, who was blocking his path. "I have determined that your operation of this café has turned out to be quite disappointing, so I've decided to sell it to these fine property investors here. We shall ink and seal the deal next week. Thirty days after that you must vacate the premises, and then the whole structure shall be demolished," he said, a rush of satisfaction elating him. He felt like beating his chest.

"Why are you doing this?" demanded Joseph. "I thought we had an agreement! You got the violin, exactly as we agreed! Wasn't that enough?"

"Dear brother! You slander me and demean my good reputation in front of these men by making such false accusations. I haven't a clue what you're talking about! I remember no such conversation. I also know you're upset, brother, but remember," he said, calming his voice and resting his hand on Joseph's shoulder. "It's just business! Relax! Someday, when enough time has passed, we'll have forgotten this whole thing, right? However, now I must kindly ask you to step aside, lest I send for the constable and have you arrested for obstructing my freedom of movement."

When they arrived back down in the cafe, Marcie was pacing about at the bottom of the stairs, arms folded.

"What do you want with us? What's your reason for coming in here with these men?"

George noticed nearby customers looking on at Marcie's interrogation. He squinted his eyes at her and frowned, pretending not to understand her question. He liked using this tactic in court or during the negotiations of some business deal. He'd often ask for further clarification, making the person who asked the question feel stupid and uncomfortable.

"I have no idea what you mean," he said. "Besides, I don't see how this is any of your concern. These are serious business issues, woman, and business is something you know nothing about."

"George is closing us down Marcie. He's selling the land to these businessmen and then the café will be torn down. We have little more than a month to leave."

She glared at George. "How could you do that to your brother? He's your own flesh and blood! You're a horrible man, George Delmott!"

"Woman, mind your tongue."

"You've got to be joking! I'm going to say what I want and I'm going to say it loud and clear and I want to make sure all these good people hear it!" Marcie said with renewed energy. "You, sir, are an egocentric, self-serving, horrible excuse for a human being. You would sell out your flesh and blood, your very own brother and his daughter, in order to line your pockets. Your brother has slaved away in this place all these many years and has made a good living for his family. You cut his livelihood out from under him and then just think you can walk away. I hope everyone finds out what kind of a shameless scoundrel you are!"

George felt his palms sweating and pulse racing as customers looked on. Nevertheless, with minimal effort he could hide his discomfort by making his face as cold and expressionless as one of those statues on Easter Island. However, judging by the faces glowering at him, it would take much more than that. Word would soon spread around the small town, to each person's family, to everyone's friends. He was even sure it would be talked about after mass the following Sunday. George, seeking support, turned towards his companions, yet they only stared at him as if he were a monster.

* * *

Midafternoon found Joseph pacing back and forth in front of Alexandra's school. This would now become a new routine. From now on Joseph would bring her to school and take her home afterwards. Joseph believed some of the townsfolk would probably think it was just an excuse for him to escape the busy café, but they could never know the truth behind his motives – he wanted to protect his daughter.

The schoolyard was filled with children of all ages happily running to their homes. From a distance, Joseph could see Alexandra and Emma walking together. Once Alexandra spotted her father, she parted ways with Emma and came running up towards him.

"Hi, Papa!" she said. "Are you coming with me to my music lesson?"

"Yes, I hope you don't mind, Angel. I'm sure I can keep myself entertained during the lesson."

As they walked, the large, fallen leaves of the great sugar maples littered their path and the smell of autumn filled the air. They strolled past white picket fences, elegant homes and gardens all dressed in their autumn finery.

Joseph kicked at some of the leaves as he walked. "I also wanted to talk to you. Your uncle came to the café today."

"Surely he didn't have anything to eat or drink," said Alexandra. "He never does. What did he want?"

"Well, he came through with some other people. They went through the whole place and looked at everything," he said, sighing.

"Your uncle is closing the café and selling the property," said Joseph. "We'll have to leave. But don't worry, the news isn't entirely bad."

Alexandra stopped. "Oh, Papa! Why is he doing this? Where will we live?"

"That's my next news," he said. "We're going to build a new house on London Street and also a new restaurant right next door. It'll be much more than a café and things will be much busier. We'll start building first thing in the spring when the weather breaks. In fact, I bought the property quite some time ago and was waiting for the right time to begin construction."

"That part is good news, but what about Marcie? And Bill? And Sophie? What's going to happen to them?"

"Well, I can't do anything about them now, unfortunately. If they find other work by the time we open for business, I'll have to hire new staff. In any event, it's the best we can do in a bad situation. In the meantime, the Maestro has plenty of room in his house for us. I explained everything to him, and he said we can stay with him as long as we want."

Alexandra and Joseph continued walking. "Papa, I never knew that people could be as mean as Uncle George. I know that when you were little, Pépé gave you and him new quill pens. Uncle George lost his pen, but one day when you weren't home, he took yours in the back garden and used it to stab at a piece of wood. He kept doing it until the nib broke off."

"Is that a fact?" he said, recalling that he couldn't have been any more than ten when the incident happened. "I'd almost completely forgotten about that. What other things do you know?" Joseph was impressed at his daughter's knowledge, and often wondered how much she really knew about the people who'd heard her play. It seemed she was like a vault locking away many secrets, with only her knowing the combination to enter, as well as the true value of what was inside. He wondered if she entered this vault from time to time to amuse herself.

"Well, I know that when you and Uncle George were teenagers you both took a farm wagon apart and put it back together on the roof of someone's barn!"

Joseph burst out laughing. "Your uncle and I got along well in those days! That was old man Gagnier's barn! I wish I could've seen the look on his face when he woke up the next day!"

Alexandra laughed.

"You do know lots of things about other people, don't you?" asked Joseph.

"Oh, yes, Papa, I know many things!" she said, smiling shyly and clasping her hands together.

"Things such as...?"

"But Papa! It's not polite to tell secrets about people! If I tell, it's the same thing as telling gossip. That would make me one of those horrible gossips – even worse than Mrs. Labonte or Mrs. Tellier! You know I don't like gossips; they are the most dreadful people in the world, gossiping all day and every day, all night and every night about this and that. I hear them every day in the café and they make me crazy! They're like a bunch of old chickens in a henhouse, *cackle cackle cackle!*" she said, flapping her elbows like a bird.

Joseph laughed at her antics. "All right, Angel, I agree with you. I won't pry."

Chapter 22

At dawn the following day, Alexandra awoke to the tapping of rain falling on her window sill. The day was damp and the ground sodden, yet the falling raindrops created a melodic, soothing pattern, accented only by the different objects they struck after their descent from the heavens. She also recalled, with pleasure, how drenched she was on that day five months ago when she first met the professor – and it brought a smile to her face. Despite the weather, her bedroom was quite warm and comfortable. It was obvious that her father had lit the big stove.

She donned her housecoat and trundled down into the café. "Papa! Are you here?" she called. No answer.

Looking toward her father's table, she saw two empty coffee cups atop a mess of papers. She picked the cups up, intending to take them to the kitchen. She paused. Each cup was warm. She noticed the assortment of papers on the table. These were certainly not the usual financial papers her father always worked on. These papers had random capital letters, small numbers and geometric symbols handwritten on them. Certainly her father would not write such things as he was a man not given to making such doodlings.

Sighing, she brought the cups to the kitchen and went upstairs, one lazy step at a time. Rather than going to her own room, she stopped at the door to her father's room. His door was open a crack and she tapped on it with her knuckle. No answer. She eased the door open, peering in to see if anyone was there. These days she never went into this room; she had no reason to. However, when she was a little girl, she used to like running into her parents' room and jumping up and down on their bed to wake them. They'd usually groan at first, but she'd be insistent. In the end, they'd tickle her in revenge and she'd squeal with peal upon peal of giddy laughter. It was a merry way to start the day, and she missed those times – and her mother.

Entering the room, she looked around at the large four-poster bed, the ornate vanity with mirror, the Queen Anne's divan, the changing screen.

Not escaping her attention were two photographs standing on the night table. One of them was of her mother. In that sepia toned photo, she had a solemn look on her face, as was typical of formal photographs, but with just a hint of the same mischievous smile Alexandra herself was known for. Alexandra picked up the photo and examined it carefully. She noted her mother also had the same oval face as she, the same eyes and hair, the latter of which made a striking contrast to her fair skin. With a great deal of care she placed the photo back down on the table. She couldn't help wondering if her father looked at it every night before he fell asleep.

In the second photo were all three family members. Alexandra even remembered the day the photo was taken. She was four years old. It was so hot that day in the studio and she had to wear a dress with a stiff collar that nearly choked her. To that day she hated wearing collars or anything else tight around her neck. The photographer was trying to be patient, but Alexandra remembered getting anxious and the poor man's patience was wearing thin. In any event, the job got done and the moment became frozen in time forever.

She replaced that photo too and went to her mother's vanity. Carefully opening a drawer, she was startled to see that her mother's jewellery was still there, along with her necklaces and tiny, ornate bottles of perfume. She examined the jewellery and removed the cap from a bottle of perfume, daintily holding it between her thumb and index finger. She raised it up to just under her nose and savoured its scent for a few moments. She smiled, replaced the cap and put the bottle back in the drawer.

She looked at all these little things, trying to reason why her mother would have left them all behind. They certainly weren't large, in fact they could easily be packed in an overnight bag. Alexandra wondered if her mother had left them behind for her. Despite the number of times she played for her father, there was nothing in his memory which could explain, with any amount of certainty, why her mother had left. His memories were full of regret at her departure even to this very day, yet Alexandra knew he possessed the unique ability to hide his feelings and emotions under that mask he presented so well to the outside world.

At that moment, Alexandra could hear the front door of the café open. She ran to her room, got dressed, and went downstairs. When she entered the café, her father was there with Sir Charles – who was already sipping on a cup of coffee. The table was clean and the strange papers were gone.

"Good morning, Sir Charles, how long have you been here?" she said as she approached him at his table. He interrupted his coffee in mid-sip and placed it back down on the table.

"G'day, m'lady! Oh I've been here for a while already; I arrived early and your father's been keeping me company."

"I'm sure he enjoys the company, Sir Charles! How much longer will you be in town?"

"I'll be here until Thursday. Oh that's the day after tomorrow already, isn't it?" he laughed. "However, until then I've got plenty of things to do – chief amongst them visiting you fine people in the café as often as possible."

"Oh, Sir Charles! I'd really love to play a song for you! May I? Please?"

"My goodness, child! Relax! Rest assured, there'll be plenty of time for that later."

* * *

Sir Charles Stanley did indeed have many things to do in Windsor. One item of business he desperately needed to tend to was to pay a visit to the legal offices of Delmott, Cord & Brewster. Carrying a small parcel, Stanley arrived at the law firm unannounced that Tuesday morning. Having been told by the secretary that George Delmott was in a meeting, Stanley promptly dismissed that excuse as rubbish. He walked right into the office where he found Delmott sitting alone at his desk.

"You could've at least knocked," said Delmott.

"Here's your package," said Stanley, tossing it onto the desk. "Make sure you follow the instructions exactly."

"Took you long enough to deliver it," said Delmott.

"You're lucky you got it at all. That concludes our business, Mr. Delmott. I never want to see you or hear from you again."

"I assure you, you won't. Don't forget your payment," said Delmott, handing Stanley a wad of money.

Stanley took the money and threw it in the air, and the bills flittered to the floor. "I don't want your money. Good-bye, Delmott, and good riddance," he said as he walked out the door.

When Stanley left the office, he recomposed himself before speaking to the bewildered secretary. "Thank you very much ma'am," he said, tipping his hat. "I'm so very sorry to have troubled you. Have a good day."

* * *

Wednesday morning found Alexandra up extra early. It was her 13th birthday and she couldn't wait to start the day. In fact, she reasoned that starting a new year was much better than starting a new day. It was like a clean page in a book – three hundred and sixty-five clean pages in fact – and there she could fill it up with endless possibilities. When she arrived downstairs, Joseph and Stanley were there, and Marcie had been there long before them both. They all lined up as if greeting royalty.

"Happy Birthday, Angel!" said Joseph, beaming.

Stanley chimed in next. "I couldn't depart for England without first bestowing my very best birthday greetings to you!"

"*Mon petit oiseau* is all grown up today! *Bonne fête! Alles Gute zum Geburtstag!* Happy Birthday!" said Marcie, hugging the girl tightly.

"Oh thank you all so much! I must still be sleeping, really, this all has to be a wonderful dream, and I don't want to wake up!"

"I assure you it's not a dream," said Stanley.

"Sir Charles is right! As a matter of fact, we're closing the café early today. Also, there'll be no music lesson for you as the Maestro is coming here, as well as Robbie and Emma. We're having a little party."

"Oh thank you so much, Papa!" she said, springing up and down. She hugged him and kissed his whiskered cheek. "This is going to be the best birthday ever!"

In short order she was ready and on her way to school, accompanied by Joseph. As they walked, the morning sun shone radiant against the magnificent yellows, reds and oranges of the trees along the usual route to school. Alexandra skipped a bit as she walked and occasionally bent down to pick up and admire a perfect specimen of a golden maple leaf.

"Do you think autumn is a good time to have a birthday, Papa?"

"Honestly, I haven't given the matter much thought. I suppose it's just as good a time as any. Besides, as long as you're here, it doesn't make much difference."

"I don't mind it. We never have a choice as to when we're born or to whom we're born to. I'm just glad I was born at all, and I'm glad I was born here to you and mama. I only wish she could be here to celebrate my birthday. Everything would be so perfect! Do you wonder if she's thinking about me today? Could she have completely forgotten?"

Joseph sighed, his pause weighing heavy in the air. "You've been asking me the same question every year since you were four, Angel.

I'm quite sure she hasn't forgotten about you. Honestly though, I can't make excuses for your mother."

"Yes, Papa, of course you can't. But sometimes I think that Mama died. If so, it would be so wonderful to think that the very last words she uttered were, 'I love you, Alexandra!' Oh, it would be so tragic, yet wonderful to believe!"

"I can't say I haven't thought of that myself," he said as they approached the school. "However, we'll make the most of what we have. Now I see your friends coming, so I'll go home. We've got to get things ready; there's so much to do."

Alexandra smiled and, hugging her father as tight as a belt, kissed him on the cheek and bid him goodbye.

Upon entering the school grounds, she was greeted by Robbie and Emma. Owen was nowhere to be seen, but that didn't seem strange. The boy's habit now was to arrive at school mere minutes before the bell rang, which gave everyone the impression that he didn't care to spend any more time than necessary in useless socializing.

Regardless, Alexandra excused herself from her friends and purposefully sought the boy out. After several minutes she saw him shuffling along toward the school, alone, from the direction of his home. She went straight up to meet him.

"Hi, Owen! Today's my birthday!" she said as he entered the schoolyard. They both stood alone, out of earshot of the other students.

"Yeah, I know," he said.

"I wanted to see you. My father has planned a party for me today after school, and I would really like it if you could come. Owen, I want us to be as we were when we were little. I really miss those days. You know, my father says that the future is a really big place with so many grand and wonderful possibilities. I believe him, and I can't bear the thought of going into that big place with these problems standing between us."

Owen stood there in the schoolyard listening to her, but looked down at his feet, using the toe of his shoe to play in the dust on the ground. Alexandra was dismayed he wouldn't look at her, yet she continued with her olive-branch overtures.

"Also, I can't see any reason why things have to be so bad between us. I can only imagine that events in your life are making you miserable."

"What makes you think so?" he said, glancing up.

"It's not hard to figure out! Anybody can see it. For example, take what happened at the Premier's Competition. Owen, it was only for fun. I never expected to win it, the Maestro entered me into it and I went because I wanted to play and meet other musicians. Your father wanted you to go too, but you didn't really want to. You're getting so much pressure at home, so much pressure to succeed, and you're finding it all too difficult. Anyway, I want my cousin back! No, that's not correct. I *really* want my cousin back! He was always like the brother I never had. Maybe in some time I could even play a duet with him. I know he's a talented musician! Please, Owen, let's just forget all those bad things. Please come to my party. I want you there!"

"I've been really horrible to you, Alexandra. I can't understand why you'd want me at your party. I'm a bully, and everybody knows me as one. Besides, I don't know that my father would allow me to go. Are Robbie and Emma going to be there?"

"Yes, of course. But that doesn't matter. They'd like us all to be friends again. Everything in the past is water under the bridge. Please come?"

Owen stood quiet for a few moments, still not raising his head. "I'll think about it," he mumbled.

"Very good. I hope the answer will be yes!" She smiled at him though he was still looking down at his feet.

When it was time for school to begin, the bell sounded and the students filed inside. Upon entering her classroom, Alexandra was surprised at what she saw. The old nun had put up a few decorations and even baked a cake. Alexandra vaguely remembered having a dream about this very situation and thinking back to that wonderful, yet horrible day when she played for the class. She even remembered the sickly-sweet words of the old nun. The embarrassment she'd suffered that day had never completely gone away, and today it returned for a horrible encore.

Once the students took their seats and said their morning prayers, Sister Rose began, heaping unwelcome praise upon Alexandra. To further add to her irritation, Alexandra noticed that Owen was sitting in his place doodling something in his book with a pencil. He appeared to be disconnected, his little drawings taking shape along the margins.

"Hello, Aydy, and happy birthday!" said Sister Rose, exposing her yellowing set of imperfect teeth.

Alexandra didn't know what was worse – having the nun make a big fuss over her, or tolerating her using her nickname. Sister Rose had never celebrated anyone else's birthday. Alexandra hated this kind of attention. She wished she could just quietly disappear, perhaps become part of the walls, or the furniture. Sinking into and becoming part of the floor would be even better.

"Thank you, Sister Rose for the birthday greetings and for decorating the room so nicely. I honestly don't feel I've done anything special to deserve it, but thank you just the same."

The old nun stood in front of the class as if she were analysing Alexandra's words. "Now I hope everyone heard that. You've just heard the words of a very humble person. The Good Lord enjoys humble people and despises anyone who thinks too highly of themselves. He has seen fit to bless us all with a very devout Catholic, exceptional student and talented musician. You should all strive to be like her."

The old woman dryly enunciated each word and began clapping her hands and, with a bit of hesitation, the other pupils did too, including Emma and Robbie.

"Thank you again for your kind words, Sister Rose. However, I must respectfully disagree with you. I feel I am not worthy of such praise; I haven't done anything special. I just happen to love music, but anyone can love music."

Meanwhile Owen, who had been doodling throughout the entire discourse, smiled and placed his pencil down. He looked straight at the nun, a look of satisfaction on his face.

"Is something the matter, Owen?"

"She finally said something that makes sense, Sister."

"Master Delmott, why must everything you say always be so rude?"

"But Sister Rose, I can't understand why you've gone to all this trouble for her. She really doesn't deserve it. She's nobody important; moreover, she's a fraudster and a liar."

In her mind's eye, Alexandra could see Owen standing in a vast field, laughing and tearing to shreds her invitation and letting the pieces scatter about in the wind.

"How dare you say that about your cousin!"

"Sister Rose, today marks the anniversary of the birth of a liar and thief. To my mind, that's no reason to celebrate. Firstly, she has no mother. There's got to be a reason for that! Now it would be understandable if her mother had died, but no," he said. Then he turned to Alexandra and continued. "She left her and her father in order to get a better life for herself. And who can blame her? She couldn't stand the whiney little girl and her boring restaurant-keeper father – or whatever he is. He treated his wife like a slave in that café. My parents talk about it all time! He made her do all the work and refused to hire anyone. So if her mother really loved her, she'd be here right now with her on her birthday, but of course she isn't. That's proof in itself! She couldn't stand her, so she left to get a better, more exciting life – a better life with a common, foulmouthed womanizing sailor! Can you imagine?"

Alexandra sat not only in numbed disbelief at Owen's words, but at the spiteful and venomous way in which he spoke them. She imagined him as a lawyer levelling his accusations against his opponents or, even worse, one of those politicians her father had told her about.

The old nun stood motionless in front of the class, solid as a monument. "Owen Delmott!" she finally barked. "Haven't you got any decency at all?"

"It's true, Sister Rose! Alexandra's mother left them to go away with a sailor who used to come in to the café whenever he visited town. One day, she just got fed up with everything. She up and left, and near as I can figure, she never visits, never writes, never does anything. If Alex's mama doesn't even love her, how could anyone else? No one can stand her!"

"Owen Delmott! You apologize to your cousin immediately! How can you be so cruel – especially when it's her birthday!"

"Sister Rose, I cannot and will not apologize to that witch! Truly she is a witch, did you know that?" he said, his voice becoming a sinister, whispering hiss. "Shh! She's a keeper of secrets! Every time she 'plays' her violin, she gets little secrets from people! She collects them all, and she knows everything about everyone. Sister Rose, she probably even knows secrets about you!"

Alexandra was struggling to remain composed, a wretched sickness gnawing away in the pit of her stomach. Thinking back, she was sure she hadn't said anything to anyone. She turned to look at Emma, who shrugged her shoulders and frowned.

The old nun spoke again. "Owen, you are clearly a miserable, angry boy who is given to making silly, ridiculous fabrications. How absurd! A keeper of secrets! I've never heard such rubbish in all my life!"

Alexandra raised her hand and looked patiently at the nun. "Sister Rose, may I speak?"

"Well of course you may speak my dear!" the nun said, softening her voice.

"Sister Rose, I must confess that Owen really is telling you the truth. I do get visions of people, yes, and I get them every time I play my violin. However, Owen is only telling you half the story! He missed the most important part! What he's not telling you is that I also have wings hidden under my clothes and that I'm really, in all truth, a bird! Why didn't you mention that part, cousin?" she said, turning to face Owen. "In fact, I can sing and fly like a bird too! I fly around the whole town and county, peeping into all the windows and watching all the good and bad little boys and girls, then I report all this to Father Christmas so he can make his list. I've been watching Owen Delmott very closely and I can tell you he's getting a lump of coal in his stocking for Christmas this year!"

The children sniggered and giggled. Even the old nun, prim and proper though she was, raised a hand to her mouth to restrain a laugh.

"Alexandra!" the nun said. "Such a fanciful story! It's about as believable as Owen's."

Alexandra grinned.

"What about her mother?" said Owen, his voice full of scorn.

"Well, you're only partly right there too, Owen," said Alexandra. "After she ran off with the sailor, I was so upset that I flew everywhere hunting her down. When I caught her, I pecked her to pieces and ate her. That's the reason she never visits or writes!"

Several students sniggered, and the old nun raised the corners of her mouth into a smile, arms folded across her chest. Owen slumped down in his seat.

"Enough of this nonsense, the both of you!" said Sister Rose. "Let's get down to work."

In the end, Alexandra could take comfort in the fact that Owen was widely known to be a liar, and she reasoned that this particular story would come across to everyone as a futile attempt to malign her. Yet, she still wondered how he could have found out about the visions. Surely, Emma wouldn't have said anything, and her father definitely wouldn't have. She wondered if her uncle knew that she had visions and he told that fact to Owen. Worse than the knowledge of the visions, though, was his story of how her mother left – if it were, in fact, true. However, his story made no sense to her. Her father had always told her that her mother left the family in order to get some rest. She thought she must have been really ill, but would never run off with anyone, especially a sailor. She dismissed Owen's story immediately, believing it to be the product of a cruel, spiteful boy.

Chapter 23

The only disappointment Alexandra had with her party was that Sir Charles had missed her play her violin. By the time he arrived she had already finished playing and had forgotten to play for him.

From up in her bedroom the following morning she could hear the brass bell on the door clanging. She was already up and getting dressed by then, and could hear people talking downstairs. She was anxious to finish getting ready so that she could go down and join them.

When she arrived downstairs in the café, Stanley was standing near the counter talking to Marcie. His packed suitcase sat near the door.

"Today's the day, right Sir Charles?" she interrupted.

"I'm afraid so, my dear."

"He was becoming a regular here!" said Marcie, chiming in.

Alexandra then switched on her best British accent.

"I'm going to miss you, Sir Charles. I miss you even now and you haven't even left! Oh wait! Before you leave can I play you a song, please? Our agreement, remember?"

"What about your breakfast? We have to hurry and get to the train station!"

"It won't take more than a minute!" she said, clapping her hands together and bouncing on her feet.

"Dear Lady! Did you know it's actually good to leave some business unfinished? This way we have something to look forward to! If we were to finish all our business today, then all matters between us are closed and we have nothing to look forward to, no loose ends to tie up! So yes, of course I do want to hear you play, but I want to hear you when you come to visit me in London. Understood?"

Alexandra pouted. "Well, I do want to come see you in the big London, so let this be our new agreement – I shall play for you there."

"All right then, agreed!" said Stanley, chortling. "Now let's eat and be on our way!"

Marcie stood nearby. "When Alexandra comes to visit you, send her home with some fine silk, would you? I'd like that as a souvenir. Don't forget to write us, and don't forget the little café!"

"I can't forget. I'll miss you all, but no need to worry. As we said before, we'll write each other often. Oh wait! I have a little something for you, Miss Alexandra!" Stanley walked over to his bag and returned with a small brown parcel.

"For me?"

"Yes, it's just a small gift. I should have given it to you yesterday, but here it is nonetheless."

Alexandra smiled and began peeling back the brown paper, which contained a small book. She examined the cover. "Oh thank you, Sir Charles! I love poetry, and I'm sure this will be a wonderful book! I've heard about this poet, Robert Browning, and I shall read it from cover to cover!"

"You're most welcome, my dear! Browning is one of our finest and most respected poets. I hope you'll enjoy his works."

"Yes I will, Sir Charles, and thank you thank you again, ever so much!" she said, pleased he had the foresight to get her a gift.

Joseph joined them, and right after breakfast they left for the train station. They walked Stanley up to the train, even right up to his first class seat where he settled in comfortably. "Safe travels Stanley, and thanks again for coming all this way. Please give our best regards to your missus," said Joseph, tipping his hat.

"Goodbye, Sir Charles. Write often and don't forget us!" sniffled Alexandra as she bent down to hug and kiss the man.

After they left Stanley, they watched as the great steam engine pierced the morning sky with a plume of black soot. The train slid down the long silvery tracks, the usual fanfare of whistles blowing and bells clanging, taking its precious cargo of humanity into the distance.

Alexandra and her father watched the train disappear before walking away from the empty platform. "I suppose if we hurry we might just get you to school before 9:00 a.m."

When Alexandra entered her classroom, the decorations had been taken down and everything was back to normal, except for one thing – Owen was absent, his seat next to Pierre, empty. Alexandra was delighted, but confused. Owen was usually late, but he was never absent. Did his father chastise him about the goings-on of the previous day and so decided to keep him home? Did he get into another fight, but this time with someone much stronger? Perhaps he's ill? The questions burned in her mind all day – so much so that she could barely concentrate on her studies.

* * *

Joseph returned to the café and sat at his usual table sipping coffee over the café financial ledgers. While he was working, one of George's partners in the legal firm walked in the door – Clive Brewster.

After quickly scanning the café, Brewster walked over to Joseph at his table.

"Hello, Clive. What brings you here?" asked Joseph.

"I've got some bad news for you, Joseph. I'm here to tell you that your brother suffered what appears to be an attack of apoplexy last night – or at least that's what the doctors think. He's been taken to hospital where his condition is being monitored round the clock."

"My goodness! Please, please sit down and tell me more!" said Joseph, motioning to an empty chair. "What exactly happened?"

"The doctors don't really know," said Brewster, sitting down. "It's too early to tell. He collapsed at home last night after dinner and was taken to hospital almost immediately."

"I'm sorry to hear that. I know we've had our differences, but –" Joseph thought a moment before continuing. "I know. I shall go there right away and visit him."

"Don't. Clara doesn't want him having any visitors. Besides, there's nothing you can do. Everything is in the hands of the doctors – and God," Brewster said, a grave tone darkening his voice.

"What do you suggest I do?"

"Look, Joseph, it's important for you to know that I've been given power of attorney, which means that since your brother has become incapacitated, I am authorized to act on his behalf and manage his affairs. However, between you and me, you should know that your brother has become very difficult to work with over the past few months. Then he told me his plans for this place! To my mind it's not only a bad business decision on his part, but it's being done out of pure spitefulness. There needs to be some level-headed thought to this and it certainly shouldn't be done in such haste. Furthermore, I'm not anxious to put you and Alex on the street nor to put the café out of business. Therefore, I'm suspending the sale pending his recovery. If he doesn't recover in, say, six months or, God forbid, if he dies, we can deal with it all then. In other words, now is not the right time."

"Well, all right, I understand, and thank you, Clive. Please tell Clara and Owen that I hope George recovers quickly. Also, please keep me informed of any changes in his condition. If there's anything I can do, please let me know."

"Very well," said Brewster, getting up. "Good day to you."

"Good day, Clive."

Brewster tipped his hat and departed the café.

After a few moments, Marcie joined Joseph at his table, a worried expression on her face.

"I couldn't help overhearing George's business partner! What on earth?" she said.

"Now, now, Marcie, let's just take each day at a time. Our plan is still in effect. We're still building a new restaurant next year. If this café remains open until then, we'll all keep right on working. In the meantime, let's hope George recovers. From what I know about apoplexy though, each one is different but the damage can be life long."

"Well, boss, I truly know about apoplexy, that I do. My little brother, God rest his soul, died of apoplexy when he was only ten."

* * *

During lunchtime Alexandra found the perfect opportunity to talk to Emma. They stood outside near the corner of the building where Alexandra was sure no one could overhear them.

"Do you know how Owen found out about the visions?"

"No, I don't," Emma whispered. "I didn't tell him anything! Honest!"

"I didn't think you would. I'd just like to know how he could've found out about them."

"I don't know. For a while I was worried you were going to blame me, but when I went to your party yesterday we didn't even talk about it. So no, I didn't tell him, I didn't tell anyone! In fact, Owen didn't even ask. Perhaps he found out about it another way."

"You're a good friend, Emma. I knew I could trust you. I also know you didn't say anything."

"Oh," Emma said, squinting one eye, "you probably had a vision about me yesterday when you played! I understand. Do you get visions everytime you play?"

"No, but I did have a vision about you yesterday, and not just you. But honestly, I don't get visions everytime and I don't get them with everyone. I really can't explain it."

"Oh? You got some visions yesterday?"

"Well yes, of course, but don't ask me to give you details! I won't ever do that! I told Papa – and I'm telling you – that I could never become a gossip like old Mrs. Tellier or Mrs. Labonte," she said, shuddering her shoulders.

Emma laughed as she spoke. "I'm just glad you didn't put Mrs. Brindle on your list!"

Alexandra smiled at Emma and looked down. After a few moments she looked up again and continued. "I don't want to get a bad reputation like Owen has. It's really awful. Also, Papa told me that if the police find out about my visions, that I could spend my life playing music for criminals and getting horrible visions about what they did."

"Maybe that's not bad," said Emma. "You would be helping people, solving crimes, doing good things in the world!"

"But I can do good things in other ways. I still want to be a concert violinist, Emma, and I want to travel around the world and see all the great sights. I want to go to London, the one with Big Ben, and visit Sir Charles and his wife. After that I'll go Paris, Vienna, Salzburg, Venice and all the other great capitals of Europe!"

"Oh, it's great to have a wonderful dream and talent, Aydy!"

"I never wanted to be ordinary," said Alexandra. "I can't be happy with an ordinary life. So many people have such dull, boring and predictable lives. It's even worse for women. It seems most become teachers, seamstresses or secretaries, while others become nuns, waitresses or housewives!"

"What's wrong with that? Many women like those jobs. My mama is one of them!"

"Oh many do! But it's not for me. I love music, dancing, poetry and art. I also like people with creative imaginations. It would be horrible if I got married to someone with no sense of adventure, someone who wants a quiet family life in Essex County, someone who's never been anywhere more than ten miles from his home and has no desire to go anywhere or do anything. It would be the same as a beautiful songbird kept in a cage."

Emma stood with her eyes fixed on Alexandra.

"What's wrong?" said Alexandra.

"I've never thought anything like that," said Emma. "It's all too strange for me. But I was wondering something. Do you think the Maestro would take on another student or two? I think I'd like to try playing the violin, and we both know Robbie does. Could you ask the Maestro if he'd take us on?"

"Oh Emma, I'm so happy! Of course I'll ask! I'll ask him real nice and I'm sure he'll say yes!" she beamed, hugging her before they both returned to their classroom.

When the school day finished, Alexandra was pleased to see her father waiting for her, as always. He paced back and forth as if he were nervous about something.

"Hi, Papa! Something's wrong. What is it?"

"Your Uncle George suffered an attack of apoplexy last night. Do you know what that is?"

Alexandra wrinkled her nose. "No, I don't."

"It can be different things, but in this situation it's a sudden stoppage of blood to the brain. If it can't be treated quickly and properly, it can be very, very dangerous," said Joseph.

"Oh my land! Is he going to be all right?"

"No one can know right now. The doctors are doing all they can. I've offered to go visit him, but he's not being allowed any visitors at the moment."

"That explains why Owen wasn't at school today. Do you know how it happened?"

"Not all the details. Uncle George's business partner came to the café and said he'd collapsed at home. He also said that because of this, the sale of the café has been delayed."

"Aunt Clara didn't tell you herself?"

"No, I expect she's at the hospital with your uncle. Knowing her, I wouldn't be surprised if she's been up all night."

* * *

Clara had indeed been up all night, somehow managing to function without any sleep. However, her physical exhaustion had little bearing on her will as she sought not only her husband's survival, but his recovery. At that time she saw fit to pay a visit to the café with Owen.

"Are Joseph and Alexandra in?" Clara asked Marcie upon entering.

"I expect they'll be here soon. Please, have a seat. Can I get you anything?"

"Yes, I wouldn't mind a cup of coffee – but please make it twice as strong – and black," she said as she sat down next to Owen at a table near the window.

"I'll have it for you shortly," Marcie said before going to the kitchen.

Clara turned her attention to Owen. "I expect you to stay respectful, young man. If we ever make it through this it'll only be by the grace of God." In a matter of minutes Marcie returned with the requested cup of coffee. As Clara sipped the bitter drink, she saw the door of the café swing open and Joseph and Alexandra enter. They walked straight up to her table.

"Clara, I'm sorry to hear about George," said Joseph, his arm around Alexandra, who had a worried look on her face. The girl said nothing.

"Thank you, Joseph," said Clara, still feeling haggard and worn. "He's in hospital, resting, but we don't know what'll happen next. Joseph, and Alexandra, I have to ask you something."

Father and daughter looked at each other then took chairs opposite Clara and Owen, Joseph pulling a chair out for Alexandra to sit on. "Go ahead," said Joseph.

"We know Alexandra gets visions when she plays her violin. There's no use denying it."

"Really? What makes you think so?" Joseph said, cocking an eyebrow.

Clara immediately recognized that gesture. It was the same one George made whenever he pretended not to understand someone's question. "Don't get coy with me, Joseph. I know because George told us all about it. He knew it all along. He told us his father used to get visions when he played the violin, and now Alexandra gets them. These visions are about different people and that she probably got one about him and what happened in the farmhouse many years ago. He also said that the instrument has probably bewitched your daughter and that's why she plays so well. Think about it, Joseph, really, nobody would listen to her if she played badly, so in order for people to *want* to listen and for her to get into their thoughts and memories, she would have to play it well."

Joseph interlocked his fingers together on the table and leaned forward. "Look, even if what you say is true, how does it matter? Suppose she does get visions. Would she tell everybody about them? Who'd ever believe her? Besides, ever since she was a little girl she's always wanted to play music and become a professional musician. She has a God-given gift and by God, she's using it."

Clara cut straight to the point. "Joseph, she could ruin us if she starts spreading rumours and gossip. Now I want to tell you what happened last night at our home with George."

Joseph leaned back in his chair and motioned towards her to continue.

"Very well," she said. "First of all, Owen came home yesterday and told us everything that happened at school. He was very upset by Alexandra's rude behaviour and the awful way she mocked and belittled him in front of the whole class – especially when he tried to wish her a happy birthday!"

Alexandra pursed her lips and hardened her eyes into two narrow slits. "Well, Owen, if you don't become a lawyer, you'll probably have a fine career as one of those horrible politicians," she said, voice red with anger.

"Alexandra!" said Joseph. "Mind your tongue!"

"Papa, he's lying! Can't you see? That's not what happened at all!"

"It's not the time or place, Alex. We'll talk about it later. Let your aunt continue."

Owen sneered at his cousin, but Clara ignored it. "You know, Joseph, we are honest people. My husband – your brother – is an honest man. We don't resort to witchcraft or magic tricks to get ahead in this world. We've earned everything we have and don't owe anyone anything. It has never been easy for us. We've taken a lot of risks in our lives and we continue to do so. George told us some time ago about the visions which are connected with this violin, and last night he wanted to prove it by opening the case and showing us the violin. He said if you looked carefully at it, you could *see* the magic. But as soon as he lifted the lid, he collapsed."

"My God," said Joseph, voice full of mockery. "What a coincidence! Has it occurred to you that apoplexy strikes without warning? Or maybe you're suggesting an antique violin caused George to collapse? I'm sorry to hear about all this, Clara, but what can I do?"

"I don't want *you* to do anything, Joseph. I want Alexandra to go to the hospital and play her violin in front of George. Then I want her to report to us what she sees."

Joseph sat back in his chair laughing. "She'd go there and do *what?* Play her violin for a sick man? Steal his memories, as you say?"

"Joseph, please don't make light of this," she said, barely able to restrain tears. "The doctors are doing all they can, but if he dies, the opportunity to find out what magic, or even vision, made him collapse will be lost forever. How could you live with that?"

"Would you know the truth if you heard it?" he said, but casting an accusing look at the boy seated next to her. "More than that, would you even believe it? Clara, I'm very sorry George has taken ill, but I cannot and will not permit my daughter to subject herself to these ridiculous fantasies of yours."

"Aydy! There you are!" said a happy, barrel-chested man walking into the café. "Where've you been? Can you play a song for us, please?"

"It's not the best time, Mr. McKay," said Alexandra.

Clara studied the girl. "Well, why don't you play something for him? We'll listen."

Owen made an attempt to stand up, but Clara put her hand on his shoulder, pushing him down. The boy huffed but remained in his seat.

"It's up to you, Angel," said Joseph.

Alexandra nodded, rose from her chair, and departed for the stairs. While she was gone, Joseph shook his head at Clara. "Don't expect anything from her."

Alexandra returned with her violin and stood at the man's table. She started playing some peppy Irish dance music, which Clara thought was a strange contrast to the girl's mood. Nevertheless, the music had the effect of brightening the mood in the café – especially where the Delmotts were seated. Clara, still feeling drained, looked on as the girl smiled and went from table to table, playing with an easy, effortless grace.

As she watched, she allowed her mind to wander away with Alexandra's music. Her thoughts soon left that of her husband, and began dwelling on a simple truth: Joseph was indeed doing a splendid job raising Alexandra. Moreover, he was doing it alone. Clara looked at the man as he watched his daughter with pride. She studied him, developing a new sense of respect for him. She soon thought about her own situation, of how she and George were raising Owen. True, Owen did have her and George, but despite this fact they were doing a terrible job. She realized that Owen was being neglected as their energies were being focused on social standing, a big career and property acquisitions. Their Owen was, in fact, growing up without any parents at all and she and George were merely caretakers. She could see the result of their parental failure sitting right next to her – a jealous, spiteful, lonely bully who was becoming exactly like his father.

When Alexandra performed at the Delmott table, she stood and played a cheery melody. Clara watched as the smiling girl played; her violin singing with crisp, bright freshness.

After Alexandra finished, she smiled and curtsied. Customers politely applauded her, including the large man who had asked her to play. Clara stood up and motioned for her to come closer, embracing the girl with an affection she hadn't shown her in ages. "Well done, Alexandra," she said, still embracing her. "Very well done."

Alexandra cupped her hand around Clara's ear. Her voice was warm and fresh. "It's not too late for them."

Chapter 24

The next several days saw no changes in George's condition. He was unable to speak, move about or even feed himself. When he wasn't sleeping, he spent long periods of time with his eyes open staring into the blankness of space. Clara, upon the advice of George's doctors, made the painful decision to transfer him the hundred or so miles to hospital in London, where he could receive better care. As the autumn months passed by and December arrived, she and Owen would take the train up on Fridays where they would spend each weekend together, returning on Sunday nights.

In the meantime, Delphis' violin remained safely stored at George and Clara's house. However, Clara and Owen wanted nothing to do with it, fearing any special powers it might possess.

*　*　*

After the café closed one night, Joseph went up to Alexandra's room to bid her goodnight. He knocked and entered, finding everything as usual. Her lamp glowed on her bedside table as she lay in bed reading a book. Joseph sat on the side of her bed, and Alexandra put the open book face down in front of her.

"How's the book?"

"It's a book of poems by Robert Browning; it's the one Sir Charles gave me. Browning writes such lovely poetry; it's almost the same as music, or even art. You can get   lost in it," she said, smiling.

"Is there anything there I'd be interested in?"

"Oh yes, there are so many wonderful poems – and lots of philosophy. I'm sure you'd enjoy it! But now I want to tell you about the visions I had of Aunt Clara and Owen when they came to the café."

"All right, Angel," he said, "but why did you wait two weeks to tell me?"

Alexandra shuffled herself up to a sitting position. "I can't explain it, Papa. I had a strong feeling that it wasn't the right time to tell you. Believe me, I wasn't trying to hide anything from you."

"All right," he replied, puzzled. "What was your vision about?"

"You know, Papa, one of the good things about having these visions is that nobody can lie to me, not even Owen. Sometimes I might not understand everything I see, but what I see feels so real. So, let me begin: Owen was at home and he told his parents what happened at school that day. Of course he lied to them about most of it, and of course they believed him. Uncle George tried to explain to Owen that the violin really did have powers. Then Uncle George went upstairs and brought the violin down – case and all – and put it on the table. As soon as he opened the lid, he fell down on the floor. But he didn't suffer an apoplexy attack, Papa. That's what everyone *thinks* happened."

"Do you know what really happened?"

"Yes."

"What was it?"

"Does Uncle George have a heart condition like Pépé did?"

"Well, yes, he does. However, he takes medicine to control it."

"He had taken his evening pills before he tried playing the violin. These were new pills he had just been given," Alexandra said.

"Do you know where he got those pills from?"

"No, there was nothing about that. If I played for Uncle George, maybe I could find out. Is it important?"

"For us it's not important. We can't change anything anyway and besides, I can't see any good time for you to play for your uncle. Two visions from him are enough."

"What about what Aunt Clara said? I mean, if Uncle George dies, we'll never know what really happened, I mean, if it was the pills that caused it or the violin!"

"True enough," said Joseph. "No matter what caused it, we can't do anything to help, so we need to let this matter rest and allow things to take their course." Joseph could barely believe he had said those words and wondered if he was becoming cold and heartless like his brother. At the same time, with George laid up in hospital, he could allow himself to breathe easier over Alexandra's safety. "You should get some sleep, Angel, it's getting late. Put the book away for tonight."

"May I finish this part? Please, Papa? It's not long," she said, picking up the book and pointing out the passage with her finger.

"All right," he said, giving her a kiss on the cheek. He stood up and walked towards the door. Before leaving the room, he turned back towards her, as always. For the first time, he was struck by how similar she looked to her mother by her facial expressions, hair, even her posture. He felt ashamed at why it had taken him so long to notice. He hesitated. He wanted to tell her of these similarities, yet feared doing so would bring up more questions about her mother. More than that, though, it made him miss his Helen even more.

"Is everything all right, Papa?" said Alexandra.

"Yes, Angel. Everything is all right," he said, sighing. "Don't stay up long. Goodnight."

Alexandra smiled up at him before returning to read the lively, glorious words painted across the pages of her book.

* * *

One evening in December, Owen was home when he heard someone knocking on the front door. He thought it must be a stranger because anyone they knew always called at the back door. Perhaps it was a doctor who'd come to deliver bad news about his father. Regardless,

Owen opened the door a few inches to find Clive Brewster rubbing his hands in the cold.

"Good evening, Owen," said Brewster. "I would like to see your mother."

"I'm afraid she's not home. She's out with her group of ladies from the church. She'll be back soon." Owen stood gazing at the shivering man through the crack in the door.

"May I come in and wait?" asked Brewster.

Owen nodded and opened the door wide.

"Thank you," said Brewster, stepping in and removing his hat and overcoat. "I never did fancy the cold." He walked into the parlour where he made himself comfortable in George's favourite chair. "I must say that your mother is a very busy woman," he said to Owen, who sat in the chair near him. "She never stops doing good for those less fortunate."

"Mr. Brewster, everyone says that. However, she just does it to look good in front of people. I don't know that what she does even helps anyone, though. My father told me that people of weak character deserve to be poor. He says if people keep helping them, they will come to expect it all the time."

Brewster gazed at the boy. He leaned forward, lowered his head and rubbed his eyes and the bridge of his nose. After a few moments, he looked up. "I'm here today because I want to give your mother her weekly report about the law firm. However, I'm glad she's not here because it gives us a chance to talk," he said.

"About what?"

"We can talk about many things. For instance, what would you like to do in the future?"

"The same as anyone," said Owen, irritated at the question. "Get married and start a family."

"What about your profession?" asked Brewster. "Would you like to be a musician?"

Owen felt an immediate jolt of adrenaline. *Is Brewster going to be another one who compares me to my cousin?* he thought. "No. I'm not talented enough to be a professional musician," he said.

"What would you like to do?"

"I'm not sure," said Owen, relieved that the conversation was turning away from music. "My parents want me to do something that will make them proud."

"You're a young man with your whole future before you, Owen. Naturally it's good that you want to please your parents, but whatever you do, you need a profession you enjoy and which can support your family."

"Of course," said Owen, rolling his eyes.

"Owen, when I was young I was in a similar position as you find yourself today, though mine was much worse. My father died of consumption when I was eleven. My mother had to raise four children, including me, all by herself. She did any work she could find, including cleaning houses, doing peoples' laundry and minding their children. Despite all that, it still wasn't enough. She had to accept charity from the good people at her church on many occasions or we'd have never survived."

Owen looked at this finely-dressed lawyer sitting in front of him. He could hardly imagine that Brewster and his family had once languished in poverty.

"Our situation slowly changed and as I grew, my siblings and I took on a number of jobs to help our family."

"What kind of jobs did you do?" asked Owen.

"I did many, ranging from cleaning cattle sheds to working in tobacco fields. I even worked on ships as a deck hand and fireman, and almost got myself killed when our ship ran aground going through the Pelee Passage."

"Really? What happened?"

"It was night, and we were steaming along in a paddle-wheeler, headed west, when the weather became very foggy – so much so that we could hardly see where we were going. It was my turn to be a fireman, so I was below deck shovelling coal into the boiler. That's what I was doing when I felt the jolt and saw the floor split. Water immediately began gushing upwards from between the floorboards. We later determined that we'd probably hit some rocks near Pelee Island."

"What did you do?" asked Owen.

"We tried bailing and pumping the water out, but it was just coming in too fast. Eventually the captain gave the order to abandon ship and I was asked to help the passengers into the lifeboats. While I was lowering a boat, the ship suddenly rolled onto its side and lurched downwards. People were panicking and I had to work quickly through a tangle of ropes while flotsam was bobbing everywhere. It was chaos. Soon the ship settled and disappeared under the surface. I had to swim to shore – thank goodness it wasn't far – but I bloody near froze to death as it was early April. I still hate the cold to this day. After I reached shore, some people were still in the water, so I went back in again and again to pull them out and bring them ashore. Sadly, I couldn't help them all."

Owen was surprised that Brewster was telling him these things. He wondered why the man had put his own life at risk by returning to the frigid waters of Lake Erie to rescue people – especially after his own safety had been secured.

"After that experience, my mother forbade me to work on the ships, so I returned to Toronto. By then she had taken on steady work as a governess for a prominent lawyer's children in Toronto. I met this lawyer and was immediately impressed and inspired by the way he could help people through their legal difficulties – and make a good, honest living in the process. We often had long conversations deep into the night, and he explained to me all about the virtues of honesty, integrity and accepting responsibility for our actions. I soon decided to be a lawyer as well, and he helped me enter law school. So you see, giving help to, and accepting help from people is nothing to be ashamed of," said Brewster. "I enjoy what I do and have no regrets."

"Aren't you the same kind of lawyer as my father?" asked Owen.

"Not exactly. Your father and I use our professions to pursue different ambitions in life."

Owen wanted to question him about this when he heard the back door open.

"Owen! I'm home, dear!" said Clara. "Where are you?"

"I'm in the parlour, Mum," said Owen, sighing. "Mr. Brewster is here to see you."

* * *

By mid-December the weather had become quite cold and a fresh blanket of snow now lay on the ground. Small snowflakes drifted down as Alexandra walked home from Emma's house early one Saturday evening. She had been helping Emma, her sisters, and her mother bake cookies. Mrs. Brindle was very good at baking, and made sure to send Alexandra home with a basketful. "These are not to sell to your customers," she'd said, "but you can share them with your father and Marcie."

The walk home from the Brindles was icy and brisk and the cold stung Alexandra's face. By the time she entered the café, her cheeks burned with the cold. Despite her discomfort, she was pleased to see the café full of people and that Marcie had already started decorating the place for the holidays by hanging glass ornaments on various fixtures, draping tinsel around the windows and door, and even setting out a small Christmas tree in the window. "This is how my grandparents used to decorate," she remembered Marcie saying.

After warming herself at the big stove and having a bowl of Marcie's soup, Alexandra began playing a merry assortment of tunes. She seldom used the corner Joseph had cleared for her to play on as a stage, preferring to stroll through the busy café and play to each customer at their tables.

At one of the tables near the window sat a small group of strangers, two young men and a woman, maybe travellers who'd stopped by for a bite to eat while taking refuge against the cold. They looked to be in their late teens or early twenties. "Would you play a song for us, too?" asked one of the young men, the one with the closely cropped black hair. He was dressed in a dark suit, but with the neck of his shirt open as if he'd just removed his tie. He looked relaxed and comfortable.

"What would you like to hear?"

"We like the music you've been playing. Perhaps you could entertain us with more of that?"

"I certainly can," she said before placing her fiddle on her shoulder and playing a rendition of "Maid Behind the Bar."

The young strangers at the table all smiled, clapped their hands and stomped their feet in rhythm to her playing.

Upon finishing, Alexandra curtsied politely, as always. Squinting her eyes and squeezing her face into a half-smile, she looked inquisitively at the group as if she were studying them. "You're all musicians, aren't you?"

"Ah, yes we are!" said the fellow in the suit. "How'd you know that? We're from across the river. We've heard all about you, Aydy, and we wanted to come hear you play!"

"Thank you for coming by!" said Alexandra. "I'm so happy to meet you! What are your names?"

"My name is Nick," said the man in the suit. "This young lady is my sister Natalie and she plays the fiddle. This guy here, this is our cousin David. He plays every instrument known to man, and he's also the intellectual one. Today he's our violist."

David quickly added, "Some would call me the brains of the group, while Nicky here likes to think he's our bassist, sometimes cellist, so we indulge him this little fantasy!" The four musicians laughed, including the bass player Nick. Alexandra wrinkled her nose.

"Don't listen to them Aydy, they're always teasing me and making jokes because I play the bass! I'm actually pretty good at it and they know it!"

Alexandra beamed at the lively bunch of musicians, taking their jokes as simple friendly banter.

"It's really so nice of you all to come here! Where are your instruments?"

Natalie spoke up. "Our instruments are at the hotel. We've just come back from playing a wedding in Chatham and thought we'd stop by."

"A wedding! Oh how wonderful!" remarked Alexandra, who was already taking a liking to the strange young woman with the toothy smile. "I've never played my violin in an ensemble, but it's my dream to do so. Would you mind if –" She was interrupted by Nick.

"Do you mean if we would go back to our hotel and get our instruments so we can play together?" said Nick, winking.

"Oh please, please do that! I'm sure my papa won't mind. It's his café."

"See?" said David. "I knew this was going to be fun!"

After having explained the offer to her father and receiving his consent, Alexandra returned to the table with the news. The two young men got up and went out into the snowy, brisk evening to retrieve their instruments. When they returned, they set about getting ready and tuning up.

"We'll play some common folk tunes, Aydy. You probably know them already," said Nick. "Just follow Natalie's lead and you'll do fine."

Alexandra was delighted to play with them and did exactly as Nick asked. She felt her dreams about orchestras, symphonies, ensembles and quartets were all starting to come true.

She wondered if her pépé would be proud of her and her musical ambitions. She stretched her memory back as far as could, to the gentle man who spoke to her in his soft voice while helping her tune her instrument, showing her where to place her awkward fingers on the strings, how to hold the bow and how to play the fast notes. She felt sorry she hadn't done more to remember him, especially all the small details. However, her fondest memory was of her little duets with her pépé. They'd stand together in front of their modest audience and she'd look way up at him and he'd smile down at her as they played. The people would always clap when they finished, and he always took her hand and bowed to her. She loved all the memories of her pépé, but this one was her favourite. She felt a deep sense of loss at the fact that never again would they play another duet together.

The rest of the evening was a pleasant mix of different melodies, and Alexandra was pleased her father decided to keep the café open longer so the group could continue. After the café closed that evening, the group continued playing well past midnight, until Joseph reminded everyone how late it was and they should quit for the night.

Chapter 25

When school was dismissed before the Christmas holidays, Alexandra set off to visit the professor for her last music lesson of the year. It had started snowing again by the time she left, and the icy cold stung her cheeks.

Despite this, the walk to the professor's house was quite pleasant – and absolutely silent, except for the crunching sound of her footsteps. The clean, white snow drifted down in large flakes in the late afternoon light, making it difficult to see anything more than a short distance ahead. It built up on everything – slender tree branches, park benches, hand railings. Alexandra thought that at least for a time, the world was a clean, pure place. She stood for a moment and listened to the silence, wondering how millions of drifting snowflakes could fall and land without making a single sound.

After tracking through the deepening snow, she finally arrived at the professor's home and knocked on the door.

"Welcome, Alexandra!" said the professor, answering the door himself. "I'm pleased to see you, though I didn't expect you'd come in this weather!"

Alexandra stepped into the warmth of the professor's home and closed the door, bringing winter's freshness in with her.

"I'm happy to come, Maestro! I was afraid the snow might stop me from attending our last session of the year. Heaven forbid I should miss this! We've had such a good year, and to finish it by missing a session would be perfectly dreadful. I don't think I could ever forgive myself if I disappointed you on account of a silly little thing like the weather!"

"You know, Alexandra, I wouldn't have blamed you if you hadn't come. You could've cancelled our lesson by telephone. I think you're really quite stubborn when it comes to music!"

"Oh not just music, Maestro!" she said as she removed her coat and shoes. "I'm stubborn in so many ways. Sister Rose knows it, and so does my papa. Marcie says my stubbornness is like an anchor holding a ship! Papa also says I can talk the hind leg off a mule! I even bothered Sir Charles so much that he said I made him want to drink!"

The professor chuckled. "I've had to resist that urge myself! Come now, let's not waste an opportunity to play some music!"

The two entered the professor's study where the big fireplace was lit, its warmth spreading throughout the room. As always, Alexandra played different selections of music, including some of the new Christmas tunes in keeping with the spirit of the holiday. She played several duets with the professor, who sometimes accompanied her on the piano, and other times on the violin.

Meanwhile, the weather had turned into a full-blown blizzard, the wind whipping the snow into drifts and cresting sloping triangles in the corners of the window panes. When the professor stopped playing, he got up and walked to the windows. He stood, hands on his hips, gazing at the spectacle swirling around outside. He huffed. "I can't allow you to walk alone in this weather. Let's call your father and ask him to come get you."

Alexandra sat nearby and listened as the professor spoke into the contraption mounted on the wall. "Joseph, yes, I understand. I can't trouble you to come that late, but your idea is much better. Just a moment, please. I'll ask her." He held the telephone receiver down and turned to the girl. "Alexandra, your father requested you spend the night here. He can come get you in the morning after the storm passes. I have many a spare room, and you'll be comfortable and warm."

"Are you sure, Maestro? I don't want to impose on your kindness!"

"Nonsense, my dear! There's no imposition. Here, please speak to your father."

For the first time in her life, Alexandra had to use the clumsy device in order to communicate with her father. To her it didn't seem real that his voice could come out of that thing, yet there it was and it was indeed him on the other end. When she finished speaking, she handed the earpiece back to the Maestro, not knowing what to do with it. The professor took it from her unsure hands and placed it up to his ear.

"All right, Joseph, we'll see you tomorrow. If you like you can call here in the morning. I do hope the weather won't affect the telephone lines."

Finally, he hung the telephone earpiece on a hook, thus ending the call.

"Have you eaten anything today?"

"No, well, I had breakfast and a few bites for lunch," she said.

"Hmm, well, Cora made some dinner before she left. Thank goodness she doesn't live far from here or she'd be spending the night as well. Come on, let's eat."

The Maestro's kitchen was not as large as would be usual for such a home. Alexandra assumed he usually ate his meals in the dining room, so a large kitchen wouldn't be necessary. Regardless, it was a cheery place with white-painted cupboards arranged neatly in a row. Each cupboard door had polished, slightly concave rectangular knobs in which you could see your reflection upside down. In the centre of the kitchen was a simple table covered with a checker yellow table cloth. The professor heated their meal in the stove which occupied one corner of the kitchen.

"Guess what, Maestro? We had some guests at the café the other day, and they turned out to be some musicians from Detroit! We even played some songs together!"

"Very good my dear. Are they professional?" he said as he set out their meals.

"I believe so. They play at weddings and such events. They even asked me to go to Detroit and play with them, but my papa won't let me," she said, frowning. "He says I'm too young. Do you think I'm too young to go to Detroit by myself, Maestro?"

"Well I happen to believe your father is right; I think it would be better if they came here instead. In fact, when you do get together, I'd like to come hear you. By the way, I wanted to tell you that your friends Robert and Emma approached me about taking violin lessons," he said with an air of frustration in his voice.

Alexandra stopped chewing and looked up at the professor. "I'm so sorry Maestro! I completely forgot to ask you about that! I was talking to Emma in the schoolyard and —"

"You know it's been a long time since I've taught anyone to play the violin."

"You're teaching me, though, Maestro!"

"It's not the same thing, young lady, and you know it! They're absolute beginners! I'd be teaching them from scratch!" he said gruffly, a pained look crossing his face. "In any event, relax, child. I decided to do it. I've determined that this will be a professional challenge for me. However, I won't be doing it alone. You're going to help me, and we're going to start after the New Year. It'll be a good experience for you as well."

"How can it be a good experience for me, Maestro?"

The professor laughed. "It'll give you good experience with amateurs and how to teach them. I'm no fool my dear, never forget that. Consider this as teacher training for you! Remember something — you never know where your musical career can lead you, and it's just as well to be prepared. I'll be the first one to tell you that. Now finish your dinner before it gets cold!"

When they returned to the warmth of the professor's study they could see a blowing frenzy of swirling snow through the grand windows beyond the piano. The fire crackled in the fireplace and the professor poked at it with a metal rod. Red embers glowed anew from the wood under the flames.

The furniture in the professor's study was arranged with two small couches facing each other at right angles several feet from the fireplace. A coffee table separated the two sofas. Alexandra sat on one sofa and the professor faced her on the other.

"Thank you again for allowing me to stay the night. You're always right, Maestro. I couldn't have survived that walk."

"Well, you almost died on me once, remember?" he said, chortling.

"You mean that rainy day when I came into the café all wet?"

"Yes, I shall never forget that!"

Alexandra smiled and leaned forward, intent on changing the topic. "Tell me the story, please Maestro, of how you got your violin!"

"I've already told you that story, my dear."

"But you only told me *when* and *where* you got it and not so much how. I'd like to know all the details."

The professor settled back on his couch. He rubbed his eyes and the bridge of his nose. He drew in and released a deep breath. "Well, my dear, it's a very long story."

"I've got all night to listen," Alexandra said, smiling.

"Very well then. I believe you to be a trustworthy person who won't go about telling this to everyone. All right, as you know, I played in many different orchestras in Europe. At one time I knew a very special lady. She was a member of the orchestra I was playing with in Kiev. She was a Ukrainian woman, very beautiful, extremely intelligent and wonderfully talented. In our spare time we would often play duets together. After a while we fell in love. Her name was Valentina."

Alexandra restrained a knowing smile. She always felt the Maestro had been in love. That knowledge hadn't come from any vision, it was just good old-fashioned intuition.

"She gave me this violin for Christmas one year. In honour of her, I decided to name it Valentina. When she gave it to me, she told me that every time I played it I would think of her. Oh how right she was! I played love ballads for her on that instrument; I must confess I've done my very best work on it. It inspired me. She inspired me. I continued to meet her regularly in cafés, restaurants and in any public, respectable places. I made up my mind I wanted to marry her, spend the rest of my life with her, have a family with her.

"About a year after we met, we went into our regular café. We liked that place; it was familiar to us and very comfortable. We were having a lovely time, a wonderful conversation. Everything was going so well. Then she told me she wanted to 'interrupt' our relationship. She had other plans, other ambitions she wanted to pursue in her life."

"Oh Maestro, I'm sorry to hear that."

"So, here I am years later with this wonderful violin. It's not the most expensive instrument in the world and I wouldn't get much if I tried selling it. However, it's valuable to *me*. Whatever shall I do with it? In a way, I feel I am cursed with this instrument and cannot part with it. It's all I have left of my dear Valentina."

Alexandra sat still, mesmerized by the Maestro's tale of lost love.

"I'm so sorry to hear that, Maestro," she sniffled. Regardless, he sat across from her dry-eyed and emotionally weathered.

"I do think about her every time I play that violin. Anyway, I don't often get to tell that story to anyone and quite frankly, I seldom get asked about it. So now you know the story behind my violin. I trust you won't tell anyone what I've just told you."

Alexandra looked across the table, focusing on him with understanding eyes. She smiled. "Your secret is safe with me, Maestro."

* * *

Alexandra and the professor spent another two hours sitting up talking. He told her, in great detail, all about the splendid symphony orchestras of Europe, the magnificent and ornate concert halls and the wonderfully talented musicians he'd met. He concluded by telling her that despite all this, his heart always yearned to be home.

Finally exhausted after a long day, Alexandra went up to the bedroom appointed her by the professor. It was a well-kept, tidy little bedchamber with a dresser, table and chair, and a bed just big enough for her. She had the feeling that despite the cleanliness of the room, it hadn't been slept in by anyone for years. After bidding goodnight to the professor, she promptly readied herself and went to bed, quickly falling asleep, oblivious to the glorious white wonderland whirling and dancing just outside her window.

When dawn broke the following morning, Alexandra rose and peeked out the dormered window. She was pleased to find that the snow had accumulated to impressive depths and had covered every possible thing – including the professor's prized rose bushes. She could hear him downstairs playing the violin. She got herself ready, fixed her hair, and went down to meet him.

She walked into the professor's study, the source of the music, where she found him happily playing his violin near the grand windows. He promptly stopped when she entered the room. "Good morning, Miss Alexandra, I trust you slept well."

"I heard you playing that wonderful melody, Maestro! It reminded me of Christmases past and I couldn't wait to come down and hear you play it."

"Well, I was hoping the music would wake you, actually. You know it's already well past 9:00 a.m. and I've been up for almost three hours myself. In fact, I've already called your father and he's on his way. I expect he'll be here soon. In the meantime, we can have some breakfast. Believe it or not I can cook. I'm not entirely helpless!"

Alexandra laughed. "I'll help if you get into trouble. After all, I'm no stranger to cooking, either. You'll just have to show me where everything is."

They went to the kitchen and began preparing breakfast with Alexandra gathering the necessary flour, eggs, butter, milk, and so on.

While she was scooping the batter into the frying pan, Joseph rapped on the door. The professor promptly walked over and welcomed him in – along with an icy blast of air.

"Please, won't you come in and warm up. Your Alexandra is making breakfast for us all and you're just in time."

They entered the kitchen and Alexandra served their plates.

"So sorry I'm a bit late, Angel. The snow is really deep, so I bought you a new pair of boots."

Alexandra looked at the boots. They were black leather with a dozen small buttons neatly arranged in a row which closed up a central flap. "They're beautiful, Papa! Thank you so much! Wherever did you get them?"

"On the way here I stopped in at Clarke's Shoes. While I was there, I ran into Mr. Nesbitt and he talked my ear off for the longest time."

Alexandra remembered Mr. Nesbitt and how he used to have a jewellery store in Windsor. When she was really little, her mother would often walk past that shop with her and sometimes they'd wander inside and dream of the sparkling items on display. Now the man was selling shoes at Clarke's. It turned out that George had convinced Nesbitt to buy large numbers of shares in a company which later went bankrupt. Following that ordeal, Nesbitt was forced to sell his shop and take on any work he could find in order to support his family.

"How is Mr. Nesbitt doing?"

"He's doing better now. His wife took a job as a seamstress and their oldest son quit school and got a job to help the family finances. It's remarkable what people will do to survive!"

They sat down and began eating. Joseph seemed eager to say something. "My visit here today is two fold, Hergie. Not only have I come to pick up Alexandra, but I've also come to personally extend an invitation to you."

The professor looked at Joseph, one curious eyebrow raised.

"Marcie is having Christmas dinner at her home, and she has invited Alexandra and me to come over. In fact, we go there every year; it's become a tradition. It'll be a grand feast, done Marcie-style of course, and she wants to know if you'd like to join us. I'm sure it'll be a merry celebration. Oh yes, one more thing – if you can come, she'd like you to bring your violin. Perhaps you and Alexandra could play a duet."

Professor Herbert Hergicksen sat there confounded. There would be noisy children running about, disorder, dirty dishes, plenty of commotion. He didn't know how he could possibly socialize with, and later entertain, all those unruly people.

"I'd love to come," he said, smiling. "Of course I'll bring my violin."

Chapter 26

Owen and his mother spent a great deal of time visiting George in London, spending many long hours at his bedside. Though his condition had improved, he still couldn't speak. He slept most of the time, but during his waking hours he either stared at the ceiling or made brief eye contact to those who spoke with him. He could also turn his head and make small, jerky movements with his arms and legs. Despite his condition, Clara decided they should spend the holiday together.

As the days passed, Clara came to the conclusion that all the social activities she was involved in were contributing nothing to her family. To the dismay of her many associations and social groups, she quit them all. Now with more time, she redirected her energies to encouraging George to get well. More than that, she also felt it was the perfect time to concentrate on changing Owen into a good, honest, and respectable adult as she couldn't bear the thought of him growing up to be like his father. Finally, through all this time, the words she last heard from Alexandra constantly replayed through her mind – "It's not too late."

* * *

When Christmas Day arrived, Alexandra and Joseph attended early mass at St. Alphonsus Church. They weren't surprised to find George's pew empty, save for a small bouquet of flowers someone had placed there.

Following mass, several members of the congregation, as usual, made small talk with Joseph outside on the steps of the church. The conversation always swung round to asking him about his brother's condition. The answer was always the same – the doctors were doing all they could, he's getting the best treatment, we all wish him a speedy recovery and we thank you for your thoughts and prayers during this difficult time.

Soon after they arrived home from church, Joseph walked behind the counter and retrieved something from one of the shelves.

"This came for you the other day, Angel," he said, handing his daughter a small envelope. Affixed to it were several red and black British stamps featuring Queen Victoria in her jubilee year.

"Sir Charles!" she said as she sprang on her feet. She slit the side of the envelope open with a knife and mumbled her way through the letter.

"Papa! I'm so happy he remembered to write! He says he's on the board of a music academy in London and has met so many interesting people! He also reminded me about the music festival in Ottawa in the spring! Wouldn't it be great to go? Can I? He says the Maestro will know all about it!"

"Well, I suppose anything is possible, Angel. Spring is still a long way off. Anyway, we should get ready because Professor Hergicksen will be here soon and we don't want to keep him waiting."

Alexandra put the letter upstairs in a special wooden box her father made. She kept all her small little treasures in that box, including some mementos from her mother.

Professor Hergicksen pulled up on the snow-packed street in his sleigh, pulled by a single horse.

"Bundle up tight, we've got a long way to go!" said Joseph.

Soon they were off in a southward direction, the horse prancing along smartly, hot puffs of air streaming from his nostrils.

The farm fields of Essex County were laid out in a blanket of crisp white snow that extended as far as the eye could see. As they passed by the old family farm, Alexandra looked at the house, at the fallen shutters, missing shingles on the roof, the weathered paint. She craned her neck until the house passed from view.

"I do miss that place," her father sighed. "It's a pity the new owners have let it slide into such disrepair. I have such fond memories there."

After another mile or so, the trio arrived at Marcie and Denis' home several miles to the south of Windsor. It had a long, tree-lined laneway which reached deep into the property. Several pieces of rusting farm machinery sat partly covered with snow near the barn and the little blacksmith's shop Denis had set up. Footpaths over the trampled snow connected everything to the house.

Marcie's husband, Denis, was there to greet them. A tall, thin man with a regal nose, he kept his black hair rather long, most of the time gathered up in a low, neat ponytail.

"Welcome, everyone. I'll put your horse in the stable. Marcie is in the kitchen cooking. Please walk in."

"Thank you Denis," said Joseph. The professor tipped his hat and Alexandra offered her usual smile.

The aroma of roasted turkey and stuffing greeted the guests as they entered the house through the side door. No one except Robbie ever used the front door in Essex County farmhouses, and Alexandra wondered why they had them at all. Perhaps they were only ornamental, or used for special occasions such as the unlikely event in which the king or queen might drop in for a visit.

"It seems you never get a break from cooking, Marcie!" said a happy Joseph upon entering.

When the smallest three of Marcie's children saw Alexandra, they clamoured to get near her. They wrapped their arms around her legs and squealed with delight so that the girl could hardly walk.

Meanwhile the professor, having just stepped inside the door, appeared agitated by the noise and horseplay of the small children. Regardless, he seemed to tolerate the little creatures. Alexandra wondered if he missed the family he never had.

"Thank you, Marcie," said the professor. "Thank you for inviting me to your lovely home. It is truly charming; you have such a lively family, too. Never a dull moment, I'm sure!"

"I've already warned them to be on their best behaviour!" she said as she peeled the vegetables.

The older children greeted their visitors as they helped with the myriad tasks involved in putting on such a large feast. Marcie's oldest child – and biggest help – was fifteen year old Bernice. She set the table.

"These dishes were brought from Germany by my great-grandmother," she explained. "We only use them at Christmastime or when there's a very special occasion. It's too risky to use them more often."

The professor scanned the room. "That's quite a large table, Denis."

"I made the frame in my blacksmith shop," he said. "The top came from some wood I gathered up here and there. A good clean up, sanding and polish and now it's a table."

"That's not the only thing he does!" said Marcie. "He also has a glass furnace in the shop! He likes making ornaments too! He can also make bottles, cups and even drinking glasses – anything and everything you could make by melting and forming glass. He's pretty good at it."

When everyone took their places, Denis said the blessing and dinner was served. The conversation was filled with lively banter and wound its way around to the happy memories people had in their lives. Alexandra loved hearing people talk about their memories. She relished the stories and could listen to them for hours. She was especially pleased to hear people volunteer their stories because she didn't feel like she was trespassing into their thoughts. The memories flowed free as water and all she had to do was to sit back and listen.

"Do you remember the time Henry ate the butterfly Bernice caught? Eww! You could see its legs sticking out of his mouth! Or the time Helen wanted to run away? Ha! She was only three! How about when mum found a dead lizard in John's pocket? Or Father, 'I'll give you a nickel if you tell me where Mum hid the fruitcake!' Oh wait, wait! Remember when John was walking the dog and Mum saw him fall into a hole in the ground?"

It seemed each person round the table had some interesting tidbit to share, some small story to tell. Even the professor regaled the group with his childhood story of how he survived a camping expedition with his friends in the dead of winter.

"After that dreaded encounter with nature, I decided an outdoor career was not for me, so I became a musician," he said, chuckling.

When dinner was finished, the professor and Alexandra took out their violins and prepared to play. They stood side by side with their backs to the Christmas tree, which the family had decorated with tinsel, strings of popcorn, and Denis's glass ornaments. The candles and gas lanterns in the room completed the effect, their light glinting and twinkling off the ornaments and other shiny objects in the room.

"Don't you two make an odd pair!" Denis said to Alexandra.

The professor turned to Alexandra. "Let's play 'The Skaters' Waltz.'"

She smiled and nodded.

Even the squirmiest of the children listened as the duo began. Alexandra started by playing the lead, with the professor playing harmony, and after a while they seamlessly switched. She played the waltz with a crisp, wintery freshness, smiling radiantly at the professor before turning to face the little audience, which sat enraptured. The entire house was filled from top to bottom with music.

As Alexandra played, she again felt herself become one with the music. The sweeping rhythm of the bow, the articulation of the sound, everything combined together to create that wonderful, perfect magic everyone so loved to hear, but only she was privileged to see.

Then, the myriad sparkles that glittered and twinkled here and there in the room began growing impatient. They soon majestically lifted themselves off wherever they were, floating freely through midair, one by one. They gravitated toward Alexandra, gaining momentum as they whirled around her in a lively circle, each sparkle playful and alive. They were soon followed by more and more sparkles which lifted off various glass ornaments, polished surfaces, tinsel, everything, until there was a grand exodus of sparks caught up in a magnificent, whirling and swirling cyclone around the wide-eyed, awestruck musician. It seemed every impossible star in the entire cosmos had wrapped itself around her in one vast, glorious, spinning orbit of space and time.

In the midst of all this, a well-dressed man carrying a violin entered the room. He was much older than the Maestro. He had a thick, well-groomed moustache which spanned his face to both ears. He smiled pleasantly at Alexandra. The professor, upon seeing this man, graciously stopped playing and stepped aside.

Amid the swirling frenzy of silent stars which encircled them both, the older man raised his beloved, and well-worn, violin up and began playing in harmony with Alexandra. It was obvious that he loved this music and this violin. It was also clear that he loved Christmastime and that he loved her. It pained them both to be separated, yet somehow the music, the sweet music was uniting and connecting them over impossible distances of time, space and circumstances. He spoke no audible words. Yet she could see in his face and hear from his music what he had so long ago wanted to say:

"Remember, my little protégé, that these lives of ours are much more than a collection of memories. Love is our greatest Gift. It stretches clear across all eternity. My life here is finished while yours is just beginning. Remember, you're free to choose the memories you want to make. You are free to love and to make these memories, and they will be your very own. Though time may fade some, it is the love you have which will last forever."

Alexandra looked pleasantly at the man, at his kind face, his deep blue eyes. She listened carefully to his silent words. The two continued playing their duet, engulfed together by the magnificent, swirling cyclone of shimmering stars flying around them; the glorious Christmas music continuing to fill the house and environs with sweet, pleasant sounds.

When they stopped playing, Alexandra curtsied politely to the man and smiled. In return, he bowed to her, taking her hand and thanking her for such a fine performance.

At that moment she was stricken with panic. Without saying a word, she pleaded with him to stay, but he smiled and told her a secret – a secret meant only for her. She smiled in return. Alexandra Delmott whispered in the man's ear. "I love you, Pépé."

Chapter 27

When the sun rose on the first day of January, the calendar showed a new year – 1888. Alexandra liked that number because there were three eights in a row. *That's got to be lucky!* she thought. She was also amused because the next three in a row wouldn't occur until 1999. After that it would be a new millennium. She wondered what life would be like then – especially music.

The turning of the New Year also brought her return to school, and after about a week, the fulfillment of the promise the Maestro had made about teaching Emma and Robbie to play the violin. "Make few promises, but always keep them," Alexandra remembered him saying.

The brass bell on the café door clanged loudly on that crisp, first Saturday morning in January. "I can't wait to have my first lesson with the Maestro!" exclaimed Emma. She stomped the snow off her boots just inside the door while Alexandra sat at the table eating breakfast with her father.

"I'm sure everything will be all right," said Joseph.

"Robbie is going to meet us there. How long is our lesson?" asked Emma.

"I suppose about an hour or so, but with you two it'll probably take all day!" Alexandra said with laughter in her voice.

"I'll clean things up here, Angel. You'd best run along now."

Alexandra didn't need to be told twice. She washed her hands, donned her woolen coat and new boots, kissed her father goodbye, and left.

When they arrived at the professor's house, Robbie was standing near the road, waiting. His arms were wrapped around his body and he was shivering.

"Where were you? What took so long?" he asked.

"You needn't be afraid of the Maestro," said Alexandra, her cheeks stinging from the cold. "He looks tough on the outside, but he's really kind-hearted. You could've waited for us inside where it's warm! Come now, let's go in."

* * *

George Delmott's condition continued to improve as he lay in hospital. The weekend visits by Clara and Owen had continued, and occasionally George would even get a visit from one of his law partners. With help, he could take short, shuffling steps and be taken in his wheelchair to the hospital atrium for a change of scenery. The doctors had been unable to discover the root cause of whatever had stricken the man, but were nonetheless pleased that he seemed to have overcome the worst of it and that his progress could now be measured on a daily basis.

Clara continued to feel that her decision to quit all her groups had been the right one. Owen, having spent so much more time with his mother, also seemed to have become less angry, yet problems remained: the boy was still a habitual liar and bully.

* * *

On that first Saturday morning in January, Owen and his mother were in London, as usual. "Your father could use a new robe," said Clara. "There are some shops nearby. Let's go."

Owen readily agreed. It was a good way to break the monotony of the hospital visit. They went to several shops in downtown London, yet Owen felt his mother was being overly picky in her selection of a robe. Bored with being dragged from shop to shop, he spoke up. "I'll just go outside for a walk, Mum. I'll be back directly. I think I need some fresh air."

Owen departed the clothing shop. As he walked past the exquisite shops and boutiques of London, he got to thinking of a long list of people who had done him wrong – about Alexandra's superior attitude and how she robbed him of first place at the Premier's Competition, how Prof. Hergicksen had expelled him, how Robbie hadn't even tried to fight him that summer day on the street, thus depriving him of another chance to beat the boy up. When that didn't happen, he had to endure the mockery of his friends. He even thought about how Sister Rose had embarrassed and belittled him in front of all his fellow pupils. These individuals, he reckoned, bore responsibility for the problems he had, and now here he was – stuck with his mama and bedridden, helpless father. He felt the whole world was against him and that the world was therefore responsible for all the problems he faced in his life.

He continued walking down the sidewalk in London's shopping district, those old familiar feelings of aggression and resentment rising up through his chest, making his blood hot and filling his face with heat. He thought that to be tough, he needed to show that toughness to that world which ridiculed him. He felt strong people should never compromise their positions or opinions – even if they're wrong – for to do so would surely be a sign of weakness. He walked tall and proud, his back straight and chin high. If someone happened to be walking the other way, he refused to turn his shoulder to allow them to pass. He often banged shoulders with people, the hard, blunt thuds making them turn their heads back, cussing and cursing. He felt this physical expression of supremacy and power to be most satisfying because people had to give way, to surrender to him. It made him feel powerful and in control.

Then he banged into the wrong person.

While Owen was strutting down the sidewalk, a finely dressed young couple approached from the opposite direction, strolling arm-in-arm. As always, Owen refused to give way, and banged his shoulder into the girl's with a deadening, unforgiving thud. The impact almost sent the girl and her bags crashing to the icy ground.

"Hey! What the hell was that about?" said her angry companion, turning back.

Owen stopped in his tracks. "What? Oh! She was in my way. Does she own the sidewalk? It serves her right."

"You apologize to her, now!" stormed the man, face red with anger.

"Go to hell," said Owen. That was the last thing Owen Delmott remembered until he awoke sometime later, with his nose bloodied and eye swollen, in a snow bank. He had no idea how long he had been there, but was surprised to find his mother tending to him. Her shopping packages sat in the snow. A small circle of strangers stood by, some offering help. Tasting his own blood, he was indignant that someone should strike him without warning.

"Come on, let's get him on his feet," said one of the bystanders, and two men helped a dazed Owen to stand up. He stood a moment, dabbing at his nose with a blood-soaked handkerchief.

"Thank you very much for your kind assistance, gentlemen," said Clara, but Owen said nothing.

"You're welcome, ma'am," said one of the men. "We hope he'll be all right. Don't forget your parcels."

Clara and Owen walked the ten minutes or so back to the hotel, where he spent the rest of that night nursing his eye and stuffing his nose with cotton batten. Clara said she didn't think it was broken, but it did have a nasty bruise which turned a bluish-black colour under his left eye which was, itself, bloodshot. When he looked in the mirror, he saw what a sorry sight he was.

The following morning found Owen eating breakfast with his mother in their hotel room, as usual, but with Owen nibbling gingerly on a piece of bread with jam.

"How are you feeling today, son?"

"I'm feeling a little better today, Mum. I can't understand why that horrible man hit me. I can only think he didn't like the way I looked at his girl. He seemed to be the jealous sort."

"Perhaps you can tell me what happened?" said Clara, a look of maternal concern on her face. "I'd really like to know."

Owen's excuse was ready. "I went outside for a walk. I was enjoying the fresh air and sunshine when a couple walked towards me on the sidewalk. I happened to take a glance at his girlfriend, and he punched me in the face!" he said, crocodile tears forming in his eyes.

Owen remembered when he'd fall and hurt himself when he was little; he'd come crying to his mother, and she always soothed and healed his wounds. "Come now, my son," she said as they stood up. She embraced him in her warm, motherly arms.

He sobbed on her shoulder, careful not to get any blood on her clean Sunday dress. He felt the corners of his mouth rising into a smirk behind her back.

Clara took a deep, ragged breath and, breaking the embrace, looked Owen straight in the eyes. "You are a liar, Owen Delmott."

Owen froze. His mother had never called him a liar in her life, so he thought his story was not believable enough.

"But Mum, it's true! He punched me in the face! Do you see this? Did I do this to myself?" he exclaimed, pointing to his injuries.

"Again, Owen, you are a liar. I should've seen it a long time ago," she said, shaking her head. "I just didn't want to believe it. Don't tell me your stories. I'm sick and tired of hearing them and I refuse to put up with them any more. I love you, yes, but I hate what you're doing. I hate what you're becoming."

For the first time in his life, Owen felt that he had been caught red-handed in a bald-faced lie and that this time there'd be no escape. Yet, he still tried. "Mum, honestly, I was walking along the sidewalk and that horrible man just swung round and punched me in the face. I can only think that he thought I was looking rudely at his girlfriend."

The disbelieving look on his mother's face told him she was having none of it. "I came out of the shop and was looking for you, Owen. I saw a group of people standing round in a circle near the crossing, and I knew you were in there, I just knew it. I felt it in the pit of my stomach. I ran over and sure enough, there you were, knocked out cold. I asked someone what happened, and a young man told me you had shoved your shoulder rudely into his girlfriend as you passed. What's more, he wasn't the only one. There were others there who said you'd done the same to them. To my mind, and may God in heaven forgive me, you damned well deserved what you got."

Owen felt like he had been stripped naked by the cutting words of his mother, with not a single shred of clothes left to hide his disgrace. Not even his father could have dealt such a humiliating blow. He stood there and said nothing, knowing from that moment on his mother would never again believe anything he had to say. Now with no safe refuge within his family, he had a strong desire to run away. However, the winter was biting cold, he had no real money except for ten dollars in his wallet, no friends and no place to go. Frustrated, angry and bitter, he slumped down on the floor next to his bed and sulked, trying to come to terms with his new reality.

Owen spent the rest of the day soul searching and hardly said anything to his mother. Despite that, they returned to the hospital together to say goodbye to George, who by then had already been moved back to his room. Owen looked at the wreckage of the man his father was. He wondered if an old violin had the power to cause such devastation, and why no harm came to Alexandra, or their grandfather, when they played that same instrument.

The first half of the train ride back to Windsor proved uneventful. Owen was surprised that after his mother's brutal chastisement she still wanted to sit next to him. He pondered the events of the last two days in his mind. He thought everything happening in his life was making him weary, exhausted, and frustrated. He wondered why other people were happy and successful and why all this had eluded him. Finally, he came to the conclusion that it was actually he who was making himself weary and miserable and it was getting him nowhere. After a while, he made a decision.

"Mum, I'll try to improve."

Clara was quick as lightning and hard as steel with her reply. "I hope you do. But you've got a long way to go to earn my trust again – if you ever do. I never want you to lie to me or anyone about anything ever again, Owen. That means all lying – big or small, white or black. You must also be ready to prove everything you say, because you'll never know when I may ask for it."

"Understood."

"Oh, but I'm not finished! This doesn't just end with you giving up lying. You've got to stop being a bully. I never in my life want to see another horrible sight like I saw yesterday, nor do I want to hear another story of you bullying, picking fights, speaking badly about people and so on. When you can do all that, you'll have regained my trust – and my respect."

"I promise I'll try, Mum," he said with his head lowered.

"However, I must admit I can't blame you entirely for this situation," she said. "Your father and I must also accept our share of responsibility for what you've become. We are your parents and we're supposed to be raising you. We weren't there to guide and lead you when you really needed it and I turned a blind eye to many of the horrible things you've done, hoping you'd somehow improve on your own. On my part, I accept my responsibility. If your father recovers, he'll have to accept his as well. We both love you."

Owen thought about his mother's words. At that moment, he felt two opposing forces pulling at him, nearly tearing him in half, the old one wanting him to remain on the same path, while the new one was tugging on him to embark on a vastly different course. The old one reminded him he could well blame his mother as the very reason he was failing so miserably at life. It told him that now would be the perfect time to jump in for the kill, hold her to account, bring the woman to her knees. She deserved it. The opposing force told him he could change his life-path, part with the old and welcome a new, bright future. The choice belonged to him alone and he made it with absolute certainty.

"Mum, thank you for telling me this. I hold no bad feelings towards you. I also want to thank you for putting me right. I even remember one time Professor Hergicksen said, 'Sometimes we need a good kick in the teeth to set us straight.' I got mine from that man in London for real. However, I really needed it – and got it – from you. I want you to know that I, too, accept responsibility for what I've done. I'm so sorry. I've not been a son you can be proud of, and I'm so ashamed of myself. I don't know how you can ever forgive me."

At that very moment, Owen Delmott died.

A new, completely different Owen now sat in the train next to his mother, a single tear forming in his eye and running down his bruised face.

"I'm also willing to work at it and prove it," he said.

"How is that? What do you mean?"

"To begin with, I will apologize to Alexandra. I'm also going to give her back Pépé's violin."

Chapter 28

The following Monday morning found Alexandra lining up with the other students at the classroom door, waiting to enter. She had been whispering to Emma when she looked down the corridor and saw Owen. When he got closer, the noisy students fell into a hush. It was clear to everyone that the boy's face was bruised, his eye was blackened and the white was bloodshot. He stood at the back of the line.

Sister Rose was, of course, standing at the door scrutinizing each pupil as they entered. After Alexandra took her seat, she turned back just in time to see the nun's arm go up in front of Owen. "Not you," the nun barked, closing the door and leaving her and Owen in the corridor. After a few moments, the students began murmuring.

"He's got into another fight! Did you see that shiner?" said one.

"Ha! He looks much better now!" mocked another.

"I wonder what the other guy looks like!" said yet another.

Alexandra was about to say something when the door to the classroom opened. Owen entered and sat at his desk. He was soon followed by the old nun, who seemed to ignore everything and whisked herself straight up to the front of the class. They said their morning prayers, as usual, and the nun began speaking to the class in her dry, parched voice. "Master Delmott has a few words he'd like to say," she announced.

All the students were hushed as Owen, appearing humbled, rose from his seat.

"Um, I was going to say this to Alexandra in private but, ah, I changed my mind. You see, since I insulted her in public, I thought that in public I should also apologize."

Alexandra's attention was fixed sceptically on the boy with the battered face. She couldn't help but wonder what kind of trouble he'd gotten himself into this time and what brought him to this pivotal moment.

"I've been horribly cruel to you, cousin," he said, sputtering his words. "I've been mean, spiteful, jealous and envious. It was wrong for me to say such horrible things to you, especially when it was your birthday. So please accept this as my apology, and I'm also sorry it took so long for me to make it. Maybe in time you can forgive me."

"Bully!" grumbled one person.

"Devil!" snapped another.

"Shh now!" said Sister Rose with an air of irritation in her voice. "Let him continue, please!"

"I deserve your words, yes, for I've often spoken them myself to others. I'm not finished, though. To anyone else I've offended by my rude behaviour or bullying, I apologize to you as well – and especially to you, Robbie Stuart."

Robbie sat in his place, eyes narrowing as he looked at the boy who just prostrated himself before the world.

After he finished speaking, Owen sat back down in his seat and sighed deeply. A great, powerful silence filled the room.

The students started murmuring again. "Was that really Owen? Did you hear that? Is it a joke? Who kidnapped Owen?"

Alexandra raised her hand to speak. The old nun nodded. "Sister Rose, I'd like to thank my cousin for his apology and I hope everything will be better in the future. Perhaps we can try playing a duet for the class sometime."

The old, dry nun nodded her head once in agreement, the faintest trace of a smile forming at the corners of her mouth.

* * *

When Alexandra returned home after her music lesson that evening, she found Marcie sitting at a table talking to Owen. He was there by himself, his mother nowhere to be seen.

Marcie got up from the table and approached Joseph. She spoke to them both in a low voice. "What on earth happened to Owen?" she asked before turning to Alexandra. "Well, no matter. It's you he wants to speak with, *Vogelein*."

Alexandra removed her hat and coat. She slouched in the seat across from her cousin, arms folded warily across her chest.

"I wanted to come here today to apologize to you in person and to return something which belongs to you," said Owen. He reached under the table and handed her an object of familiar shape and size. Alexandra straightened up and, with uncertain, yet grateful hands, accepted it.

"Thank you, Owen. I don't know what to say. It feels like a dream, really, I –"

"It will never make up for the way I've treated you, yet I believe now that our pépé wanted you to have this all along."

"Thank you so much, Owen, and now I have my Nellie, too. I've come to love that one as much as this. Our pépé's violin shall be a great family heirloom, and I hope someday I can pass it along to my children."

"I also wanted to apologize to you, in person, for those horrible things I said in the classroom on your birthday," he said before lowering his face.

"I forgive you for that, Owen," she said, rubbing the boy's shoulder. "Especially when you said my mother ran off with a sailor. I knew all along it wasn't true."

Owen offered no response. He sat silently, gazing down at the table. Alexandra studied him as an icy chill spread through her arms and legs. "That wasn't true, was it?"

As he continued looking down at the table, Alexandra noticed tears dripping down onto the tablecloth. He raised his head and looked at her. His bruised face was now glistening and wet, and his voice cracked as he spoke.

"I'm so sorry, cousin. I was so cruel to you. I should have never said that. It was the cruellest, most wicked thing I've ever said to anyone."

"But was it true?" she asked again firmly.

"I'm afraid it is."

"How do you know that?"

"I heard my parents talk about it often. They said that a sailor only came to the café two or three times and that one day your mother ran off with him."

Alexandra was trying to formulate another question when her father came and sat in the seat next to her. Casting a scornful glance at Owen, he placed his arm around Alexandra's shoulders.

"What's the matter, Angel?"

"Is it really true, Papa?" she said, voice breaking. "Did Mama really leave us for a sailor?"

Joseph sighed and, after a few uncomfortable moments, spoke.

"Angel, please forgive me. I'm such a coward. I've always wanted to protect you from harm, and from this harm I wanted to protect you from most of all. I'm sorry to say that it really is true. I can't explain it all myself, really."

Owen sat silently, looking at neither Alexandra nor Joseph.

Alexandra made a weak attempt to hit her father's chest with her upturned fists, but quickly pressed her head into him. His arms engulfed her as she began weeping.

After several minutes, her crying was reduced to whimpering, and finally to numbed silence. Joseph continued holding her in his arms, stroking her face and, using his fingers, moved the tear-soaked strands of hair away which hung near her eyes and tucked them behind her ears. Eventually she sat straight up and wiped the remaining wetness away with the backs of her hands. She sniffled as she spoke.

"Owen, I want to thank you for telling me the truth, but it's horrible you had to tell me this way. I also want to thank you for returning Pépé's violin. I forgive you, but don't you dare do anything to hurt me again."

"I won't, I promise," he said, glancing up.

Turning her attention to her father, she continued. "Papa, why didn't you tell me what really happened? How could you let me believe she just went away to rest? It's so horrible to be living in false hope and finding out the truth – from Owen!"

"Angel, I –"

Marcie approached and stopped just short of where Alexandra sat. "Can I get anything for you, *Vogelein*?"

The answer came immediately. "Yes. You can go upstairs and get my violin. I want to play a duet with Owen."

The boy looked up at Alexandra. Marcie set off up the stairs to the room where the girl kept her most valuable possession.

"I don't have my violin here, Alex," said Owen.

"You'll play Pépé's violin."

"It won't play for me, remember?"

"It will now," she said.

Joseph squeezed her shoulder once just as Marcie returned with the instrument. She carefully handed it to Alexandra, who delicately plucked at the strings to check the tuning. Alexandra watched as Owen opened the case with D.C.D. on the cover and removed the heirloom. He picked and plucked at the strings too, and the instrument sounded in perfect tune.

Alexandra took up her bow and played a short series of notes. After she finished, she looked on as Owen raised their pépé's violin up to his neck.

"Don't be afraid," she said. "Nothing bad will happen. Trust me."

Owen nodded, and focused his attention on the instrument. He sighed once and pulled the bow across the e-string. It resonated through the café with a crisp, clear sound. He did the same with the other strings, and they all sounded true as well. Finally, he played a short series of notes, which sounded bright and colourful.

"Do you like Strauss?" asked Alexandra.

"Yes, I know some of his music."

"Let's try Vienna Waltz?" Alexandra suggested.

"All right."

The two cousins stood opposite each other and held their bows up to their instruments. Alexandra began first, drawing her bow back across the strings, crisply playing the first few introductory notes of the waltz. Owen joined in moments later, and the sweet sound of the waltz spread through the whole building. Joseph sat at a table and watched, while Marcie watched from behind the counter. The few customers remaining in the café stopped talking and looked on. The two cousins played the song through from beginning to end, and Alexandra felt as if they'd been playing together for years.

When they finished, Alexandra curtsied to Owen and he bowed to her and to their modest audience. Everyone in the café politely applauded the duo as they stood down and began packing up their instruments.

"I'm glad to have my cousin back," said Alexandra.

"So am I," replied Owen, smiling, as he returned their pépé's violin to its case and gave it to Alexandra.

* * *

As the weeks turned into months, Alexandra enjoyed helping the professor teach Robbie and Emma to play the violin every Saturday. Soon they even received practice instruments – second-hand violins the professor let them borrow. Alexandra was happy to see them making slow, steady progress as they worked diligently on their craft practising scales, bow movements, correct hand positions and so on. She was pleased when one of them could learn a new technique and improve on it. "It's called professional satisfaction," the Maestro would say. She really admired how he was so full of such useful little tidbits. One of her favourite expressions from him was, "if you really want to learn something, teach it," and another, "you really don't know something well enough until you can teach it to another person." The Maestro was wise indeed, she thought, and she knew deep down who he had meant these lessons for.

Alexandra's musical pleasures continued almost non-stop. Though the old nun hadn't yet asked her and Owen to play their duet, there was still plenty to do. Her new friends, the group of musicians from Detroit, often stopped by. Whenever they did, they always played together – much to the delight of the diners in the café.

One of the greatest pleasures she received, however, was when she played her violin with Owen. The boy had indeed done a miraculous turnaround and seemed so much happier in his new life. At one point he even defended Robbie when someone tried calling the boy Rabbit Stew. "That's not his name," he said. As the weeks passed, he visited the café more often, especially with his mother when they were either on their way to, or taking the train from, London.

On a particularly rainy and foggy Friday afternoon in mid-April, Owen and his mother stopped by the café to say hello. The two cousins played a couple duets, as usual, with Owen using their pépé's violin.

After they finished, Alexandra had an idea. "Owen, why don't you bring Pépé's violin up to London and play a song for your father?"

"Should I?" the boy asked his mother.

Clara paused a moment. "How do you feel with the violin, Owen?" she asked.

"It's fine, Mum, really. You've seen me play it and everything is all right. I don't think it caused Father to have his problems. It's just an old violin."

Clara hesitated. "I suppose you're right. I can't see any harm in it. You may bring it."

Alexandra packed the instrument carefully in its case, gave it to Owen, and bid them both bon voyage.

*　*　*

The big black locomotive from Windsor to London plunged steadily along through that foggy, drizzly April evening, belching vast plumes of spray out from under its churning wheels with their giant piston arms sawing back and forth.

When Owen, violin in hand, and his mother arrived at the hospital, George was not in his room, but was sitting in a wheelchair in the hospital atrium. He was staring straight ahead, eyes focused nowhere.

"George, dear, it's Clara and Owen. We've come to visit you!" she said in a higher than normal tone as she straightened the collar on his shirt.

Owen knew that special voice, that artificially bright one his mother always made whenever she was trying to comfort someone in distress. She could produce that tone under any circumstances, even for someone on their deathbed, painting that scene with bright, rosy colours.

George continued staring blankly into nothing.

"Owen has brought your father's violin! He'd like to play you a song! Isn't it wonderful? I've already asked the head nurse, and she said it would be fine if he did."

"Yes, Father, if you don't mind, I'd like to play a song for you," added Owen as he took out the family heirloom.

For some reason he could not explain, Owen felt a strong desire to play "Vienna Waltz," the song he had first played with Alexandra. He held the violin up to his neck and relaxed his arm. Taking a deep breath, he began to play, the sounds coming from the instrument being sweet and delicate indeed. He soon closed his eyes as he enjoyed the rhythm and flow of the music. Without a doubt, the melody pouring forth from the strings of the instrument was truly magic, enchanting, captivating. Several couples in the atrium even started dancing and twirling about, especially the older people; the pleasant sounds taking their minds back many decades to the carefree, memorable days of their youth.

As he continued, Owen's mind was taken up too, transported, travelling the countless eons through time and space. It was a magical journey; in fact he had never experienced anything like that in his life. Eventually he found himself in his father's oak-panelled law office, a distant spectator in a great, seminal moment in the life of his family.

A young George Delmott was standing in that office with another young man. He had a legal document on his desk.

"Sign the contract, I'm warning you, this is your last chance," said George.

"I will never sign it. The property is mine and I will never sell it – especially to the likes of you!"

"As you wish. You shall rue this day forever."

Owen continued playing the melody, mesmerized by its delicate sounds and intrigued at the vision which played through his mind. Some couples danced merrily, swirling about just as they'd done in their younger days, while other people gathered in a circle around the young performer to watch and listen.

Owen stood gazing as his father set fire to various objects in a little shop in the middle of the night. Following that, he stood on the street corner with two other men and watched the flames grow in intensity, soon spreading to the neighbouring buildings and beyond.

Owen felt the passage of time. Secrets and silence: George spoke nothing of this for many years.

"How dare you swear an affidavit to the magistrate!" George stormed to a young woman. "I told you about the fire in confidence and you betrayed me! You were taking steps to have me prosecuted, weren't you? You'd have me thrown in prison,

wouldn't you? Well, no matter, I've taken care of it. The magistrate belongs to me. Now you listen and you'd better listen well: Take only a few items of clothing and one small bag. Tonight a merchant seaman will take you on a voyage to a place only he and I know about. If you return, contact your family, or ever try to prosecute me again, I swear that your fate – and theirs, will lie in ashes as well. Of this you can be absolutely certain."

The music and dancing came to a sudden halt. Owen's eyes bolted open as he looked in horror at the man in front of him. George's entire body was shaking and his fists were clenched so tight that his knuckles were turning white. He struggled to speak, sputtering a few pitiful sounds as drool ran down his chin.

"George! What is it?" shouted Clara as she held the man up by his shoulders. "Quick! Please! Somebody get a doctor!"

* * *

Clara was relieved that it took only a few minutes for the doctors to arrive, but it took a good hour to calm George down. One doctor suspected he'd had an epileptic seizure, while another thought maybe he'd suffered the side effects of his new medication. Eventually though, George was taken back to his hospital bed.

"That's all we can do for him tonight. We'll keep a good eye on him; you've nothing to worry about. Please, get some rest and come back in the morning," said the doctor.

Clara and Owen walked in silence to their hotel room. The hour was growing late, yet Clara was curious to know what happened. She hung up her coat and hat and sat in one of the rather uncomfortable looking wooden chairs. "I haven't seen your father like that since –"

"Since that day he accidentally heard Alexandra play the violin," said Owen.

Clara remembered that day clearly. Though the time and situation were different, both events somehow had the same strange feel, the same strange atmosphere to them.

"Yes, since that day. Now why did you choose to play that particular song for your father?"

"I'm not sure why I chose that, Mum. I played it recently with Alex and it was the first thing that entered my head," he replied, sitting on the foot of the bed.

"Do you believe your pépé's violin is magic, Owen? I have to ask because I have never in my life seen you play any violin like that. I've also never seen people dancing with each other to your music, too. You've played in the past Owen, and God knows you've done it well. But this time was much different. I also saw the look on your face as you finished the song and how you looked at your father. You were horrified."

"Yes, but it wasn't at the way he looked. In fact, I wasn't even surprised. It was because of the vision I had of him as a young man."

"What? Are you trying to tell me you're having visions, too?"

"Songs bring back memories in people, Mum. Think of it, you hear a song that you used to hear when you were young. Memories come back from that time. Alexandra could see them in other people. She could see them ages ago but I couldn't until now."

"Tell me what you saw, Owen. I'd really like to know," she said in her false, cheery voice.

Owen leaned forward, elbows on his knees. "Perhaps it was the same sort of vision Alexandra gets, I don't know and I can't be sure. I don't even know if it was real, but it sure seemed real to me. Perhaps you can help me make sense of it."

"Maybe I can, but I want you to tell me, and God help you, you'd better tell me the truth."

"Why not? In my vision I saw Father when he was young. He was trying to make someone sign a contract. I think Father wanted to buy some property from that man. I don't know who the man was; I'd never met him. When the man wouldn't sign, Father threatened him. Later that night, Father made good on his threat by setting fire to the neighbouring building. He wanted to make it look like an accident.

However, the fire spread quickly and ended up burning half the town."

Clara stretched her memory back to the night of the fire. She remembered well the chaos, panic, the smoky air, the cries of the women and children. She also recalled George coming home and walking into their bedroom in the wee hours of the morning. She remembered his defiant attitude and heartless remarks, which he spouted over and over: "Serves him right, he had it coming. His problems are only beginning now, ha!" Yet somehow despite all this, she naïvely believed that through love, time, and patience she could change him. She accepted it as a personal challenge – to mould him, form him, and shape him to her ways.

"To make matters worse, there was something else. You knew all along that Father had done it. You never spoke about it with him, but you knew. You kept silent and said nothing to anyone."

"Stop!" she said, on the verge of tears, her voice real. "I don't want to hear any more."

"But Mum, there's more! It's very important! I have to tell you!"

"I don't want to hear it, whatever it is!" she said, sobbing. "I also don't want you playing that thing ever again. In the morning, I want you to do what you do best."

"What's that?"

"I want you to destroy it."

Chapter 29

Bang! Bang! Bang!

Owen and Clara were startled awake by the sound of a pounding fist on the door of their hotel room. It was 4:00 a.m.

Clara lit her lamp, donned her robe and walked to the door. Owen sat up in his bed, curious as to who might call at this hour.

"Who is it?" asked Clara through the door.

"I'm from the hotel staff, ma'am. I have an important message for you."

Clara opened the door a crack. Owen could barely see a man standing there dressed in hotel livery. "I'm so sorry to disturb you ma'am, but the hospital just phoned. There's been a change in your husband's condition."

"What change?"

"They wouldn't give all the details, ma'am. They only said he's got up from his bed and walked straight up to a nurse in the corridor. He's speaking. He asked about you and your son. The hospital wants you to go there quickly."

Owen and his mother wasted no time getting dressed and leaving the hotel for the hospital. "If your father can indeed speak, and dear God in heaven I hope he can, I want you to say nothing about last night's events – or about the visions you had."

"I understand, though I can't help thinking about what I saw him do."

"Hold your tongue, young man! Your fantasy proves nothing, especially now," said Clara.

Upon entering the foyer, they were greeted by an anxious young nurse. "He just about scared me to death! He remembers nothing from last night and wants to go home."

"Thank you," said Clara. "Where is he?"

"He's in the atrium. This way, please."

The nurse escorted them into the atrium where they saw George sitting in an armchair. He was fully dressed and looked ready to leave. The big room was devoid of anyone except two nurses and a cleaning lady.

"Clara, my dear! Owen!" said George upon seeing them. "I'm so happy to see you! Where've you been? What is this place?"

"George dear, you've had some medical problems. We nearly thought we'd lost you. I'm so happy you're back with us! You know, we're at a special hospital in London. Didn't the nurse tell you? We sent you here so that you could get the very best care."

George turned his attention to the boy. "Owen, how've you been, son? I'm pleased that you've come with your mother all this way."

"Hello, Father," said Owen, looking at the man through new eyes. "Lots has changed since you've been away."

"Well, it's high time I go home, don't you think?"

"I'm sure we can, George dear. We can take the early train back to Windsor. However, I was told that the doctor should check you over and sign your release forms. You've been through a terrible ordeal, and we must be sure everything is all right before you leave!"

After hesitating a while, George agreed. They sat talking as the night gave way to the first rays of morning sunshine. Finally Clara, not willing to leave George, sent Owen back to the hotel to check out and collect their meagre things. She also sent him off to do as she bid with the violin.

As he retraced his steps to the hotel, Owen's mind dwelt on the permanence of the task set before him – and the guilt he would suffer the rest of his days. He also thought about how Alexandra was delighted to have the instrument back, to save it, preserve it, and pass it on to her children someday. She also loaned it to him in good faith and if he destroyed it, any trust he earned from her would be destroyed as well – and that, indeed, would be worst of all. Nausea churned in his stomach.

Despite everything, Owen Delmott always considered himself a clever boy. He entered the hotel room and sat at the table. He took two pieces of paper and quickly scrawled a few lines on each one, slipping one of the notes inside the violin case. He collected all their belongings – two small suitcases plus the violin, and took everything to the front desk. "I would like to check out," he said to the young man tending the reception desk. "I would also like you to do me a favour, if you please."

"Yes, of course."

He handed the second hand-written note to the desk clerk, along with a sum of money and the violin.

"I'd like you to package this instrument extra well. It is extremely valuable. Then I want you to mail it here. I hope this will be enough money."

The clerk took the note and read it aloud. "Alexandra Delmott, Goyeau Street, Windsor, Ontario. Very good."

* * *

"Good morning, Angel!" said Joseph from his paper-strewn table one day in late April. "Today's the day!"

"What day is it today, Papa?"

"Why, it's Thursday today, of course!" he said, laughing.

"What's so special about Thursday?" she said with a hand on her hip and laughing.

"Ah, don't you know that Thursdays are special days?" he took his glasses off and winked. "Only good things happen on Thursdays! It's my favourite day of the week!"

Alexandra thought the man had lost his mind.

"Ah, before you think I'm crazy, I wanted to say we're breaking ground on the new house today. Everything is all staked out. Here, have a look at this," he said, motioning toward a large paper spread out across the table.

"Our new house! Oh Papa, it's so exciting! I can't wait for it to be built!"

"Look here," he said, pointing at the blueprints. "Do you see this? This is where your bedroom will be, and it's twice the size of the one you have now. This is also our kitchen, a real kitchen, so we won't be sharing it with the restaurant any longer, and this is the parlour. Also, on this next blueprint we have the new restaurant. It, too, is twice the size of this one and it even has a special section where you and other musicians can play."

"Papa, really, this is like a dream come true and I can hardly believe it. I'd like to go there after school with Robbie and Emma. Maybe even Owen could join us, though he hasn't been to school at all this week. Would you mind?"

"Well, of course you may! But I think there won't be much to see except for workers digging a hole in the ground, but you're welcome to go."

"I will. When I go, I'll take a mind-photo so that I can remember it always. I'll stand across the street, look at the empty lot and remember exactly what it looks like. Then, I'll close my eyes. In a few months, when it's all complete, I'll return to that exact same spot and again I'll close my eyes. When I open them, everything will be finished!"

"You're just as crazy as I am, girl," he said, chuckling. "Now I know where you get it from. By the way, you've received a letter in the mail, and a parcel," said Joseph as he walked behind the counter and retrieved the items.

Alexandra looked first at the well-wrapped, distinctively shaped parcel with postal markings on it.

"*Another* violin? Who sent me a violin?"

"Well, why don't you open it and find out?"

Alexandra unwrapped the parcel only to find the familiar case with D.C.D. on the lid.

"It's Pépé's violin! But I loaned it to Owen! Why –"

"I have no idea, either," said Joseph. "Owen must be the one who sent it. Perhaps there's a problem and they're stranded in London. Perhaps your uncle's condition has declined, so Owen felt an urgency to send the violin back to you. I don't know."

Alexandra squinted. She held the case up, examining it for damage. She saw none. Then she opened the lid and saw a handwritten note lying on top of the instrument. "Papa, there's a note here! It's from Owen! It says, 'Alex, No time to explain. Hide this violin and don't tell a soul you have it. Owen.'"

Alexandra stood in the café holding the scribbled note. She read it again, but the second reading revealed no more information than the first. She removed the instrument from the case and examined it carefully. It was in perfect condition.

"Why would he mail it back? It doesn't make sense!" remarked Joseph. "Well, I think you should do what he says, at least until we find out what's happened."

"Yes, and he can explain why he's not been at school all week, either."

"You have one more letter. Actually, it came several days ago but I forgot to give it to you," he said, passing her the envelope.

She slit the side of the envelope open and extracted the contents. She unfolded the paper and read the typed letter quickly through. "Papa! It's the music festival Sir Charles and the Maestro have been telling me about! I've been invited! Oh please, please, can I go?" she said, bouncing up and down.

"Oh, another trip in the works, eh?" Marcie said as she approached.

"Yes indeed! This time to Ottawa!" Alexandra responded. Then turning to her father, she asked again, "Please, Papa, can I go?"

"You know, Alexandra, it will cut into your study time at school, and Ottawa is truly a very long way from home. Ha! Do you actually think I'd deny you the chance to move your music ahead? Of course you can go. In fact, we'll all go. Why not? We could use the break. Besides, Ottawa will be lovely at that time of year. What do you think, Marcie? Can you come with us? Can you pry Denis away so he can come too?"

"Please, Marcie, please come!" Alexandra pleaded, holding the woman's hands and bouncing up and down. "You'll have a holiday! Imagine! *You* will finally be the one to stay in a grand hotel, have people serving *you*! Waiting on *you*! Oh it'll be so wonderful!"

"Well now, we've been saving up a bit of money, perhaps for a trip to Niagara Falls. But why not Ottawa?"

* * *

When Friday arrived, Alexandra set off happily for school. She wore a plain dress, but since the weather was pleasant, she left her coat at home, choosing to wear the mustard yellow sweater. The grass was now starting to green up, and crocuses were peaking yellow, white, and violet blooms from between shrinking patches of snow. The air was filled with springtime freshness, and trickling meltwater formed little streams which sparkled in the April sunshine.

Upon entering the schoolyard, she immediately spotted Owen. "Hello, cousin! Where've you been? Are you all right? Thanks for mailing the violin to me, but you could've just brought it back with you, I wasn't that anxious to get it back!"

"Hi, Alex. I'm all right, but there's so much I have to tell you. There was a good reason to post the violin to you."

"Please tell me! I have time!"

"Of course, but now is not the time or place. Have you done what I asked?"

"Yes, of course."

"Good. Meet me here after school and I'll tell you everything."

"All right, but I have a violin lesson with the Maestro. You can walk with me there and tell me everything."

* * *

Following the students' dismissal, the two cousins began wending their way to the professor's home.

"My father has come back from the dead, Alexandra, and now he's home. But this is no happy resurrection."

"What do you mean?"

"Let me start by saying that I played Pépé's violin for him in hospital. When I played it, I got a vision. Now I know without any doubt that there is great power in that instrument."

"What did you see in your vision, Owen?"

"It's not so much what I saw, but what I now know. It wasn't just a vision. It was a revelation."

"Go on."

"Alexandra, my father started the great fire many years ago because he was angry with someone. He kept the whole thing a secret all this time. My mother also knew what he'd done, yet she did nothing and said nothing."

"My goodness, Owen," she said matter-of-factly. She had no reason to doubt his words. To her, concrete proof of his sincerity had been delivered in the mail the previous day.

"I began by telling my mother about the vision I had of the fire. She got very upset and told me she didn't want to hear any more, and that I was to destroy the violin. In the end, I wouldn't do it. That's why I mailed it to you. Again, you must not tell anyone you have it. She thinks I destroyed it."

"Thank you, Owen, for that," she said, finally realizing how close the heirloom had come to destruction.

"Oh I'm far from finished, Alex. There was much more to the vision. I was going to tell my mother about that too, but now I'm glad I didn't. Alex, my father bragged to someone about the events surrounding the great fire. That person was taking legal steps to have my father put in jail. However, when he found out, he put a quick stop to it. The person who was trying to do this was – your mother."

Alexandra stopped dead in her tracks. "My mother? But Owen, you said she had run off with a sailor!"

"Those facts had been twisted by my father over the years to make it *look* like your mother had just deserted you. The so-called sailor was actually a merchant seaman. He was nothing more than a worker on a ship. They had no romantic interest in each other at all."

Alexandra stood on the sidewalk, trying to come to terms with yet another new reality shaking up her life. "Why hasn't she written?"

"My father warned her against it. He told her that if she ever tried to visit, contact you, or if she should try to have him prosecuted again, that everyone's fate would lie in ashes."

"Oh Owen! Do you know what this means?"

"What?"

"It means my mama still loves me! Papa was right all along! She is loving me from afar!" she beamed, taking the boy's hands in hers. Shortly afterwards though, her joy became decidedly muted. "Owen, my mama will never come here. She won't allow any harm to come to me."

"Yes, I know, but don't worry. She won't have to come here."

"Why?" Alexandra asked, puzzled.

"Because you're going to her."

* * *

Alexandra felt it best not to say anything to Owen about her other visions – especially the one about their pépé in the kitchen of the farmhouse. The two cousins now had an unspoken agreement between them. Alexandra plainly knew that Owen was aware of her visions, yet she wasn't prepared to fully trust him. *The past is a hard thing to undo,* she thought. She needed to discuss these matters with her father before deciding what to do next.

When the café closed later that evening, Alexandra had an idea. "Let's go for a walk along the river," she suggested to her father.

Joseph locked the café and they set off, strolling leisurely along the riverbank. As they strolled, they watched the ferries go back and forth across the river.

"Papa, please tell me how you met Mama," Alexandra asked, watching her father's face for a reaction. He raised the corners of his mouth into a half smile, his eyes thoughtful and dreamy.

"Let's see now. Your mother worked for your Uncle George's law firm in those days. That's how I met her. One time I visited my brother at his office, and there your mother was, all smiles. Oh she was such a pleasant lady! Sometimes she'd come to the café, and if I was there we'd have lunch together. We soon fell in love and got married, and two years later, you were born."

"That sounds so romantic!" Alexandra said before changing her tone. "Now I have to ask you, please tell me how Mama left."

Joseph sighed. "Well Angel, you were only four years old. Your pépé had died that spring, we still had the farm and your mother worked in the café. I was trying to manage the harvest – it was the last harvest before we sold the farm – and the weather was horrible. The farmhands and I were struggling to get all the work done. In fact, I had been out there for two weeks straight. I felt so bad, honestly, because your mama had to run the whole café by herself, plus she had to look after you. It was a really difficult time in her life, and I felt guilty because I wasn't there to help. Then one day, your Aunt Clara arrived at the farm by coach with you and Owen. She said that the café was closed and your mother was gone. Are you sure you want to hear this?"

"Yes, Papa, I have to hear it. I remember Mama taking me to Aunt Clara's. I thought it was just going to be a visit. I also remember riding out to the farm that day, but I want to know more. I want to know everything, especially the details."

"All right then, I immediately went back to the café. It was closed, just as your Aunt Clara said. I went inside, and there was a note for me on the counter in an envelope. I still have the note, as a matter of fact. I memorized every word."

"What did it say?"

"It said, 'My Dearest Joseph, It breaks my heart to tell you that circumstances have forced me to leave you and our daughter. I wish you both a very good life. I wish things could have turned out differently. I love you and will never forget you. Helen.' " Joseph drew in an exasperated sigh. "Quite frankly, I was devastated, but I understood why. I wasn't there when she needed me most. I can't help but feel it was my fault because I left her overworked. She was later seen boarding a ship in the company of a sailor. In fact, there were several people who saw her."

Alexandra dabbed her eyes. "Thank you for telling me this, Papa, but that's not the real reason she left. I know what really happened."

"What do you know? Did you get a vision about that?"

"It's about a vision, yes, but it's not my vision."

"Whose vision?"

"Owen's vision."

Joseph looked at Alexandra, squinting his eyes.

"Papa, when Owen was in London, he played Pépé's violin for Uncle George. You do know that the visions never lie."

"The visions never lie. I understand that," said Joseph. "But Owen lies. We can't trust him."

"Maybe, but I need to tell you about it anyway, Papa, especially if it's true."

"Well, all right then, go ahead – if you think it'll help," said Joseph.

"In Owen's vision, Uncle George was responsible for the Great Fire of Windsor. He bragged about it to Mama and she tried to report him, but he found out and was very angry. He told her to leave town, never contact us and never try to report him again, or 'our fate would lie in ashes.' Papa, she was really afraid of Uncle George. He's a horrible criminal, Aunt Clara knows it too but she doesn't want to admit it. Also, I know that Mama still loves us. She didn't want anything to happen to us, so she left with some worker on a ship to go to some secret place. That's what happened."

"It never ends, does it?" said Joseph, shaking his head. "Where did she go?"

"I think only Uncle George would know for sure. Do you want me to play for him? Maybe we can find out?"

"Under these circumstances, I do. However, even if you played for him, there's no telling that your mother is still where he sent her. That was nine years ago! Anything could've happened, but it's a start; it's something. I'll have to figure out how to get you close enough to your uncle so he can hear you play, because he will never voluntarily listen to you. Is it possible for you to take this information from his memory? I mean, could you take it from him as if you were asking a question? If so, we might be able to find your mother!"

"Papa, the visions just come to me. I don't have any control over them and can't choose which memories from people I want to see. The only thing I can do is try, and hope I can find out."

"It's all we can ask for. Good. I'll work on a plan to get you within earshot of your uncle."

Alexandra and Joseph returned to the café, their plan beginning to take shape. She went up to her bedroom, reached up on the shelf and took down the small, decorated box in which she kept all her valuable things. She placed the box down on her bed and took the items out, one by one. She examined each one carefully – especially the ones her mother had given her. She wondered if things could talk, what stories would they tell? With no one to speak on their behalf, every precious item in the box just remained some old thing, a passing curiosity at best. She longed for the answers to her questions, but the items remained silent, quiet reminders of days forever gone.

Chapter 30

The following Monday morning, Clara and George stepped outside into the bright spring sunshine. They were on their way to the law offices of Delmott, Cord & Brewster.

"I'm so glad you're finally home dear and that you feel well enough to visit the office today," said Clara as they walked. "The staff at work will be very happy to see you. So much has happened! People come and go and, in fact, Windsor even has a new police chief!"

"Yes, yes," he said. "I'll be meeting him soon enough. Before that, I've got a lot of work to do, people to see and, of course, unfinished business with Joseph, his kid, and that damned café that needs tending to."

Clara shuddered at his remark. "You know dear, Clive has been doing a wonderful job managing your affairs. He has been real faithful about reporting to me every week. He even said that profits are up and that everyone at the law firm is so much happier."

He scoffed at her words. "Are you saying it's a happier place because I haven't been there?"

"Why not at all George! Everyone misses you!" she said, catching herself in the very act of lying.

As the two continued their walk, Clara listened as George continued speaking about the myriad tasks that must be awaiting him after such a long absence. She knew as a businessman he hated surprises, wanting to know as many things as far in advance as possible.

The couple walked up the steps to the law firm and into the reception area.

The secretary was at her desk, as usual, and several office staff were busy with the daily goings-on of the law firm. When everyone noticed George, they stopped and stared at him as if he'd just returned from the dead.

George looked at everything – the new furniture, drapery, freshly papered walls, paintings, and even the new electric lighting. Clara stood next to him glowing as he surveyed it all.

"I designed it myself!" she said. "I knew you'd recover, so I thought I'd brighten things up a bit and welcome you back in style!"

George huffed. "Redecorated? Exactly who did you think would have to pay for all this?"

Clara's face fell. "Why of course, you did, dear," she said matter-of-factly. "Actually, it was your company that paid for it."

"I can't believe it! I get ill and everyone goes behind my back on a spending spree wasting my hard-earned money on frivolous extravagance! Who approved all this?"

"I did," said an offended Clive Brewster, walking out of George's office. "I see you've returned and brought the sunshine back with you."

* * *

Owen left school early that day to help his mother prepare a special dinner at home, and soon the house began to fill with the smell of roast beef. Owen knew his mother had taken particular pride in planning the meal. When George returned home that evening, the three family members sat at their usual places at the table.

"Delicious meal, Clara," said George.

"Thank you, dear, I know it's your favourite," she replied, smiling and passing him the platter of meat.

George turned his attention to Owen. "You've hardly spoken two words to me since I returned, son. Is something the matter?"

Owen looked at the man who ate his dinner as if nothing at all was wrong in the world.

"I've just been thinking a lot about the future."

George put down his fork and gazed at the boy. "Really?" he said. "You're actually *thinking* about something? It's high time you've given serious thought about doing something with your life. So far you've been nothing but a bitter disappointment to your mother and me."

"Now, now George," said Clara.

"Was I talking to you, woman?" he snapped.

"Of course I know what I want to do with my life," said Owen.

George was incredulous. "Perhaps you'd care to share this divine revelation with the rest of the world?"

"Of course I would. I'd like to be a lawyer."

George sat back in his chair laughing. "You really do have no concept of reality at all, do you? Only smart people can be lawyers. You're living in a dream world of fantasy and illusion. You're a walking, talking failure, Owen. There's nothing about you that convinces me you could be a lawyer at all."

Clara did not speak, nor did she turn her head to look at George. She glanced in his direction but quickly lowered her eyes.

"I'll be a lawyer all right," said Owen. "In fact, I want to be a lawyer like Clive Brewster."

"You're rather rude, aren't you? Why like Brewster? What's so special about him?"

"I like and respect Mr. Brewster. He's an honourable man."

George froze for a moment, glaring at Owen. Enraged, he stood straight up, grabbed the table ledge and with one mighty thrust, heaved the whole end of the table up and over, sending their dinner, dishes, cups and cutlery crashing to the floor.

"What do you mean? Is that your way of saying I have no integrity?"

Owen sat defiant in his chair as his sobbing mother tried to salvage their spilled dinner and collect the broken pieces of china from the floor. "I –"

"Now you listen carefully to me, you rude little boy," shot George, face red, pointing his finger straight at Owen's face. "You know nothing of how the world really works and how ruthless people can be! You have to rule them with an iron fist! You can't give them any ground at all or they're going to walk all over you for the rest of your life. The sooner you understand that, the sooner you'll succeed. What's gotten into you, anyway? You've changed and I don't like it."

"Well, Father, while you were in hospital, I decided to change the course of my life."

"Hallelujah! It's a miracle!" said George, throwing his arms in the air and sitting back down in his chair. "Whatever on earth inspired you to do that?"

"It all began by deciding to tell the truth, Father. From there it moved to not twisting all the facts around. I also decided that, while I'm at it, I would never force people to do things by threatening them. I'd also never get revenge on people by burning down their homes and offices."

"Is that your way of saying I've done all these things, Owen? Is it, boy?"

"Only you would know that for sure."

"What makes you think so? Oh, wait, I know! You've been getting that little witch to perform her magic tricks in front of me while I was laid up in hospital, haven't you?"

"No," said Owen, rising confidently from his chair. "I played Pépé's violin there. I saw the whole thing and I saw what you did. You will never get away with it."

"George," said Clara while making a pile of broken china. "I made him destroy the violin."

"Good. At least you've done something useful in your lives, the both of you. Now you two remember well these words: if you know what's good for you, you will not breathe a word of these things to anyone. Furthermore, we will never talk about this again, for if you do, I shall personally ensure your fates are exactly the same as those people you saw in those visions."

* * *

"The world will laugh with you, but it's not going to cry with you." Alexandra remembered the words of the professor as she lay awake in bed late that night. She reasoned that people might sympathize with her plight, with the fact that her mother was living in a faraway place, but no one would do anything to help her and she'd somehow have to do it all herself. She also reasoned that hers was a much different situation than the professor had. His Valentina left because she *wanted* to. However, Alexandra knew that her mother left not for any selfish reasons, but because she really feared her brother-in-law, feared how powerful he was and what he could do. She probably felt it was the only way to protect her family. Furthermore, the vision of her Uncle George refusing to help her pépé was as troubling to her as Owen's vision must have been to him.

Sometimes, evil wins.

* * *

Alexandra, deeply troubled, didn't fall asleep until late that night. She was grateful her father allowed her to sleep in on Tuesday and miss school, but by mid-morning she was up and in the café having breakfast. Charlie and his friends were in their usual places, Mrs. Labonte and Mrs. Tellier were gossiping as always, and Marcie and staff were tending to the customers.

"I'll have a little fiddle music with my coffee, please, Miss Aydy!" said a jovial Charlie as Alexandra picked at her meal.

She looked at Charlie; he was always such a happy man. Despite how she felt, she didn't have the spirit to refuse him and sour this good man's mood. Sighing, she went upstairs to get her violin. When she returned, she decided she'd play an assortment of music which reflected the time of year – sunny, bright and colourful. Perhaps if she played this music, her own mood would change as well.

Alexandra raised the violin up to her shoulder, but before she could play, the brass bell on the door clattered angrily. She looked over at the intrusion to find her uncle standing there. He was not alone. In fact, all eyes were focused on him as he stood talking with the new chief of police, a constable and several men. A strange, middle-aged woman joined them a few moments later.

"Is Mr. Joseph Delmott here?" said the chief.

At that moment, Joseph appeared from the kitchen. "What's going on here?"

"Are you Joseph Delmott?" said the chief.

"I am."

"Mr. Delmott, you are under arrest for arson."

"Arson? What do you mean?"

"Mr. Delmott, you're under arrest for causing the Great Fire of Windsor back in '71. These witnesses have come forward placing you at the scene of the crime. Please do not make this any more difficult than it has to be. You will be granted a fair trial."

"George! What have you got to do with this?" said Joseph.

"Remember, dear brother, nobody crosses me. This day was a long time in the making, a day we can proudly say justice was served."

Alexandra, still holding her violin, ran up to her father and wrapped her arms around him. "Papa, no! It's not true!" she said, crying. Turning to the chief, she continued. "My Uncle George is lying! My father would never do such a thing!"

"I'm afraid that will be for the courts to decide," said the chief.

"That's right," said George. "You know, with the complexity involved in prosecuting this case, it could take years."

"What about Alexandra?" said Joseph. "What will happen to her if I'm in jail?"

"No worries, Joseph. Mrs. Crawford is here to take her to a residential school in Toronto." He turned his attention to Alexandra. "We all know how fond you are of Toronto, right? There you can learn all the useful skills for a woman. You know, practical things such as cooking, sewing and cleaning."

"Can't wait to get back into action, can you George?" said Marcie.

George scowled at her. "This has nothing to do with you, woman! Do not interfere with these proceedings."

"Play for me, Aydy," said Charlie, but looking at George.

"We want to hear a song!" said Mrs. Labonte and Mrs. Tellier.

"Please, Alexandra, some music!" said Marcie.

Alexandra looked at her instrument, wondering if it would be appropriate to play it under such dire circumstances. Then she noticed the little nick in the neck of the instrument, the worn ebony, the darker colour of the wood. She realized she had taken the wrong violin and now all eyes were focused on her to play. She looked up at her father for approval.

"Play a song for us on your violin, Alexandra," said Joseph. "And make it sing."

"What for?" said George. "She's wasting time!"

"I don't see any harm in her playing a song," said the chief.

George stood in the middle of the café glaring at the girl. "Well," he scoffed. "It doesn't make any difference now."

Alexandra performed a concert-level rendition of "The Blue and the Gray." As she played, she closed her eyes. The song was soft, enchanting, and the melody carried with it the essence of bygone days, youthful ambitions, sacrifice. Everyone in the room became entranced by the magic developing around them as their memories from that time came flooding back. Even George was not immune, the haunting notes finding a place in his memory. The magic of the music was making it difficult for him to concentrate. He soon found himself being pulled back through time, through space, all the way back to that fateful night of 1871.

With just the faintest hint of dawn creeping through the window and into the bedroom where his wife slept, George Delmott turned the doorknob and entered the room.

"Where in God's name have you been?" Clara asked, sitting up in bed.

"Do you remember Max Barker?" said George, unaware that he was speaking aloud in the café. "I taught him a damned good lesson for crossing me. He refused to sell me his property, so I settled accounts with him."

"Who's Max Barker?" asked Clara in the vision.

"Max Barker? He's the man I was trying to buy the property from in Windsor! It was a real estate transaction. You know I had my eye on that property for a long time. I wanted him to sell it to me, to sign the contract, and he refused to do it."

"What did you do?"

"So I set fire to the little shop next door! I have strength, I have courage, I'll tell you that! I set fire to the shop knowing full well it would spread to Max's building and I'd get my revenge. No one would ever suspect it!" he said, boasting.

"Did anybody see you, dear?"

"Unfortunately, Bill Rennon and Hugh MacPherson saw me. However, they'll stay quiet. I'm quite sure of that. I'll keep them in my pocket. If the situation ever arises, they'll just come forward and say that Joseph burnt it down. Joseph didn't like Max either, so the story is credible."

Alexandra played the melody all the way through, but everyone's attention was focused on George. The whole café was hushed, save for a few people murmuring to themselves. After Alexandra stopped playing, she held the violin at her side and stared at her uncle.

"Did everyone hear what he just said?" remarked the police chief.

"I'd have never believed it!" said one.

"The truth comes finally comes out!" said another.

"It's true!" said MacPherson. "He came to us the other day and said he needed to collect a favour. He threatened us if we wouldn't cooperate!"

"Well, this puts things into whole different light," said the chief. "Joseph Delmott, you're free. Thank you, George, for your confession. You are under arrest for arson and intimidating witnesses."

"What? But how?" said George, emerging from the vision. "Oh you tricked me! You little witch!" he cried, glaring at Alexandra. At that moment he lunged towards her and she darted behind her father. Joseph rushed forward and pushed back against George, locking his hands around the man's flailing wrists as he tried taking wild swings to get at the girl. "I'm going to kill you, you witch!" he cried over and over. Charlie had already sprung from his chair and began forcing his way between the two brothers. The constables and the chief pulled George back and pushed him to the floor, face down. "You ruined my life!" George screamed. "I'll make sure you pay with yours!"

"Attempted murder and uttering a death threat," added the police chief with deft professionalism. "You all witnessed that, too. All right George, calm down, calm down. We're going to the police station," he said as the constable handcuffed the sobbing man. "You've got a lot of serious explaining to do."

* * *

The human mind is difficult to understand with thoughts moving in and out like breezes waving and fanning out across a grassy field. With this thought in mind, Alexandra rationalized that she really had no control over the events that led to the arrest of her uncle. She had simply played her music, but the thoughts and memories belonged to him – he created those memories himself and he alone was responsible for them.

Alexandra did not go to school at all the day her uncle was arrested. Instead, she and Joseph decided to step away from the café and go for a walk to check on the construction of their new house and restaurant.

As they strolled, a streetcar would occasionally pass by, rattling and screeching along its rails. Joseph and Alexandra rarely took the streetcar, for everything they needed was fairly close by. Besides, it was a lovely spring day and perfect for walking.

"How can bad things happen on such a lovely day?" Alexandra wondered aloud to her father. "I've never understood that. I see the bees buzzing in the flowers, carrying on with their business. The grass grows, the birds sing, the sun shines. They know nothing of what's going on in the world today."

"Yes, well I'm sure that even they realize the world is not a perfect place. It never will be. There are always going to be problems of some kind somewhere. If we wait for everything to be perfect, we're going to miss out on the everyday beauty we see around us. However, our world is filled with love, joy, hope and countless wonders – all the small things we see around us every day. This is one of the problems with us adults. We get caught up in our busy lives and never pay attention to the interesting details. I'm glad you notice them, and I hope you always will."

"I hope so too, Papa. I also have hope that someday I'll see Mama again."

"What did you see in your vision today? Was there anything there about your mother?"

"Papa, if you can believe it, I didn't see anything because I didn't have a vision at all."

"But how could it be? You heard your uncle George in the café confessing his guilt!"

"Yes, he did. I've never been able to understand everything that happens, but maybe that's not so important – except for one thing."

"What's that?"

"I was hoping to get a vision of where Uncle George sent Mama. He must know where she is."

"If visions won't tell you, it's going to be almost impossible to get your uncle to tell us. I know my brother. He won't do or say anything to make his problems any worse. That being true, we do have some hope. Your uncle's arrest will no doubt make the national papers. I can only pray your mother reads one of them and realizes it's safe to come home."

Chapter 31

When Alexandra and her father arrived at the building site, the workers were just as busy as the bees Alexandra had described earlier. The air was filled with the smell of freshly cut wood and the irregular, clanking sound of hammers could be heard everywhere.

"There's so much progress, Papa!" Alexandra said, looking around.

"I'm glad to see it too. If they keep up at this rate, we should be open by summer," said Joseph, surveying the framework of the newly erected structure. "Do you see that window there?" he said, pointing to a framed-in dormer on the still-open roofline. "That's where your room will be, and mine is across the corridor."

"Can I go up and have a look?"

"Yes, but please be careful and mind your step. This is no place for a woman in a dress."

Alexandra smiled and, amid the clutter of building materials, walked up to the new house. She navigated her way through where the main foyer would be and then up the stairs, which still had no railings to protect clumsy people from falling over the side. She arrived at the top and looked up at the sky from between the roof trusses and down a corridor in front of her. There was a bedroom on each side of the corridor, and she looked towards the room which would soon be hers.

Her new bedroom would be much larger than her current room. Despite this, she sighed when she noticed that her father's room was much smaller than hers. The man must have thought he had no need of a large room because there was no one to share it with. In any event, she looked through the framed-in window of her father's room towards the street. From her vantage point she surveyed the whole construction scene and spotted her father talking to some workers. She was about to shout and wave to him when another sight caught her eye – Aunt Clara and Owen approaching from down the street. She gasped and turned round quickly, dashing back down the stairs through the partially built home. She joined her father just as Clara and Owen arrived.

"They told me I'd find you here. Look, Joseph, it's clear that George is in serious trouble. I have to be honest with you; I married your brother for better or worse, but recently things have been virtually intolerable with him. I never in my life thought it would turn out this way. Even now the police are at George's office, poring through his documents and taking them away in boxes. They are like vultures picking through the bones of a corpse."

"Clara, I'm sorry it turned out this way," said Joseph.

"I should really be upset with you," said the wounded aunt, turning her attention to Alexandra and scanning her up and down. "However, I cannot be. In fact, I even owe you a debt of gratitude. I had been living far too long in the hopes that your uncle would become an honourable man. I've decided to sell our house, pack our things, and move. Owen and I will live with my sister in Barrie."

"If there is any way I can help, I will," said Joseph.

"Thank you, but not now."

"Well, we're here if you need us. However, there is a way *you* can help *us*."

"Help you? How?"

"By asking George where Helen is," he said, a glimmer of hope rising in his voice.

"How would he know where Helen went?"

"Mum, I tried to tell you about that," said Owen, breaking his silence. "You know that whole story Father told us about Aunt Helen running off with a sailor? It wasn't true. That was another one of his many lies. In the vision I had, he bragged to Aunt Helen about the fire and she set out to have him prosecuted. He found out and told her to leave with a merchant seaman and never return. If she didn't do it, he said he'd reduce them all to ashes."

Clara stood there in the spring sunshine, shaking her head. She sighed. "I'll ask him. Why not? We certainly don't have anything more to lose, but you have everything to gain. Don't get your hopes too high though, even if he does know, he won't want another witness testifying against him. The best I can do is try."

* * *

The following days found the newspapers on both sides of the border giving vast coverage to the shady business dealings of George Delmott, his pyromaniac tendencies, and his fall from grace. "Windsor Lawyer Admits Setting Fire," said one paper, "Arsonist Confesses to Great Fire of '71," read another.

Meanwhile, the two cousins continued their schooling, and even Sister Rose seemed softer, especially to Owen, and especially since he made his apology public to Alexandra.

As the month of May wore on, the trip to Ottawa was fast approaching. In fact, it was Friday and the very next day she would leave bright and early. When school was dismissed and the last of the students were leaving, Sister Rose approached Alexandra in private.

"Young lady," she said.

"Yes, Sister?"

"You know, our school year is almost finished and next year you'll be attending St. Mary's. Now that I have a moment, I wanted to say…"

Alexandra looked at the nun, whose face was flushed as she seemed to grasp for the right words. The nun cleared her dry throat. "I wanted to say that I was really quite pleased to have you in my class. Perhaps, though, I pushed myself too hard on you and embarrassed you in front of your classmates. I am truly sorry for that and hope you will accept the apology of this old lady."

Alexandra smiled at the old nun, who now displayed an unusual, yet particularly welcoming sweetness. Against all proper and acceptable protocol, Alexandra hugged the nun. Sister Rose, hesitant at first, hugged the girl in return. "There's nothing to forgive, Sister Rose. You really meant well. Please, don't think I hold anything against you for it but, if you please, of course, I forgive you."

"Thank you," said the nun. "Also, don't forget me when you're playing in all the great concert halls and with all the great orchestras of Europe, Alexandra."

"That won't happen for a while yet," she said with laughter in her voice. "But before it does, of course I'll come visit you. You can be sure of that."

"Well, God bless you, Alexandra. Have a wonderful time in Ottawa. Come home safely!" she said.

"Thank you, Sister! I suppose I should go now. I'll see you before the roses bloom again," she said as she joined Owen, who was waiting for her in the corridor.

Sister Rose stood at the classroom window and watched as the cousins walked happily together out of the schoolyard, around the corner, and out of sight. She sighed raggedly and turned back into her empty classroom, raising a hand to her wet eyes.

* * *

"I'd really like to go up to Ottawa with you, Alex," said Owen.

"Yes, I know, but I promise I'll get some souvenirs for you. I'll get some for Emma and Robbie, too. By the way, I'd like you to be the first one to play a duet with me when the new restaurant opens. Maybe you can even play with the Detroit group when they come over! They're really a lot of fun, you know. We're also meeting them up in Ottawa."

Owen sighed. "Thank you, but you heard my mum, we're moving to Barrie. That will be my new life."

"Then you will make new memories in that place! A very wise person once told me, 'You are free to make the memories you want to make.' I take this to mean that you alone are responsible for your happiness in life and the choices you make. Owen, I'm proud you're my cousin and that everything is better between us. I'm sure that wherever you are or whatever you do, that we'll always be close."

"The same here," he said as they came to the end of their stroll.

"I'll see you in a week, Owen," said Alexandra, taking the boy's hands in hers then hugging him.

Before leaving, Owen turned back. "I know that wise person who said that to you. He said the same to me."

* * *

"Welcome, my dear!" said the professor.

"Hello, Maestro!" said Alexandra, stepping into the professor's home.

"Have you packed for Ottawa yet? I'm sure you'll love it there. You know, it will be like a second spring. While our blooms have mostly fallen off, theirs should be at peak season. You know, those folks are about a fortnight behind us! Now I want to tell you a piece of very good news."

"What news, Maestro?"

"The headmaster of the England's Royal Academy of Music is going to be there at the music festival."

Alexandra beamed. "Oh, Maestro! That's wonderful news! Sir Charles wrote and told me all about the Academy! He also said that he's accepted an appointment to the board of directors! Isn't it wonderful that he's involved with music?"

"Indeed it is," said the Maestro.

"Are we going to hear some of their musicians play?"

"Yes, and more than that! They're only here with a small contingent promoting their fine institute. However, I personally know the headmaster, Professor Wilkes, and he specifically asked to hear us, actually *you,* perform onstage. Remember, word spreads quickly in the music community and they are always looking for fresh, new talent. They'll hear you now, remember you, and I believe you have every good chance of being accepted by them. I know you can do it, Alexandra. I have every faith in you. If you can do this, I know without any doubt that all your dreams about a musical career will take one giant leap forward."

"Professor Hergicksen," she said, her voice taking on a serious tone.

"Please call me Maestro," he winked.

"All right, Maestro," she said, smiling. "Thank you so very much for this opportunity. I am so grateful to you for everything you've done, all your support, all your encouragement. I promise you I will do my very best. I will not disappoint you."

"I know," he said as the two walked to the study.

The Maestro and Alexandra played many songs, including their favourite classical pieces, and even some Celtic music. The two spent their time happily with Alexandra on her violin and the professor accompanying her on the piano.

* * *

When she returned to the café later that day, Alexandra found her father at his usual table. He was there with Clara, and they both appeared to be having a serious conversation. "Alexandra, come here please," said Joseph.

"Dear," said Clara. "I asked your Uncle George about your mother."

"He told you?"

"Well, yes he did. I thought maybe he wouldn't. He said that now it made no difference. I'm so sorry to tell you –"

"That my mother is dead?"

Joseph interrupted. "Please, Angel, let your aunt continue."

"No, she's not dead, dear. He sent her away to England with a merchant seaman who would ensure her safe passage. He also said that of course, there was no romantic relationship."

"I knew it!" said Alexandra, springing up and down. "It's my destiny! Don't you see, Papa? It all makes sense! Everything makes perfect sense! Owen told me I would go to her! Remember Sir Charles? Our unfinished business?"

"Well, yes of course I remember!"

"Oh Papa, we must go there! We can find Mama there!"

"That's not all, though," said Clara. "He told me he had bribed the officials so that your mother could get a new name, new identity. He did this so that she would never be found."

"This would truly be an expedition beyond all imagination," said Joseph. "I promise you, Angel, we will do it. First though, we must open the new restaurant. I have every confidence in Marcie to handle things. Then we will go to England and stay with Sir Charles – and we will find your mother!"

Alexandra threw her arms around her papa and kissed him. She then turned to her aunt. "Thank you, Aunt Clara, for asking. I know Uncle George is telling the truth."

"For once in his life," said Clara. "Well, I do hope you find your mother."

"We will," said Joseph. "I promise you that."

* * *

Before the roses bloom again. Alexandra liked that phrase, it was one she remembered her mother using when she said goodbye and she often found herself using it, too. Roses were beautiful – both to look at and to smell. The professor liked roses as well. In fact, they were his favourite flowers. They were certainly something special to look forward to, the perfect symbol for a special meeting with someone you love dearly. Alexandra couldn't wait to take a ship across the wide expanse of the ocean with her father, returning home with her mother and vast, lovely bouquets of English roses.

That night, when all was quiet, Alexandra was sitting up in her bed reading a book. She heard a gentle knock on her door. "May I come in?" her father asked in a quiet voice.

"Yes, Papa, come in."

The door eased open and Joseph entered the room. "I'd like to wish you a good night, Angel. Don't sit up too long. We've got a big day ahead of us tomorrow."

"I know, Papa. I'm really excited about going to Ottawa, but I'm more excited about going to England. Do you think we'll find Mama there?"

"I have no doubt of it. I dream about it myself."

"Really? Do you dream about finding Mama?"

"I do. In fact, I often have dreams that's still with us."

"You do? Can you tell me, please?" she said, placing the book face down.

"Well, let's see now. Sometimes I dream about her two, even three times a week. The dreams are like she never left. She was there with you, watching you grow, always encouraging you to play your violin."

"That's so wonderful, Papa! Oh I wish I could have dreams like that too, but I think I don't have them because I wasn't old enough to remember very much," she said, a wave of sadness washing over her.

"Sometimes dreams can help us cope with the challenges we face in our everyday lives."

"I think you're right, Papa," she said, regaining some level of comfort.

"Now it's getting late. We both need some sleep so I'm going to bed. Goodnight Angel, I'll see you in the morning."

"Goodnight, Papa," she said, smiling. "Sweet dreams."

Chapter 32

Alexandra and her father were already up when dawn broke the following morning. Their bags were packed, waiting near their table. Then, the bell on the café door clanged merrily as a happy Marcie entered, dressed not in her work clothes but rather in a pink dress and matching, flowered hat. Following her through the door was Denis, dressed smartly in a suit with a gold chain which looped round, tucked neatly in his pocket.

"You shine up real nice, Denis! Just like a new penny. I hardly recognized you!" said Joseph, chuckling.

Marcie laughed. "We're going to our nation's capital today, so we thought we'd get all dressed up for the occasion. Good Lord knows when we're going to have the chance to get away again!"

They departed the café for the short walk to the train station. When they arrived, the professor met them on the platform. He had a cased violin as well as a medium sized suitcase. Alexandra immediately noticed something different.

"Good morning, Maestro! Where's your Valentina?"

"Ah, how observant of you, my dear! I decided to retire her. You know, it's time I made a break with the past and thought more about the future. This instrument I have here is also of fine quality. I'll show it to you on the train during our trip."

"I look forward to seeing it," said Alexandra, a knowing smile spreading across her face.

They took their places in the train and, after the customary "All Aboard!" the mighty steam engine headed off into the rising spring sun.

The train huffed and chugged steadily eastward past all the familiar places – Chatham, London, Toronto. Alexandra spent a good part of the journey sitting near her window watching as the scenery changed. She noticed a great deal of change after they passed Toronto.

The landscape now consisted of a lush green forest which sprouted from the rugged, hilly terrain – which itself seemed to have been formed by a great sculptor's hand. As the train wound its way through this paradise, the hills often gave way to allow a spectacular view of tree-lined lakes, their shimmering waters sparkling in the sunshine. Alexandra and her travelling companions marvelled at the rocky slopes with pine trees growing precariously from between cracks in the rocks, and how these trees formed a blanket of green, softening the ancient, lichen-covered rocks.

"Aren't you going to show me your violin, Maestro?" Alexandra asked.

"Oh yes, I'm sorry, I almost forgot!" The professor reached for the case and opened it. "This fine instrument was made by the Klotz family of Germany. It's well over one hundred years old."

Alexandra examined it in its case, but dared not touch it. "Aren't you afraid to travel with it, Maestro?"

"No, I just don't let it out of my sight. Anyway, you'll hear it tomorrow. We play at noon sharp."

At long last, the train eased to a stop in Ottawa.

* * *

The air in that part of the country was noticeably different. It had a distinct woodsy aroma to it, though sometimes one could smell the odours wafting through the air from the E.B. Eddy paper mill.

The five set off in their coach, bound for their hotel, which was a cozy limestone building overlooking the Rideau Canal. It wasn't as luxurious as Alexandra remembered the Queen's Hotel being, yet it was charming, affording the traveller everything they could hope for – friendly staff, comfortable rooms, and an elegant dining room. It would be their home for the next several days.

"Professor Wilkes from the music academy in London will be joining us for dinner tonight," said the professor. "We mustn't keep him waiting, he's a very busy man. If you thought I was busy and impatient, this man is the very definition! Come quickly!"

The small group of travellers met, famished, in the dining room overlooking the canal.

"Oh this is so marvellous!" Marcie said as she took her place at the table. "I'm so glad we were able to come! It's nice for someone to serve *me* for a change!"

"I'm glad we came too. We needed the break," said Denis. "I'm sure Bernice is taking care of everything back home."

"You were indeed right, Maestro," said Alexandra.

"About what?"

"About everything! You said Ottawa was about a fortnight behind us. I see there are still flowers on the trees here and even the daffodils are still blooming! Oh, it feels like heaven!"

The professor and Joseph chuckled just as a well-dressed stranger approached the table. The professor recognized him right away. "Wills!" he said to the man. "I trust you had a good voyage."

"I did indeed, Hergie. I've even brought along some of my young prodigies."

"I'm anxious to meet them! Please, let me introduce you. May I present Marcie and Denis Gionelli, and this is Joseph Delmott and his daughter Alexandra. She also goes by the name Aydy. She's the one I was telling you about."

"Ah, yes," he said, studying Alexandra. "It's a pleasure to meet you all. I look forward to seeing you perform tomorrow, Miss Delmott. Professor Hergicksen has put in a very good word for you."

"Thank you, Professor Wilkes. I hope I won't disappoint you – or him tomorrow."

"Nonsense, my dear," said the professor. Turning to Wilkes, he continued. "Please Wills, have a seat. I'm sure the waiter will be along soon for our orders."

Everyone enjoyed a pleasant meal and conversation in the atmosphere of the historic restaurant. However, following their well-anticipated dinner, Professor Wilkes had to excuse himself from their company in order to attend his group of students. The remaining diners went outside on the veranda, which was furnished with comfortable wicker furniture. It afforded a splendid view of the Rideau Canal.

"Oh! Look over there!" said Denis, casually pointing across the canal towards someplace in the distance. Everyone strained their eyes, and then they saw it – a single, multi-coloured hot air balloon rising majestically into the late afternoon sky.

"Those people are so lucky!" Alexandra said. "What a glorious sight! Who'd have ever thought we'd see a hot air balloon!"

The professor laughed. "Don't forget, my dear, we're in the nation's capital. Now you know where all the hot air goes!"

Everyone laughed except Alexandra, who just wrinkled her nose and scratched her head.

* * *

The following day was just as glorious as the previous one, and Ottawa was awash in springtime glory – and musicians. They came from all over Canada, with some participants arriving from the U.S. and other countries to attend the music festival located in one of the parks near the Rideau Canal. The Parliament Buildings were visible some distance away.

The whole place had a carnival atmosphere. Vendors sold their wares, concession stands sold refreshments, and people strolled about dressed in their fine apparel – women in dainty hats, dresses and carrying parasols, escorted by fine, proper gentlemen. Alexandra herself felt quite regal. She wore one of her Sunday dresses, a blue dress with small, white polka dots. Since the springtime air had a bit of a chill to it, she also wore her favourite mustard-coloured cardigan sweater.

Following a jovial and light-hearted breakfast, Alexandra decided to practice on the restaurant's veranda to ensure everything would be perfect. The practice session reminded Alexandra of performing in front of customers back home at the café.

"I think you're as ready as you can be," said the professor. "Now let's be off. We don't want to be late."

The five began their stroll through the park. Every so often they would pause and listen to a little musical group practicing, though the professor kept urging them to move along. It was difficult to do because the music from these musicians, who came in all sizes, shapes, ages and talent levels, was exceptionally good.

"Papa, if this isn't paradise, I don't know what is," said Alexandra.

"Yes, well it's good that the weather is cooperating with us today."

"Come on now! We mustn't dawdle!" the professor grumbled. "We'll be late for our performance!"

"Look!" said Alexandra. "It's the Detroit group! Oh Maestro, I want to introduce you to them, please, let's go! We have time!"

The professor checked his pocket watch and sighed. "All right, fine. But let's be quick about it."

Alexandra walked straight up to David and tapped him on the shoulder. He turned round. "Aydy! So glad you could come! We've all been practicing, especially Nicky here. He needs practice, you know. He's also accident prone. Do you know why he has four strings on his bass?"

"Because it's like a big violin?"

"No! Do you know what three of those strings are for?" he said, smirking. "They're spares!"

"Don't pay any attention to him," said Nick. "I use them all!"

The professor shook his head and chuckled. "You all remind me of myself in my younger days. All right, now let's go find the stage."

* * *

The outdoor stage at the music festival was a neat little arrangement where musicians could use the area behind it to prepare and, when they were ready, they could come up and perform their musical repertoires on a raised platform. The only immoveable piece on the stage was a grand piano. Neat rows of seating were arranged in front of the stage to accommodate perhaps a hundred or more people. Those not lucky enough to get a seat could stand. Surrounding the whole complex were rows of brightly coloured marquees to provide shade and shelter for both musicians and spectators.

Performing on the stage at that moment was a children's quartet composed of two girls on the violin, one boy on a viola and another on a cello. They played bright, happy songs and Alexandra recognized all the melodies.

"They are from the London Academy," the professor said. "There's one more group after them, and then it's our turn. It seems we've arrived just in time."

"Aydy!" said another familiar voice.

Alexandra looked away from the stage to find none other than Alfred standing there. The professor appeared agitated at the intrusion.

"We meet again!" said Alfred, smiling. "Dare I ask what brings you into town?"

"Well, I don't know!" said Alexandra, putting her hand on her hip and finger alongside her face as if she were thinking. "I heard Ottawa is quite lovely at this time of year!"

"Welcome!" he said. "I hope you'll not refuse my invitation to play together this time! We're just over there. Please, come!"

She remembered refusing the boy two times previously, though both times she felt justified in doing so. Now the situation was almost the same, but her words came back to haunt her: this time she really did have no time – in the absolute, most literal way possible. She reasoned that perhaps she could appease the boy – and the professor – by playing with his little troupe later.

"Make the memories, call them your own."

"Alexandra? Did you hear me?" Joseph said to the distracted girl. "I said you can play your violin with Alfred later. You really must go on stage soon."

"Oh? You're going onstage, Alex? We can wait. We'll be here all week. We can play later."

"Do not be afraid, Alexandra. Make the memories, make them…"

"Alfred, I'm not sure what to say," she said. "Mr. – excuse me, please. I don't even know your last name! Perhaps we could –"

"Before the roses bloom again…"

"Rickleton," he said. "We can do it later, after your performance."

"Play."

"I'm so sorry," said Alexandra. "Of course I'd be honoured to play with you and your group, Alfred." Turning to the professor, she continued. "I cannot perform on stage with you now, Maestro. I'm so sorry. I really must go with Alfred. Please, please forgive me."

Alexandra, violin in hand, walked away from her stunned companions in the company of Alfred.

* * *

The area in which Alfred's little group practiced was set some distance away from the main stage under a marquee, reminiscent of how things looked in London the previous summer.

"What has possessed that girl?" said the professor, shaking his head at the hodgepodge of different musicians – a girl on the viola, Alfred on the cello, and an older man sawing away on the bass. "I've never seen her behave like this. She knows how important this is to her future!"

"I'm sure she's well aware of that fact, Hergie."

"I have no idea how I can explain all this to Professor Wilkes!"

"Alexandra can do that," said Joseph. "Of that you can be sure."

* * *

Alexandra was, at first, apprehensive about her decision to abandon the Maestro and ruin their plans, but felt she had made the right decision. She practiced with the group while her travelling companions looked on.

"Let's try a pretty song," said Alfred. "Blue Danube?"

Alexandra always liked that song; her mother used to hum parts of it to her when she was little. She also liked the song because it had so much grace and charm, and when it was played on such an emotional instrument as the violin, it became even more so. "Yes, let's try it," she said. "I'm ready."

The famous waltz was played well by the group of musicians and Alexandra's alterations between harmony and melody resonated well. People, as usual, stopped to listen, the quartet playing the song in practice just as well as they would have played it at a performance. As she played, she gazed out over the growing number of people who gravitated there to listen. More were coming, drawn to the music, to the sweet sounds which echoed and fanned out into the park like a gentle spring breeze.

Alexandra closed her eyes as she played. She was pleased at the effect music could bring to people, at the way it could alter and change their moods – but especially how it could evoke their memories. As she continued her performance, a single red rose petal drifted down and slowed to a stop in midair, about an arm's length from her. It was luminescent, yet transparent. It lingered in mid air before being joined by another and another, each delicate petal drifting down and stopping at different levels, shining, sparkling and shimmering like the most brilliant of jewels, each radiant petal sparkling with a living memory. They surrounded the girl in a magnificent, ethereal aura.

Alexandra, a spectator through time, stood and watched as a young, dark-haired woman with trembling hands was writing a note. "My Dearest Joseph, it breaks my heart to tell you..."

The hands of time moved forward. The young woman now sought work in a new land – in law offices, banks, insurance companies – success was slow, but was earned.

Years pass. "Sunshine, you are doing very well on the violin, making fine progress," *the woman said to a girl, aged about nine.* "If you work hard, you will become a concert violinist. Your pépé would be proud of you."

Alexandra's vision continued, but now the hundreds of shimmering, floating rose petals in midair began crackling, sparks bursting out from them as one memory began connecting to another memory, and to another and another until they all connected into a whole, vast, magnificent curtain of pulsating energy.

"You can find your answers at home. I know the truth. I know what happened. Please trust me," *said the large man with the accent.* "This will be more than enough money for you."

Weeks pass. "Mama, I'm frightened," *said the girl in a British accent.* "I don't like this travelling."

Days pass. "There are so many musicians here!"

Minutes pass. "Do your best, Sunshine. If you do, your violin playing will be as good as that girl."

"Which girl, Mama?"

"Don't you see? The brown haired girl in the blue dress and yellow sweater."

Mid-way through the song, Alexandra stopped playing and slowly opened her eyes, trying to refocus them in order to see clearly. The dazzling display of sparkling rose petals began fading, dissolving into the air one by one, each sparkling a final time before disappearing. She gazed out over the vast crowd who had gathered to hear her play, her eyes searching over the people. Despite her abbreviated performance, they applauded her wildly.

"MAMA!" Alexandra's cry reached out, yet she could not see the woman. She quickly handed her violin to Alfred and started pushing her way through the crowd.

"Wonderful performance!" shouted the professor from a distance.

"Bravo! Bravo!" said Marcie and Denis, clapping next to him.

"More Aydy! More, please!" people demanded.

They kept crowding near her, but Alexandra ignored them all, determined to push her way through the massing crowd who thronged to get near her. "Please! Aydy! Play us more!"

"No! I have to find my mother!" she said before crying out again, "Mama! Mama!"

Meanwhile, Joseph was pressing his way through the crowd too, trying to reach his daughter. It was almost impossible, the vast numbers of people made it too difficult to move anywhere and no one was giving either of them any room to move.

"Excuse me, please, I have to get through!" cried Alexandra, squeezing and forcing her way between the crush of people. Finally breaking free from the crowd, she ran into open space – a large, paved promenade.

"Mama! Where are you? My God, where are you?" she wailed in exasperation, looking round in all directions. Not knowing which way to run, she threw herself down on a park bench, leaned over sideways and sobbed, her whole body shaking, almost in convulsion.

At that moment, someone came and sat next to her. "Excuse me," said a young girl in a British accent. "Please don't be sad. Your performance was most excellent. Mama says if I practice I can be just like you."

Alexandra sat up and looked at the girl. She had large, almond shaped blue eyes, auburn hair and an oval face. Alexandra thought she was looking at her younger self in a mirror. "How can it be?"

Emerging from the crowd of people, Alexandra could see her father walking towards her with a dark-haired woman. They were arm in arm.

Alexandra and the girl smiled at each other and walked over to meet them. Watching from a distance were Marcie, Denis and the professor.

The sun did indeed shine brightly on the Delmott family that last Sunday in May, 1888.

Alexandra stopped just short of her mother. "Mama? Is it really you?"

"It is, Angel, it's me," she said, taking the girl in her arms and embracing her warmly.

Alexandra sobbed anew into her mother's dress. "Mama, I've missed you so much!" she said, looking up at her mother before hugging her tightly once again.

"I've missed you too, Angel. I'm home now," she said, kissing the girl's head and running her fingers through her hair. "I have so much to tell you! But first I want you to meet your sister," said Helen before turning to Joseph. "Darling, I want you to meet your daughter. She plays the violin, too. Her name is Katie."

"Katie! That's such a lovely name!" said Joseph.

Katie smiled.

"Helen, how did you know to come here?" said Joseph.

"I met Sir Charles Stanley at the music academy in London where Katie had been taking violin lessons," said Helen.

"Sir Charles?" said Alexandra, sniffling. She loosened her hug and wiped her eyes. "You met Sir Charles?"

"Yes, I did. He was curious about my North American accent, asked me exactly where I was from, and I told him. He put all the pieces together." She turned her attention to Joseph. "He told me that you had written and told him that George was incapacitated 'by our mutual plan.' What does that mean?" she said, squinting. "He said it was safe to come home, that I should come to the music festival here in Ottawa. Joseph, he said I'd find you and Alexandra here. I'm so sorry I left you, but I had to protect –"

"To protect us, I know. You needn't worry any longer, my love. We're all together again, and now I am truly blessed," he said, looking at Helen, Alexandra, and Katie.

"What happened to George?" asked Helen.

"Well, he recovered from his affliction, but through an interesting little trick, which I'll tell you more about later," he said, winking at Alexandra, "he confessed to causing the Great Fire of Windsor. He was promptly arrested."

"Aydy!" said Alfred, appearing from the crowd with the Maestro, Marcie, and Denis. "There you are! I've been looking for you! Here's your violin!" He looked at Alexandra's mother and sister.

"Oh Alfred! Maestro! Marcie! I'm so happy! This is the best day of my life!" exclaimed Alexandra. "This is my mother – and my sister! Her name is Katie – and they've just arrived from England! Katie plays the violin, too!"

"I see where Alexandra gets her good looks," said the professor. "It's a pleasure to meet you, ma'am."

"Likewise, Maestro. Please call me Helen," she said. "Sir Charles spoke very highly of you."

"This is Marcie," interrupted Joseph. "She's the head waitress in the café."

"Alex, and Katie, would you like to come play a song with us?" asked Alfred.

"May I, Mama?" asked Katie.

"Yes, of course you may, Sunshine," replied Helen. "We'll all sit together and watch."

The group of musicians returned to the marquee to find many people still there. "Aydy! Play us a song! Please!" they said.

Alexandra Delmott returned to her place under the marquee with her sister and Alfred. The crowd burst into applause upon her return. Alexandra beamed.

"Let's reprise 'Blue Danube,'" she said. "Do you know it, Katie?"

"Yes," she said, "I can play it, and Mama hums it to me all the time."

The two sisters raised their violins up, placing them in the crooks of their necks. They smiled at each other, and began playing the first, sweet introductory notes of the famous waltz. Helen, Joseph, and their company of friends watched from rows of seating across the front.

The beautiful melody spread through the park as before, but now something was very different. Alexandra's father stood up and reached his hand to Helen. She took his hand and rose to her feet. Joseph placed his arm around her waist and they began dancing, sweeping round in elegant, graceful circles, their eyes fixed on each other.

Alexandra smiled as she played, the sweet sound of the music wrapping itself around her in a completely new and wonderful way. She saw no vision this time, her reality being right before her eyes. At that moment, she remembered the secret her pépé had told her in that vision long ago.

"Stay true to your course, my little protégé, and your deepest dreams will become your happiest memories."

What happens next? A Bonus Chapter, of course!

Visit my website at www.edwardcurnutte.com and subscribe to my mailing list. The Bonus Chapter to *Aydy's Fiddle* will be emailed to you absolutely free! You can unsubscribe any time you like.

Author's notes

Aydy's Fiddle is a story of love, hope, and family. It is a combination of many stories from many people. It was inspired, in part, by listening for hours, often deep into the night, of family members speaking about their life-experiences. It would have been a pity if their stories vanished forever when the big broom of time sweeps everything away.

The story was also inspired by a violin owned by my great-grandfather, Dolphis Hebert. Though his violin is no longer playable, it is kept in safe storage. I look at it from time to time, wondering what fascinating stories it could tell if it could talk – or sing.

Some historical events, such as the Premier's Competition and the Music Festival in Ottawa are purely fictitious. Though there's no doubt that music festivals took place during the 19th century, they did not always occur regularly and most were loosely organized – as many still are today. It is also my hope the reader may forgive me for shortening some of the geographical distances – especially around the Windsor and Sandwich area (which were greater than depicted).

Finally, I recognize that in order to become proficient at a musical instrument, or in any worthy endeavour, takes years of study and practice – all of it fuelled by a determination to succeed. Those who do, have my deepest respect.

- Edward Curnutte

Acknowledgements

I wish to express my grateful appreciation to the following people, without whose assistance, technical or otherwise, *Aydy's Fiddle* would not have been possible. To Bogdana Boyko for editing services and manuscript suggestions, Joyce Cherwak for historical information and contacts, Nora Curnutte, Jacki Curnutte-Hindman for her beta and proof-reading, Susan Curnutte-Ball, Elehna Duda, Barb Feldman for editing services, Alexandra Klymenko, Fern McKenna Walsh, Kathy Moore for her cover photo of Olivia Skinner, Marcene Renes and Dennis Kasarda for manuscript suggestions, Katerina Schedel, Vonda Wood for proof-reading, editing and manuscript suggestions, and Molly Stone Zucknick for her beta-reader review – which was the most comprehensive and complete I have ever seen.

With the exception of Hiram Walker and Oliver Mowat, the characters portrayed in this work are fictional. No other characters are meant to depict any person, living or dead, and any such resemblance is purely coincidental. This is a work of fiction.

www.edwardcurnutte.com

Made in the USA
Middletown, DE
22 September 2018